Reviewers Love Melissa Brayden

"Melissa Brayden has become one of the most popular novelists of the genre, writing hit after hit of funny, relatable, and very sexy stories for women who love women."—*Afterellen.com*

Sparks Like Ours

"Brayden sets up a flirtatious tit-for-tat that's honest, relatable, and passionate. The women's fears are real, but the loving support from the supporting cast helps them find their way to a happy future. This enjoyable romance is sure to interest readers in the other stories from Seven Shores."—*Publishers Weekly*

"*Sparks Like Ours* is made up of myriad bits of truth that make for a cozy, lovely summer read."—*Queerly Reads*

Hearts Like Hers

"*Hearts like Hers* has all the ingredients that readers can expect from Ms. Brayden: witty dialogue, heartfelt relationships, hot chemistry and passionate romance."—*Lez Review Books*

"Once again Melissa Brayden stands at the top. She unequivocally is the queen of romance."—*Front Porch Romance*

"Autumn Primm and Kate Carpenter are my favorite Brayden couple to date. This book had me laughing, crying and swooning like never before."—*Les Reveur*

"*Hearts Like Hers* has a breezy style that makes it a perfect beach read. The romance is paced well, the sex is super hot, and the conflict made perfect sense and honored Autumn and Kate's journeys."—*The Lesbian Review*

D1603070

First Position

"Brayden aptly develops the growing relationship between Ana and Natalie, making the emotional payoff that much sweeter. This ably plotted, moving offering will earn its place deep in readers' hearts."—*Publishers Weekly*

"*First Position* is romance at its finest with an opposites attract theme that kept me engaged the whole way through."—*The Lesbian Review*

"This book is thoughtful and compassionate, serious yet entertaining, and altogether extremely well done. It takes a lot to stand out, but this is definitely one of the best Traditional Romances of the year." —*Lesbian Reading Room*

"You go about your days reading books, thinking oh, yes this one is good, that one over there is so good, and then a Melissa Brayden comes along making everything else seem…well, just less than." —*The Romantic Reader*

How Sweet It Is

"'Sweet' is definitely the keyword for this well-written, character-driven lesbian romance novel. It is ultimately a love letter to small town America, and the lesson to remain open to whatever opportunities and happiness comes into your life."—Bob Lind, *Echo Magazine*

"Oh boy! The events were perfectly plausible, but the collection and the threading of all the stories, main and sub plots, were just fantastic. I completely and wholeheartedly recommend this book. So touching, so heartwarming and all-out beautiful." —*Rainbow Book Reviews*

Heart Block

"The story is enchanting with conflicts and issues to be overcome that will keep the reader turning the pages. The relationship between Sarah and Emory is achingly beautiful and skillfully portrayed. This second offering by Melissa Brayden is a perfect package of love—and life to be lived to the fullest. So grab a beverage and snuggle up with a comfy throw to read this classic story of overcoming obstacles and finding enduring love."—*Lambda Literary Review*

"Although this book doesn't beat you over the head with wit, the interactions are almost always humorous, making both characters really quite loveable. Overall a very enjoyable read."
—*C-Spot Reviews*

Waiting in the Wings

"This was an engaging book with believable characters and story development. It's always a pleasure to read a book set in a world like theater/film that gets it right…a thoroughly enjoyable read."
—*Lez Books*

"This is Brayden's first novel, but we wouldn't notice if she hadn't told us. The book is well put together and more complex than most authors' second or third books. The characters have chemistry; you want them to get together in the end. The book is light, frothy, and fun to read. And the sex is hot without being too explicit—not an easy trick to pull off."—*Liberty Press*

"Sexy, funny, and all-around enjoyable."—*Afterellen.com*

Praise for the Soho Loft Series

"The trilogy was enjoyable and definitely worth a read if you're looking for solid romance or interconnected stories about a group of friends."—*The Lesbrary*

Kiss the Girl

"There are romances and there are romances...Melissa Brayden can be relied on to write consistently very sweet, pure romances and delivers again with her newest book *Kiss the Girl*...There are scenes suffused with the sweetest love, some with great sadness or even anger—a whole gamut of emotions that take readers on a gentle roller coaster with a consistent upbeat tone. And at the heart of this book is a hymn to true friendship and human decency."
—*C-Spot Reviews*

"An adorable romance in which two flawed but well-written characters defy the odds and fall into the arms of the other."
—*She Read*

"Brayden does romance so very well. She provides us with engaging characters, a plausible setup with understandable and realistic conflict, and ridiculously fantastic dialogue."—*Frivolous Views*

Just Three Words

"I can sum up my reading experience with *Just Three Words* in exactly that: I. LOVED. IT."—*Bookaholics-Not-So-Anonymous*

"A beautiful and downright hilarious tale about two very relatable women looking for love."—*Sharing Is Caring Book Reviews*

Ready or Not

"The third book was the best of the series. Melissa Brayden has some work cut out for her when writing a book after this one."
—*Fantastic Book Reviews*

By the Author

Waiting in the Wings

Heart Block

How Sweet It Is

First Position

Strawberry Summer

Soho Loft Romances:

Kiss the Girl

Just Three Words

Ready or Not

Seven Shores Romances:

Eyes Like Those

Hearts Like Hers

Sparks Like Ours

Love Like This

Visit us at www.boldstrokesbooks.com

LOVE LIKE THIS

by

Melissa Brayden

2018

ISBN 13: 978-1-63555-018-4

This Trade Paperback Original Is Published By
Bold Strokes Books, Inc.
P.O. Box 249
Valley Falls, NY 12185

First Edition: October 2018

Credits
Editor: Lynda Sandoval
Production Design: Stacia Seaman
Cover Design by Jeanine Henning

Acknowledgments

As I approached the last book in the Seven Shores series, I did so with happy-sadness. Happy to complete the journey, yet sad for it all to end. I've enjoyed my time with Isabel, Taylor, Autumn, Kate, Gia, Elle, Hadley, and Spencer. What I came up with for book four might be a little bit different from what the readers might expect, but it's my hope that you'll enjoy the journey, twists and turns and all!

I want to extend a warm thank you to the team of professionals at Bold Strokes Books for their guidance and understanding. I wrote this book very, very pregnant, and was humbled by the behind-the-scenes creative process and how much everyone along the way was willing to give to help me reach the finish line. I also send buckets of love to my friends and family, who were there with words of encouragement when I truly needed them. It's so nice to have good people, and thereby a fantastic support system, on my side. I'm simply the luckiest.

I would be remiss in not taking a few lines to thank the little guy, who was with me each and every day as I wrote *Love Like This*, a firm reminder of what love can be. Everett made his debut in the world in the midst of the editing process and was the biggest inspiration one could ask for. I hope he'll usher me along the path to many more books to come. It looks like I have a new sidekick.

When I think of my readers and the wonderful give and take I have with you, I feel nothing but an abundance of gratitude. Thank you for sticking with me, and for embracing this series! I've had a blast taking this ride with you. I hope you enjoy this final chapter.

For the Daydreamers

CHAPTER ONE

Hadley Cooper turned the page at lightning speed. She had only four minutes before she needed to grab her bag and leave for work. Unfortunately, this also happened to be the exact moment the time machine ran out of fuel and the portal to return to the present was slowly closing on her band of new book friends. She read quickly, her eyes sweeping across each sentence, gobbling up what happened next in the story as fast as she could. Her heart leapt into her throat as the suspense climbed to a terrifying crescendo. Janika, the protagonist, mashed the buttons, playing the control panel like a piano, anything to find a backup source that would give them enough power to make it home. Hadley exhaled and rolled her shoulders to ease the increasing tension. It didn't work. They weren't going to make it. With her hand covering her heart, she checked the clock.

"Oh no," she breathed. While the characters were out of time, so was she. She sadly closed the book, reminding herself that, on the bright side, she had something to look forward to later that night. After holding the book to her chest for a few tender moments, she placed it gently on her coffee table and gathered her belongings for the day ahead.

Silhouette, the posh boutique on Rodeo Drive that Hadley proudly assistant managed, would open for the day at eleven. She would need to be there by ten to ensure the displays were updated and her staff briefed on the week ahead. She had an extra burst of energy, however, as today was the day she would meet in person with the up-and-coming designer she was convinced would help change the image of the store. The store's owner and general manager, Trudy, had been hounding her for months about revising their current list of designers. Trudy wanted new lines that weren't stuffy, weren't geared to the over-forty-five crowd exclusively, and would give Silhouette an edgier appeal. No designer Hadley had presented her with thus far had fit the bill, and the pressure seemed to grow exponentially with each day that ticked by.

But this one was different. Spencer Adair came with a design book that left Hadley drooling. She would be new on the LA retail scene and came with a cult following on social media where she promoted her work, which she sold entirely from her own website. Making the leap to retail was a big deal, and Hadley wanted to be on the inside track. She was confident that once Trudy saw the same innovation that Hadley had, she'd be thrilled with Hadley's find, and Silhouette would burst onto the forefront of the younger market, shooting it into the stratosphere of Rodeo history. At least, that's how she imagined it would all play out, and dreaming was everything to Hadley. She lived for those pie-in-the-sky possibilities.

"Someone's in a hurry," Gia Malone said, as Hadley dashed from her apartment. The two had been next-door neighbors on the second floor of the Seven Shores apartment complex for close to three years now and best friends for nearly all of that time. Gia's long dark hair was down that morning and she wore cut-off shorts and a bikini top, blending nicely with the August temperatures. In her right hand, she carried the remnants of what Hadley recognized as a protein smoothie that would usher Gia into her workout. As a professional surfer, she kept in tip-top shape.

"I got lost in my book," Hadley said remorsefully. "I should have been on the road and sitting in traffic fifteen minutes ago, but it was so good I couldn't stop."

"I have a feeling you'll smile your way out of any true consequence."

Hadley sighed, straightening her designer black dress paired with designer heels, aka her upscale work clothes, not to be confused with her more comfortable Hadley-at-home persona. "But I'm also meeting with that new designer this morning, the one Elle recommended." Elle Britton was Gia's fellow surfer on the Women's Pro Tour. The two were major competitors. She also happened to be Gia's girlfriend, and the love of her life.

"Oh yeah? I didn't realize that had panned out."

"It hasn't yet, but it will!" Hadley said with a smile and sprinkle of determination. "This is gonna be the one that gets Trudy off my back and puts Silhouette on the map." She headed down the outdoor stairs to the central courtyard of the complex. "Gonna be a fantastic day, G," she called over her shoulder.

"Yeah, it is. You're gonna rock this meeting. Hit me up later tonight with all the details. We're gonna want to hear all about it."

She realized that meant Elle would be over, which was perfect! She adored Elle.

"Off to work, I take it," Autumn Carpenter said as Hadley scurried past the adjacent coffee shop, the Cat's Pajamas, on the way to the parking lot. Hadley beamed at Autumn, another of her three best friends. Autumn stood on the sidewalk, phone in hand, wearing her work apron over her ginormous stomach. The twins she was carrying were due the following week, and Hadley was about ready to burst herself—in her case from warm fuzzies and uncontrolled excitement.

"Yes!" Hadley said, with a smile. "I have a much-anticipated meeting with a designer before opening. Any signs of labor? Contractions? Nesting?" It was her standard series of questions.

Autumn touched her stomach. "While there is certainly a one-on-one soccer match going on in there, no labor pains yet."

Hadley nodded. "You know that the second you feel them—"

"I am to call you immediately." Autumn ran a probably tired hand through her untamed red curls. "I know the drill, Had. You remind me daily."

Hadley kissed her cheek with a smack. "I adore you, so please don't spend too much time on your feet today. Call that firefighting wife of yours for backup. You need to rest up for the big day."

"Yes, ma'am. Have a great day at work."

Hadley beamed, warmed by the sentiment. "Thanks! You, too." With a final touch of Autumn's stomach, aka her future honorary niece and nephew, she was on her way to work, singing loudly to eighties music as she maneuvered through the tangled traffic of LA. Making good time, she arrived at the store just a minute or two after ten.

Silhouette was a posh boutique, decorated very simply on purpose, with a black and white color scheme. Trudy was emphatic that minimalism was the way to go. The 800-square-foot store came with retail space on a lower level and a set of four wide stairs that led to a plush sitting area of white couches around a grouping of full-length and well-lit mirrors, allowing their clients to lounge with friends as they tried on a variety of pieces, with the help of a store attendant at their beck and call, of course. A little white wine never hurt a sale either. On Saturdays, the store was strictly appointment only, with a less formal structure during the week, in which the retail space was open to foot traffic from Rodeo Drive. Sometimes that meant traffic from tour buses that never bought anything, but secretly, Hadley liked the tourist visits. The friendly faces always managed to brighten her day.

"Good morning!" Hadley said with a smile, as she strolled through the retail space.

Daisy, one of her most valued employees, was already hard at work organizing their newest shipment of designer gloves for display. The hand mannequins were always such a pain that she was grateful Daisy had taken the initiative without having been asked. Daisy was a keeper.

"Morning, Had. Hey, have you seen the new Gucci blacks?" She held up a striking pair of long leather gloves. Hadley felt herself light up all over as she took the new arrivals in her hands reverently. She examined one side and then the other, taking in the richness of the leather and the intricate stitching.

"Wow! They're even softer than last year." She took a deep inhale, never tiring of that expensive leather aroma. She couldn't afford gloves like these herself, but she could certainly enjoy being in their presence for a little while. "I predict we're out by the end of next week."

"At the latest," Daisy said with a grin. "Even with my store discount, I sadly cannot justify these guys."

"Yeah, but there are knockoffs all over town."

Daisy winked. "Don't think I'm not already putting out feelers."

Hadley had always liked Daisy. Petite in size and barely five foot one, she wore her curly brown hair in a variety of interesting styles that kept Hadley impressed at her skill with a brush. But it was Daisy's positive, willing-to-try-anything-for-the-good-of-the-team mentality that kept Hadley grateful for her support at Silhouette. They dealt with a lot of demanding clients, rich women who were used to getting exactly what they wanted. Some employees didn't do so well in that arena and balked at being talked to a certain way. Working on Rodeo Drive required a certain finesse, Hadley had learned over the years, and a willingness to bounce back from an afternoon with a difficult customer. Daisy, however, with her great big smile and patience for weeks, was the perfect person for their sales floor. In fact, Hadley saw a lot of herself in Daisy. They'd both graduated from the Fashion Institute of Design and Merchandising right there in LA. They'd both started in sales, with Hadley working her way up to management. She had no doubt that Daisy, if she put in the time, could do the same.

Hadley checked her watch. "Miranda should be in in the next thirty minutes. Get her to help you."

"Yay," Daisy said, with a modicum of enthusiasm. Miranda not only took her job very seriously, she also took the rest of the world that way. Hadley had less confidence in her ability to succeed in the high-end retail world, but time would tell. "You headed back to the office?"

"Yes. I have a meeting with a new designer in just a bit. Spencer Adair. When she arrives, will you show her back?"

"On it," Daisy said, with a smile. Her focus was immediately pulled away so she could awe at another new pair of gloves.

Hadley laughed. "One day, Daisy, we're gonna be able to afford all the gloves."

"I'm holding you to that."

Hadley excused herself to the small office at the back of the store that she shared with Trudy. Given that Trudy didn't clock many hours in the store itself, Hadley had taken firm possession of the space. As she took her seat behind the cherrywood sculpted desk, she smiled at the photo of her dads, the one they'd sent from Cabo on their most recent vacation. They looked sun-kissed and blissfully happy. She then turned to the photo of her along with her three best friends, Gia, Autumn, and Isabel, snapped on the beach the year prior. Isabel had her tongue out and Autumn was laughing at something off camera. One of her favorites. Staring at those all-important people in her life was how Hadley preferred to begin her day. She moved on to email next, including purchase orders, delivery schedules, and ad updates. Just as she'd slogged her way through a slew of recent orders and receipts, Daisy knocked lightly on her open door. "Hadley, Spencer Adair is here to see you."

"Perfect!" Hadley said, beaming. She stood and waited as the designer she'd been dying to meet appeared. Her smile dimmed slightly because Spencer's online photos hadn't done her justice. Spencer Adair was…striking in every sense of the word. Her midnight hair was parted in the middle, but she wore it swept onto her right shoulder. She had large, luminous brown eyes, perfect brown skin that she must have dedicated some serious time to, and a soft smile on her perfect lips. There was something else there, though, and Hadley had picked up on it during their earlier phone call: confidence. Spencer Adair carried herself with a ton of it for someone who was likely under thirty, as though she knew exactly what she was out to accomplish and would own this city in no time.

"Hadley Cooper?" she asked.

Oh, that was a smooth voice. Velvet-like and easy. Spencer would be great on a nighttime radio call-in show. "That's me. Nice to finally meet you in person." She extended her hand and Spencer accepted it with a firm shake. Hadley, for reasons she wasn't clear on, felt the need to wiggle her toes. Something about the warmth of the touch. She swallowed the unexpected toe-wiggling reaction. "As we discussed, I'm a big fan of your designs. You have so much talent." She gestured to the arm chair across from her desk. "Please, have a seat."

"Happy to," Spencer said. She'd brought a hanging garment bag and her portfolio along with her. "I took a look around the store, which, of course, I've heard a lot about."

"And?"

"It's a beautiful space. Impressive." She hesitated. "I'm struggling to figure out why you're interested in meeting with *me*."

"Well, to start with, because you're good at what you do, and we want the best designers we can find."

"Thank you."

Spencer had incredibly long eyelashes, which was beside the point of the meeting. Seriously, though. Look at them. She did. Oh, how she looked! Hadley blinked and refocused. "And you bring fresh, new perspective to the fashion world."

"I see." She paused. "But if I may speak freely and possibly save us a great deal of time."

"Of course," Hadley said, curious to hear what had Spencer so clearly hung up.

"Please don't take offense, but the store seems a little…white. You may or may not have noticed, but I'm not."

Hadley opened her mouth and closed it again, not sure what the correct response was in this scenario. She decided to just go with honesty. "I know exactly who you are, and I love what I've seen of your work online, from the runway videos, the shots of your customers wearing your clothes. All of it."

Spencer nodded and seemed to accept the compliment. "You think I'm a fit for this place? Because looking around out there…" She didn't finish the sentence, but she didn't have to. Her facial expression said it all, and honestly? Spencer wasn't off base. A good portion of their clientele were white women over the age of forty, and their slate of designers could best be described as…conservative, if not stuffy, to cater to that very market. But it was one of the things Trudy was hoping to adjust when she charged Hadley with the task of bringing in new lines, new designers. Their goal was to appeal to a wider market so the store had longevity, an eye on the future, and an appeal to a wider, younger audience. Their price point wasn't exactly universal, and that wasn't likely to change. But with real estate what it was on Rodeo Drive, they had to keep the lights on somehow. Spencer produced high-quality clothes that came with the sophistication that could command a high-dollar price tag.

"I understand why you would think Silhouette may not be a match for your work," Hadley said, seeing the store through Spencer's eyes. She placed both palms on her chest. "I wholeheartedly understand. But I think our interest in your designs is a signal that we're trying to move out of that unfortunate and boring niche." Spencer regarded Hadley with a dubious stare. She didn't seem sold. But the reality was, they both knew this kind of retail exposure would be huge for an up-and-comer like Spencer who'd never ventured from online sales. Retail was a hard and expensive market to break into. Rodeo Drive was where everyone wanted to be…eventually, when they could manage it. Spencer had a chance at that *now*, right off the bat. It would be career changing, and Hadley couldn't imagine her passing it up. No one would.

"Fair enough," Spencer said, reaching for her garment bag. "Would you like to look over my new line? None of these samples have been viewed by anyone yet, but you seemed so interested. I'd be lying if I said I wasn't flattered when you called."

"I'd love to." Hadley laughed. "I've been staring at that bag since you got here." A minor lie. She'd been staring at Spencer herself, which was probably rude and obvious and not at all how she was brought up to behave. But the clothes had her doing a happy dance, too. Hadley stood and excitedly came around the desk as Spencer hung a variety of pieces around her office. Hadley took her time exploring, studying the lines, which were classic in many ways, and the textures, which seemed to be a huge part of Spencer's point of view as a designer. However, it was the color combinations and the accents that made each piece pop. Spencer's work was beautiful, unique, and as always, pushing the envelope just a tad. Bare shoulders were in this season and her work showcased them, a nod to the mainstream. But in little glimpses, nothing gratuitous. She also embraced a wider pant leg in the age of slim, which in Hadley's opinion was a breath of fresh air. A step away from the overt trend. But above all else, her color choices were bold and they worked. But were they universal enough? Did they have to be? Those questions circled her brain.

"I love your use of green," Hadley said, running her hand down the soft sleeve of a peasant shirt. She wasn't afraid of riskier choices. That was clear and a hallmark of her breadth of work.

"The promise of spring," Spencer said. "I've always looked forward to that time of year when everything starts waking up again, and that sentiment was my touchstone when designing this year."

Hadley surveyed the room, catching the smallest elements of nature woven in. "I can see it throughout now that you've pointed me to it. It gives everything…a common texture. A link."

Spencer smiled. "Yeah, well, I like looking back at my work and knowing exactly what inspired me at the time. It's important to me."

"I admire that." Hadley took a top off the hanger and felt the weight of it. "What I also like? You don't cut corners with fabrics."

"No. I'm a fanatic about fabric. I only use the best, which is why my price point is on the higher side. It hasn't been great for my margins, but I'm willing to make less money for the sake of good clothes. I figure the business side of things will take care of itself eventually."

"Precarious," Hadley said. "But I get it." She studied the designs. "I love what I see here, and with your permission I'd like to hold on to a few of these to present to Trudy Day, the owner, who has the final say."

Spencer shoved her hands in the back pockets of her gray jeans. Her outfit was perfection. An off-the-shoulder cream blouse, the jeans, and taupe heels with the most interesting design snaking around the side. The heels gave Spencer the height edge, but it wasn't by much.

"What do you think the chances are she'll bite?" Spencer asked.

"Trudy? If she sees what I see, then I think you'll be hearing from me soon with good news. She's been pushing for someone just like you for a while."

Spencer's conservative smile blossomed into a full-on sincere grin. Hadley wiggled her toes. "I'll leave the samples with you, then." She extended her hand a final time. "It was a pleasure, Ms. Cooper. Thank you for seeing me."

Hadley blushed. "Oh, Hadley, please. That's what everyone calls me. Had works, too. Either, really."

"Hadley it is."

Spencer turned to go and then flipped back around as if on impulse.

"How long do you think it might take, before I hear back?" She cared and it showed.

"Give me three days."

Spencer seemed okay with that, nodding several times. "Thanks, again."

"Of course." She watched as Spencer Adair retreated from her office, leaving her alone with those fabulous pieces. Hadley had to restrain herself from trying on one of the tops then and there, though they would need to see them on people at some point before making any firm commitment.

"These are hers?" Daisy asked, stepping into the office.

"All of them. What do you think?"

Daisy walked the space, taking in each design. "I love them. Look at the asymmetry on this one. It has a camo feel, but it's not entirely that either."

"They're unique. Multifaceted."

"And amazing," Daisy said, moving hurriedly to the next piece. "Where can I buy this top?"

"Hopefully here if I can convince Trudy."

"A no-brainer. She's going to love them! How could she not?" Daisy asked, her eyes dancing with the possibility. "I could sell these clothes for days if given the chance."

"That's exactly what I was thinking." In truth, Hadley hadn't been more excited by a find in years. Yes, the designers they had on their roster were fine, and sold decently, but they were nothing to write home about. If they stuck with them, they'd never evolve with the times, and Silhouette would evolve into a strictly older women's store as their clients aged.

Spencer Adair was different, and Hadley was ready to put her on the map. She tapped her lips and smiled. A shiver moved through her. "Daisy, today is an important day. I can feel it."

The cell phone she kept tucked away while at work buzzed, pulling her away from the trajectory of the conversation. "My dad," she said apologetically to Daisy, who nodded and gave her the office.

"Hi, Dad," Hadley said, after clicking over. She spoke to her parents somewhere between once and ten times a day, depending on their supply of downtime in retirement. Dad called more often, as he was a little more sentimental, but Papa stepped it up when jealousy flared.

"Hey, Sunshine. Have you ever had a halogen lamp?" he asked, without waiting for a return greeting.

"I have. Why do you ask?"

"We're considering one for the den but didn't want to border on gaudy if we could avoid it, and with your sense of style, I knew you'd be the one to ask."

"I say go for it. They're fairly universal in terms of style, and provide a lot of light. With all the reading you both do, it would be a great source of illumination without distracting from your personal design."

"That's what I said. Speaking of, the new Stephen King is out and eight thousand pages, but I love it more than cheesecake, which you know comes with a large amount of love."

"He's been reading nonstop," a deeper voice said.

Aha. They'd passed the phone.

"Hey, Papa!" Hadley said, with a smile. "Just make sure he's stopping to sleep and eat. You know how consumed he gets."

"Well, he's eaten three slices of cheesecake since yesterday so I think we're okay."

"Four," Dad said, taking the phone back. "And I have no issue owning it. Will we see you this weekend?"

"I'll be by on Sunday."

"Great. Your Aunt Jodie will be here with her new boyfriend, the one with the unfortunate piercings, and we were thinking of cooking out. I'll get your favorites."

"Oh, you don't have to go to a lot of trouble." This was a losing battle, but it felt better to protest anyway.

"I do, too. You're my kid, and I want to. Oh, and Papa got a haircut you just have to see. I actually can't wait."

"Too short?"

"Way too short. I'm taking lots of photos to commemorate the occasion. Hey, do you want those ice skates in the garage? We're trying to clean out the space as much as possible."

She definitely did. Who knew when one needed last-minute ice skates? "Yep. I'll take them with me when I'm there."

"Perfect. I love you, Sunshine."

"Love you back. Give my love to Papa."

"I'll tell him."

She clicked off the call that was like so many others with her dads, upbeat and a little all over the map. The shorthand was everything.

It was how they communicated best and she wouldn't change their relationship for anything. She glanced around her office at the many pieces from Spencer Adair's new line and felt the excitement bubble all over again. She punched the air a few times, channeling her inner Rocky, shuffling her feet, and dodging imaginary blows like a pro. Yessiree. Things were definitely on the upswing, and Hadley wasn't about to lose momentum now.

❖

The line at Jamba Juice was insane, but then it was inching close to lunchtime, which had everyone out and about in the sunny LA weather. Spencer didn't care about the wait. She'd had a fantastic meeting with Hadley Cooper, and Silhouette, of all places, was interested in *her*. Whether she thought the store was the best fit or not, this was a lot to take in. Her phone buzzed in her front pocket.

"Hey, Mama." She smiled into the phone, her excitement from the earlier meeting still spilling over.

"You didn't call," her mother said, worry in her voice. "Is the meeting over?"

Spencer smiled. "Yes, ma'am. It went well. The assistant manager thinks I have a good shot at receiving an order."

"On Rodeo Drive. My baby!" Spencer held the phone away from her ear momentarily and smiled at the customer in front of her. "My mom," she mouthed. He offered her a halfhearted thumbs-up and turned back around.

Spencer chuckled. "We're not there *yet*, but things are looking up. Just the fact that they're interested in me is flattering. Treating myself to a smoothie."

"Of course it's flattering! When I get home, I'm going to bake you a pie. This is a big day." Her mother worked as a successful real estate broker who'd actually held her own in the housing crisis a few years back and lived to tell the tale. In addition to knowing everything about LA real estate, she also knew everything about making the perfect pie. Spencer felt this was a winning combo and had always looked up to her mother on both counts. Business and baking. To say she and her mother were close was an understatement.

"I don't know that I have time for pie, Mama. Got a lot of orders to fill once I get back to my apartment." The move to retail would be a huge one if it happened, but she couldn't forget her bread and butter, the one that had her packing a lot of boxes for her vast customer base on her online store. As a one-woman shop, she'd done a remarkable job, handling every aspect of the business without having to spend money on extra help. She'd always prided herself on being a go-getter, and maybe this time it was about to pay off.

"I'll eat it in your honor, then. Gonna go with apple spice!"

"My favorite. You're the best, Mama, but I gotta go. It's almost my turn to order."

"Call me as soon as you hear something and not a minute beyond."

"Yes, ma'am." She clicked off the call.

"Welcome to Jamba Juice! What can I get you?"

"I'll take a cucumber orange cooler with a vitamin D boost, please," she told the counter guy who had welcomed her about three times since she'd entered the store.

"Coming right up," he said with gusto, and bounced away to make her drink, like Tigger of Jamba Juice.

She'd say one thing for the place, they had the market cornered on perky. She thought back on her meeting with Hadley Cooper, deciding that she'd probably do great at Jamba Juice herself. Blond hair well past her shoulders, piercing blue eyes, and a bundle of vivacious, welcoming energy. But it wasn't put on. At least not that Spencer could tell. Hadley came off as kind and genuine, both on their initial phone call and at their one-on-one. She bought Hadley's excitement surrounding her designs, and that felt kind of…contagious. But she wasn't one to judge someone so early on. She'd been burned enough in life, especially in the fashion industry, which was pretty much eat or be eaten.

"This drink is ready for you! This drink is ready for you! This drink is ready, dear Spencer A. Your cucumber cooler loves you, too." She blinked, doing her best to put up with his ridiculous song. She'd never really been into ridiculous, being a more serious-minded individual. She smiled anyway.

"Thanks."

"Come back again," he sang, with jazz hands, to the tune of "And many more." She nodded in his direction and wondered who'd hurt him.

The cooler was a refreshing cap off to the afternoon, but her evening would be spent in the trenches, packing boxes, filling orders, sending confirmations, and making sure her social media ads were running on schedule. Oh! And she needed to post her latest giveaway. Contests always seemed to garner attention, and more attention meant more page views, and more word of mouth, and more orders, and more money. Her work was never done and she loved every second of it.

At midnight, she surveyed her apartment. With several towering stacks of boxes by her door ready for shipment, and fabrics of all colors laid across her couch, dining room table, and floor along with tape measures, scale rulers, scissors, and sketches, the place looked nothing like a residence and more like a workshop populated by elves. Spencer wore it like a badge of honor.

She gave her neck a soothing roll from side to side. Tomorrow there was lots of work to continue, meaning she better steal what sleep she could. She picked up her cat, Minnie Mouse, and gave her a smacking kiss. "That's because you were a thoughtful and quiet assistant tonight."

She trudged sleepily to her room, cat in hand. The fashion world waited for no one. As she lay in bed that night, she replayed her meeting with Hadley once, twice, and a third time for good measure. She fell asleep with a hopeful smile on her face, understanding that she had come to a unique place in her life, a crossroads of her own making. Having options was an exciting reward, and the prospect of moving beyond the empire she'd established to something even bigger triggered a shiver. The really, really good kind.

CHAPTER TWO

"So, how'd the thing go with the lady-lady?" Isabel Chase asked, two days later at Breakfast Club. Though Hadley and her best friends lived wildly different lives during the day, they did their best to meet each morning at the Cat's Pajamas for coffee, baked goods, and gossip. It kept them centered, in touch, and ready to blast off to their different professions each morning. In Isabel's case, to Paramount Studios, where she wrote and produced one of the hottest shows on television, *The Subdivision.*

Hadley studied her patiently. "What lady-lady about what thing? You're speaking early morning Isabel again."

Isabel's eyes got wide. "The lady about the thing, and the new designer with the good clothes and promise. You were nervous, then excited. It was a whole deal," she said, around a mouthful of blueberry muffin. "Anyway, how'd it go?"

Hadley smiled, translating the nonsensical version of Isabel, who was often useless until caffeine took hold. Right on cue, Steve, Autumn's number two guy and the assistant manager at Pajamas, delivered Izzy's latte, along with Hadley's sugary caramel mocha. "Thanks, Steve!" Hadley said brightly, perfectly capable of mustering the cheer before the coffee. Life was too short to be anything less than friendly and warm, principles her fathers raised her on. She turned back to Isabel. "I believe you're referencing that new designer Elle recommended."

Isabel sipped her coffee and closed her eyes, allowing it to wash over her. "And there it is." She opened them again. "Yes, that one."

"What about me?" Elle asked, approaching their table with Gia. They were both in shorts and hoodies, which meant they had swimsuits on underneath and would be heading to the beach for training after breakfast. As two of the top surfers in the world, and competitors themselves, they rarely took days off.

"I met with your friend Spencer Adair earlier this week," Hadley told Elle. "She's an amazing find and I owe you everything for the tip. I'm going to make you cookies by way of thanks. Chocolate chip ones!"

"Yay!" Elle said, fist in the air. "I love it when you bake me things."

"I'm presenting her stuff to Trudy today. Fingers crossed for me." Elle tucked a strand of her blond hair behind her ear and lit up. "Spence is gonna be thrilled if this goes through."

"And how do you guys know each other?" Isabel asked Elle.

"Oh, Spencer and I went to high school together. She's one of those people you can lose touch with but pick right back up again like no time has gone by at all. She's good people, but she doesn't mess around. She's got goals and charts and plans."

Hadley nodded. "She's clearly driven, and not at all afraid to speak her mind."

Elle grinned. "Sounds like Spencer. She's always had a firm head on her shoulders. Knew she was gay by the time we hit tenth grade. If only I'd had her self-awareness."

"Then you might not have been single and fallen for me," Gia said, in uncharacteristic meekness.

Almost as if she couldn't resist, Elle leaned over and kissed her. "It wouldn't have mattered when I realized it, I definitely would have found you. No matter what it took or where you were."

Hadley covered her swelling heart. Romance in all forms was her complete and utter undoing, and seeing Gia so happy these days with Elle had the thing ready to burst. Then there was Autumn, who'd been so happily married to Kate for almost a year now as they waited on their twins to be born. And of course, before that, Isabel had fallen madly in love with her boss, television producer extraordinaire Taylor Andrews. The two were practically inseparable. Yet here Hadley sat, alone, cheering everyone else on from the sidelines of singledom. Not that she minded. One day her person would come along. No question about it. She just wondered why it seemed to be taking them so long.

Two arms snaked around her neck from behind. She knew that hug and leaned into it. "Hi," she said, looking up at Autumn, around her stomach. "How are you feeling, Mom-to-be?"

"Like I'm ready for this all to be over and for these giant, unruly kids to be here so I can kiss their cheeks and love them. It's impossible to get comfortable. I'm about to abandon the concept of shoes altogether. You might find me lying in the courtyard like a beached whale. Call me Willy. I'll answer."

"Sit down, Willy," Isabel said, jumping up and ushering Autumn to her customary chair at their table. "We can all imagine you already hugged us. The hugging credit is there. No reason to remain on your feet longer than necessary."

"Good to know." Autumn sat down with a weary sigh. It was likely she'd come in before six a.m. to open the place, which was insane, given how far along she was. "I think it might be time to hand the store off to Steve until delivery."

"You think that might be a good idea?" Isabel said with a laugh. She'd been pushing Autumn to go on maternity leave for a while now.

"Good call," Gia said. "Time for you to do nothing but relax."

Hadley sighed in relief. She, too, had been waiting to hear that statement for weeks now, but Autumn was a stubborn one who refused to leave her business, which she loved beyond all measure, until the last possible second, throwing Hadley's worried heart into overdrive. "I'm going to bring you a basket of bath bombs later, and I order you to use them. Start with the blue glittery one. It's called Moonlight Madness and it will make your life feel like it's new again. Oh! And play some flute music while you soak. Does it for me every time."

"Bless the blond girl," Autumn said, with a hand over her heart. "Bless her sweet soul. If I didn't have pregnancy brain, I might even remember her name."

"Flute lunatic works," Isabel said.

"How's Kate?" Gia asked. "I haven't seen her around much."

"She's been picking up extra shifts at the firehouse any chance she gets, which will allow her to take more time off when the kiddos are here."

"Smart," Elle said, with a thoughtful look. "When I have kids one day, I want to do the same. Take some time for just them."

Autumn lit up. "So, does that sound like a game plan in the works?" She looked from Gia to Elle.

"I wouldn't put it on your calendar, but maybe," Gia said, with a small smile on her lips. She looked over at Elle and took her hand. "Down the road. Yeah, I think we definitely want kids."

"Who's going to carry?" Hadley asked, sold on the idea instantly. She leaned forward with her chin in her hands, eager for details.

"I think when we decide we're ready, I will," Elle said, as pink touched her cheeks. "I've always wanted to be pregnant."

"God, I can't wait to see that," Gia said, looking skyward. The glow coming off of her could light up the whole block in an outage.

Autumn pointed at her stomach, eyes wide. "If you hurry, that little one can be friends with these guys."

"Do the mysterious twins have names yet?" Isabel asked. "Taylor suggested Donald and Daisy, but I like Elphaba and Fiyero."

"Jack and Diane," Gia offered.

"Jon Snow and Khaleesi," Elle said with a grin, followed by a smolder.

Hadley shook her head. "Weirdos, no. Those are all couples. You can't name the twins after couples."

"She has a point," Autumn said. "But no names yet. I might need to meet them first. Get some experience with their out-in-the-world vibe."

Isabel dropped her head onto the table with a thud. "Fine. Thus, we wait."

They'd learned a few months back at a gender reveal party on the beach that Kate and Autumn were expecting a boy and a girl, which had Hadley shopping for them like a maniac. She'd singlehandedly purchased an entire summer wardrobe for both babies, each item selected to compliment the outfit of the other twin, obviously. She'd matched accent colors, and hints of patterns, and even tossed in a few theme outfits, her favorite. With Fourth of July right around the corner, how could she resist little red, white, and blue top hats? No one could. It would be blasphemous.

"What about you guys?" Hadley asked Isabel. Of all the couples, she and Taylor had now been together the longest. "Any thoughts of little ones? Tiny creative writer feet prancing through the studio crafting conflict? That could be fun!"

Isabel smiled. "Right now, we have two little ones with furry feet to worry about. Fat Tony is making great strides on his social skills, and Raisin has mastered 'snuggle eyes' like no one's business. I think that's enough. Plus, I'd want to be married first. Start with that foundation and build from there."

"And when is that happening?" Autumn asked, her eyes hopeful. "I'd be happy to do the coffee for the reception."

Isabel glanced at her watch. "Would you look at the time? Story meeting in a little over an hour, and with traffic, I'm already gonna be late. Gotta jet."

"Someone's scared of commitment," Gia called to Isabel's retreating form.

"If it ain't broke," Isabel called back.

Autumn turned to the remaining group. "Oh, yeah. She's terrified."

"Totally," Gia murmured. "What about you, Had?"

Hadley glanced from Gia to Autumn. "What about me?"

"Any big bang yet?"

She smiled at the use of the term that dated all the way back to her adolescence, when she'd decided that meeting that special someone would surely feel like the Big Bang they'd learned about in science class: unexpected, earth shattering, and all encompassing. Her dads had agreed and encouraged her quest. "Strangely, not in the last twenty-four hours. One day she'll come along. I think the universe just wants me to be ready for her."

"I love how optimistic you are," Autumn said. "And in my opinion, that optimism will be rewarded kindly."

Hadley returned her chin to her hand and sighed happily. "Wouldn't that just be awesome? I'm holding on for that."

"Wait," Gia said, bringing the whole thing to a stop. "When exactly does the big bang happen? Is this an as-soon-as-you-lay-eyes-on-them kinda thing, or can it happen later? For me, it was definitely later. I wanted to kill Elle, well, until I wanted to make out with her. I think it took a little time for me to get it, though, that this was my big bang."

"Same," Elle said, glancing at Gia. "We knew each other for years first."

This was a great question, and one Hadley wasn't sure she had the answer to, having never experienced the big bang herself. "I think it can happen at any point really. It doesn't necessarily have to mean that you're in love. The big bang is just that moment when you know that you're on the path to your person, that this one is different from all the others." Hadley paused and grinned. "But when it happens, you know. I'm confident of that. That's what makes it the big bang."

"Oh, I most certainly knew," Autumn said, fanning herself, her eyes darkening with lust. "It was the second time I saw Kate, when she sauntered into the coffee shop looking like Kate does with all that quiet confidence and eye contact for days." Autumn looked like she might combust on the spot from the memory alone.

"Now you're getting me all hot and bothered," Hadley said, "and I haven't even had the big bang yet."

"Somehow," Gia said, "I have this feeling that it's not far off for you."

"And after that you get to just keep banging and banging and banging," Autumn said. She and Gia shared a fist bump.

"I see what you did there," Hadley murmured into her coffee cup with a smile. Didn't sound so bad at all.

❖

Trudy Day breezed into Silhouette half an hour after she was scheduled to meet with Hadley, who'd waited patiently that afternoon, not at all surprised by her boss's disregard for time. She ran her hand through her severe dark brown bob and regarded the room with her wide-set eyes. Trudy believed that the world operated according to her schedule. Due to the money and power she wielded in high-end retail at only forty-eight years of age, it kind of did.

"Who did the glove display?" Trudy asked, with an air of distaste. Hadley studied the display, which was simple and elegant. Perfect for the store.

"Daisy, and she did a lovely job." Hadley had worked for Trudy long enough to know how to nudge her out of an unreasonable opinion. It worked most of the time.

"You don't think the beiges are too prominent on the right?" She placed a hand on her hip, signaling her struggle.

"I don't," Hadley said with a hint of serenity. "I was actually just thinking how pleasing the color layout delineation was earlier today. It's going to sell a lot of gloves."

Trudy nodded, probably zeroing in on the word *sell*. "If you think so. Which one is Daisy?"

"Friendly, petite, curly hair. A whiz at displays like this one."

"Right. The little short one. Keep an eye on her." Hadley quirked an eyebrow, unsure what that even meant. Trudy, meanwhile, stalked through the store en route to their shared office. "Well, I'm here," she tossed the words over her shoulder. "Isn't there a new designer you're just wild about? Let's get to it."

"Yes. I think you're going to love her," Hadley said, scurrying after Trudy in spite of her high-heeled Manolos. She presented Trudy with Spencer's portfolio and résumé and had the samples displayed in an order she thought showed a progression in story.

"Interesting," she said, taking in Spencer's book. "She's certainly no wallflower, is she?"

"Not at all, which is what I really like about her work. It stands out, yet it comes with an elegance we're known for at Silhouette, a sophistication that works for our clients. She's gonna be a hit, Trudy. She just needs a chance. I think we give her an order and see how it goes."

"Hmmm." Trudy flipped a few of the pages, which almost made Hadley cry out, because each page contained such vital information to who this designer was. It was important for Trudy to take the proper time in her assessment. Yet...she was Trudy, and not one for dwelling. Finally, she looked up at Hadley with a grimace. "I don't know."

Hadley nodded. She had prepared for this reaction. It was Trudy's second nature to balk at anything new and outside the box, even if it was precisely what she'd asked Hadley to find for her in the first place. It was up to Hadley to put Trudy's nerves to rest. She made sure her tone was gentle and full of understanding. "I get why you would hesitate. The bold colors, the edgier prints, some of the lines push the boundaries of what we're used to greenlighting for the store, but we're purposefully seeking out new designers that help us revamp our image, right? That's been the plan all along, and Spencer Adair is the perfect person to kick us in that new, innovative direction."

"It's a no from me," Trudy said, as if she'd just announced that the coffee was ready. "A worthy effort, Hadley, but a swing and a miss. Keep trying. Oh, and let me know when the new Dior scarves arrive. Text me immediately. It's dire." She grabbed her bag, and started for the door, probably mentally already moving on to her next appointment.

"Wait," Hadley said, following her. "Before you completely close the door on the idea, let me walk you through some of her inspiration. I think it really offers an insight into who we're dealing with on an artistic level and signals what we can expect in the future. Plus, we haven't even gone over the samples from her spring line, or the sales figures she's provided from online sales alone—where she's killing it, by the way. It's insane."

"I glanced at the samples," Trudy said, sounding bored. "The colors are just too bold, and she dabbles in prints, which you know is a pet peeve of mine. The world has too many prints! It's barbaric."

"Dior's entire spring and summer line is full of prints."

"Dior is *Dior*," she said haughtily.

"Don't be afraid of an occasional print from someone unknown."

"I'm not afraid of anything," Trudy said, straightening, and glancing around as if she smelled something unpleasant. It's what she did when she felt she was being challenged, and in a way, she was. Hadley believed in this designer and was willing to push back. She was always one to pick her battles with Trudy, and this was one she gladly selected. She narrowed her focus and dug in.

"What can I do to change your mind?" Hadley asked.

"I'd be willing to take another look if she can get me revised pieces in a month. That's not a lot of time, so I doubt it's even possible."

Hadley doubted it, too, but it was worth a shot. "Let me talk to her."

"Fine. But understand, it's a stretch."

Hadley nodded, but couldn't resist. "A stretch you wanted."

Trudy sighed, as if she'd been taxed so very much today already. "And maybe that was a mistake."

"It wasn't," Hadley said. "Give her a month."

With a curt nod, Trudy popped on her oversized Chanel sunglasses and strolled back to the front of the boutique. "Text me when the scarves arrive."

"Making a note right now," Hadley said, touching her temple. "It's dire."

"I don't like the gloves!" Trudy called without looking back. "Fire Daisy."

"Not going to fire Daisy," Hadley said calmly, as she strolled behind the reception desk.

Trudy paused in the doorway, defeated. "Then maybe less beige on the right side?"

"You got it."

Once Trudy left, Hadley placed a hand on top of her head and sighed. Hurricane Trudy had struck once again, and she now had a lot of work to do. No day like today to get started.

❖

"Minnie. We've talked about this. Leave those alone." Spencer stared hard at her mischievous cat who batted two of her Prismacolor pencils around like she was a three-year-old in a ball pit. "Do you realize how expensive those are, you maniac?" She snatched the stray pencils off the kitchen table and placed them back in the tin.

Minnie Mouse, her white cat with black ears, had pretty much adopted Spencer two years earlier simply by following her everywhere she went outside and never leaving her doorstep once Spencer went into her apartment. It was one way to find a home. Demand it. Cite squatter's rights. Refuse to leave. She admired the tenacity and had seen a little bit of herself in Minnie when she decided to invite her inside and make their arrangement a permanent one.

She turned back to her sketchpad and continued to add detail to the blue skirt, inspiration firing. She liked where this was going, biting her lower lip as she sketched. Honestly? When she imagined the fabric, she was thinking something sturdy, military inspired. Maybe with an accent of gold buttons, a concept she could run with for her entire fall line. Minnie Mouse leapt for the pencil in her hand. Spencer dodged the move handily. "Nice try, ninja cat." She reached for her phone, which had been buzzing incessantly for the last few moments.

"This is Spencer," she said, to the foreign number on her readout.

"Hi, Spencer! Hope your day is going well. It's Hadley."

Spencer sat up straighter, her senses on heightened alert. She'd been waiting for this call, for any sort of indication on whether she'd be getting an order from Silhouette. If so, there would be manufacturing details to hammer out, and money she'd have to front. Not that she hadn't planned for it; she had. "Hi, Hadley. Just getting some sketching in. How are things on your end?"

"I wondered if you had time to talk this afternoon?"

"Sure. I'm free right now. What would you like to discuss?" She held her breath, waiting for the verdict. If there was *something* to talk about, then the deal wasn't dead, right?

"I meant in person."

"Oh." A pause as she scrambled to decode what that could mean.

"I could come to you, or we could meet at the store, or somewhere in between."

Spencer surveyed her apartment/workshop/tornado central in horror. Sketches and fabric and swatches everywhere. It looked like a proper design studio had exploded. She pivoted. "Do you drink coffee?"

"Are you kidding?" Hadley practically shouted. "I know the perfect spot!"

An hour later, Spencer pushed open the door to a funky little coffee shop in Venice with a cat, of all things, playing a guitar and wearing what looked to be crazy pajamas on the sign out front. Points for creativity. She dug the vibe. If the coffee held up, she would make note of this place. She scanned the half-full portion of the cafe space and found Hadley in less than two seconds, waving with a friendly smile on her face. One thing was notably different about her, however. Gone were the upscale designer clothes, heels, and fancy hairstyle. This version of Hadley wore jeans, flip-flops, a soft purple T-shirt, with her hair down. Subtle waves caressed her face and fell down her back. It took Spencer a minute to adjust. The transformation was so…pleasing. Hadley was a person in the real world, living life, and a really beautiful one at that. This felt a little bit like running into your teacher at the mall and bracing against the impending crush.

Hadley stood, beaming as Spencer approached. "Hi, there! Any trouble finding the place?"

"Not at all. I'm pretty handy with my phone."

Hadley shook her head. "No one ever needs directions anymore. Technology is awesome. We're lucky." Hadley, Spencer realized, thought a lot of things were awesome. In fact, she was perpetually cheerful and optimistic in every conversation they'd had thus far. She couldn't decide if that was an endearing quality or annoying one. Not that it mattered. This was business. "What can I get you to drink?" Hadley asked.

"Oh," Spencer said, and waved her hand. "I can get it."

"No, no, no. I invited *you*. Entirely on my dime. I insist. I will throw a fit right here if I have to."

Spencer gave in. "To avoid the fit, I'll take a cappuccino."

"Good choice."

Hadley walked to the counter, and Spencer watched her go, only realizing moments later that she was blatantly staring. She gave her head a shake and scolded herself, deciding she needed to get out more, and maybe not check out her potential clients. She exhaled slowly, ruminating on what the next few minutes might mean for her future, her career, and her bank account, which, let's be honest, could use a boost.

"One cappuccino and one caramel mocha," Hadley said, placing the drinks on the table. The part in her hair left a strand drifting across one eye as she leaned over. She brushed it to the side, revealing her big, blue eyes. The action caused a pleasant stirring in Spencer. Hadley was really pretty.

"Thank you," Spencer said, and lifted the hot mug to her lips.

"Wait," Hadley said, eyebrows near her hairline.

Spencer froze.

"You're going to burn your mouth."

"I'll risk it," she told Hadley, and took a sip. The hot liquid settled on her tongue, and the flavor spread out strong and bold. "This place is no joke," she said, as much to the cup itself as to Hadley. She lifted the mug. "Amazing brew."

"Everyone says that. My friend, Autumn, is the owner and spends hours coming up with the perfect flavor profiles and roasting times. It's her life's passion."

Spencer nodded, identifying entirely. "I suppose we all have those."

"Speaking of yours, I have good and bad news."

"Bad first." She exhaled, not liking the direction this was heading. "Tell me."

Hadley didn't hesitate, but her features softened to sooth the blow. "Trudy didn't go for the line as is."

Just as she'd thought. Her clothes didn't fit in at Silhouette. Her gut instinct had been correct. "How is there good news after that?" Her gaze fell to the table as she attempted to recover. Her spirits catapulted.

Hadley nodded sympathetically. "I get that you're probably demoralized and a little pissed off about that, but the door isn't closed, which is why I called. She's willing to take another look at the line with a few small changes."

Spencer sighed, not sure she could stomach this. "What kind of changes? I've never really compromised myself for a client."

"A slight tone down in color, and maybe the subtraction of a pattern or two." Spencer opened her mouth to object, but Hadley held up her hand. "I get it. This is your work, your vision, *your* passion, which is why I'm offering to help."

Spencer made sure not to balk visibly, but in her head was a pretty aggressive *hell no*. "I don't collaborate. It's not my thing. No offense."

"It wouldn't be that. Think of it as a temporary consultation. I'm a fan of what you do, Spencer, and I also have a great big desire to see Silhouette move into a more accessible direction. I think I might be able to help bring those two things a little closer together."

While everything in Spencer wanted to push back, finish her cappuccino, thank Hadley for her time, and get the hell out of there, there was a viable part of her that wanted to take the next big step, and seize the opportunity. Was she capable of swallowing her pride and making a few adjustments to her work in order make it out of a niche market and into the larger fashion world? Damn it. She was actually considering this crazy thing. "We're not talking an entire redesign, because if that's the case I have to respectfully decline."

"No," Hadley said. "Some adjusting, which admittedly will take some work."

"You're telling me."

"You have a month."

Spencer nearly spit out her coffee. "A month for sketches, or a month for samples?"

Hadley winced. "Samples would be ideal."

"You realize we're talking about fashion. Clothes. Not pancakes you just sent back to the kitchen."

"I do." Hadley reached across the table and covered Spencer's hand which, in a weird way, seemed to quickly calm her. She wasn't a casual toucher, and the gesture caught her off guard. But her breathing slowed, as did her heart rate. She focused on Hadley's kind eyes and that helped focus her. "I think this could be a very good thing for everyone, and I just want to help all I can."

Spencer nodded, her thoughts shooting off in a million different directions like a batch of wayward fireworks. She ran her index finger around the ring of her mug, letting the heat from the coffee warm her wrist. She flicked her gaze to Hadley. "Can I think about it? Mull it over?"

"Of course, but we don't have a lot of time."

"You did mention that. How about I call you tomorrow?"

Hadley nodded. "Perfect. Tomorrow would be great. I will wait to hear from you and hope desperately that you say yes."

There was that contagious optimism again. Spencer stood, downed the rest of her cappuccino, and met Hadley's gaze. "Thanks for going out of your way for me. You didn't have to." She felt everything in her tighten for this next part, as she dropped her tone. "And I don't know if anyone has ever told you this, but you look killer in a simple pair of jeans."

Hadley's mouth formed a small *O*, their eye contact unbroken.

The comment seemed to have stolen her words, which was rare as far as Spencer could tell. "Professionally speaking, of course."

"Of course." Hadley blinked several times in succession.

Spencer chuckled quietly at her own brazenness. "I better go bang my head against a wall about this Trudy thing. Talk to you tomorrow, Hadley."

Hadley nodded, still not saying anything. She did, however, raise her hand in farewell. Spencer made her way to her fairly new Nissan Altima, bright red, purchased just six months ago with all the bells and whistles. This car had been Spencer's one indulgence when she started making waves, and cash, via her online store. She'd played it conservative with money in every other aspect of her life, storing away as much as she could, but this car was her own little celebration. She wondered if maybe, someday, there might be another reason to celebrate.

She pulled her phone from her bag and dialed. "Hi, Mama. You free for breakfast tomorrow? I have something I'd love to talk over with you."

❖

Hadley hadn't moved since Spencer knocked her over with that compliment and then took off. She stared out the window, watching the traffic fly past as she floated back to herself. She'd been complimented before. This had felt markedly different. The way Spencer had said it, in her lower register with a twinkle in her eye left Hadley...tingly. She had wiggled her toes both then and now. She was becoming a toe wiggler out of nowhere.

"Who was that?" Autumn asked.

Hadley blinked and then blinked again. "What? I missed what you said."

"The hot girl you were just having coffee with? Did you forget about her already, or is that who you're daydreaming about all starry eyed-like?"

"What?"

Autumn patted Hadley's head. "Who were you just meeting with, sweetie?" she said more gently.

"Oh, that was Spencer Adair. The friend of Elle's, you know, the designer I told you about? I'm still trying to get her stuff into the store. Trudy's not making that easy."

Autumn pointed at the empty chair and then back at Hadley. "That was work?" Hadley nodded, and Autumn held up her hands in surrender. "I totally mistook that for a date. I could feel the chemistry from across the room."

"No," Hadley said, smothering a grin. "Just a meeting. She is attractive, though. I can't lie about that."

"Well, I don't know what it's worth, but you two make a striking pair. Even Steve thought so."

Hadley felt the blush but didn't fight it. "She's very attractive. Very."

"Do you want to say *very* again?" Autumn asked with a tilt of her head. "Not sure you've made the point enough."

"No, I think that's plenty. She is, you know."

Autumn placed a finger on her cheek. "I heard that somewhere. But?"

"She's a client, you know? It feels weird to say she's pretty."

"Except you've easily said it three times. And she's only a client until she's not." Autumn chuckled again and headed back behind the counter where she wasn't supposed to be anymore, due to maternity leave. She always had been stubborn. Hadley followed her.

"What do you think it means when you have to wiggle your toes?"

"That you need new shoes?"

"No, it's a good wiggle. What does good wiggling signal?"

Autumn stared at her. "I have no idea what that means."

"No, and how could you?" Hadley gave her head a shake and tried to explain herself. "When I'm around Spencer, I wiggle my toes. I've never done that before, but it's rampant! I'm this overzealous wiggler who keeps telling people Spencer's attractive, like a maniac. I'm a wiggling maniac."

"Finally, we have a name for you! Interesting. Steve, do you wiggle your toes when you have the hots for some girl?" Autumn asked.

Steve's eyes went wide, and he paused mid-cappuccino-preparation. "Not that I know of. Am I supposed to? Maybe that's part of my problem. I could try." He was so cute in all his nerdy glory. Hadley wanted to pinch his cheek in spite of her present dilemma.

"Who knows?" Autumn asked. "Had does when she's all hot and bothered. She just said so."

Hadley scoffed. "I am *not* hot and bothered."

"Are, too."

"Fine. A little bothered. A tad hot. Without the two mingling."

"Semantics, Cooper, but if you prefer we can stipulate to the no mingling."

Hadley followed Autumn into the storage room behind the counter. "I don't think it means I have a crush on her, though. She just has an effect on me I haven't figured out. A physical one."

"That's fair. What do you think a possible reason might be? Let's break it down." Autumn rifled through a shelf of supplies, looking for who knew what coffee accoutrement.

"Maybe because I'm uncomfortable with how pretty she is? That could be it. What's the scoopy thing?" she asked, pointing at the thingamabob on the shelf.

"For measuring ground coffee. Does the rest of you feel uncomfortable?"

She thought on this and the answer was easy. She liked Spencer, admired her. There was no unease, though. "No."

"Do you feel excited, and tingly, and happy when she's around? I mean, you're always happy, but extra happy in any way?"

Hadley squinted. "Yes, but that's probably just the clothes that are making me happy. Don't you think? Clothes always get me worked up." She rolled her shoulders, channeling the energy the reflected passion brought on. She really did live for good fashion, and that's exactly what Spencer brought to the table.

Autumn nodded sagely. "Then maybe it's the killer combination of the two. Her looks and her talent. Bear with me."

"Bearing."

"Some killer clothes. A killer bod, which I can attest to, and some killer chemistry might have your toes a-wiggling. Ever think of that?"

"Not until right now. It's not impossible," Hadley said. She took the silver canister Autumn handed her and followed her back to the front of the shop.

"Biscotti?" Autumn offered, stealing one from the jar on the counter and biting into it herself. "I'm a ravenous pregnant woman in the wild. Pay no attention."

"No thanks. Hey, why are you here, by the way? Aren't you supposed to be temporarily retired? You promised."

"I was retired, that part's true, and enjoying it like a boss. Bath bombs, apple juice, which I've been craving like you have no idea, feet up and all. Then I just got this surge of energy, like I had to *do stuff*. So here I am. Doing all the things I can think of. The energy surge is amazing. I figured I should use it while it's here. I'm about to reorganize this whole shop. My apartment's already done."

"Oh, my goodness. Oh, my goodness!"

Autumn stared at her. "What is that about? You sound like an orphan in *Annie*."

"You're nesting! I read about this." Hadley covered her mouth with both hands. This was huge!

"Really? Huh. Hadn't considered that."

"It's real and it means that you're about to go into labor. Like, any second." She pointed once and then again at Autumn's stomach for emphasis. "They're coming."

Autumn shifted her lips to the side in thought. "I've yet to feel any signs of that, other than the twins and their usual afternoon dance party, which, let's be honest, is growing tiresome."

"Any second now," Hadley said, and stared at Autumn. And stared some more. She looked at her stomach, then back at her face. The silence felt a little awkward, and nothing seemed to be happening.

"You're being a weirdo again." Autumn shook her head and went back to her intense organization.

Still nothing had happened three hours later, as Hadley sat smack in the middle of the courtyard, waiting, holding watch like the lookout in a scary movie. This was it. She could feel it, and she was not about to miss one second of such a monumental occasion in her best friend's life. She checked her watch and glanced at her book. Reading it felt a bit like cheating, but she stole a few chapters anyway. This was book five in the Janika series. Only three more to go before she'd have to say goodbye to Captain Janika and her crew forever. She lost herself in the action and drama of the space opera until Seven Shores seemed all tucked in for the night. Quiet and peaceful. She smiled at the night all around her.

Good things were headed their way she told herself, and if it weren't for that tiny, nagging feeling in her gut, she could allow herself to fully believe it.

CHAPTER THREE

Hadley had been asleep for close to an hour when her phone rang. "On the way to the hospital," she heard Kate's clipped voice say upon answering. "You're first on the phone tree Autumn handed me."

Hadley bolted upright, a huge goofy grin taking shape on her face. She hadn't been wrong. The tiny kids were on their way! "I'll take it from here, Lieutenant!" And she did just that, blowing up the phones of her best friends and Autumn's mother, Vicki, who would be a lot to wrangle at the hospital, but Hadley was up for the job. She'd mentally prepped for this for weeks: ways to keep Autumn calm, ways to occupy Vicki so Autumn could remain calm, ways to keep Isabel from swearing too much in front of the nurses. She was born for this day!

The hospital, which Hadley had gotten an early taste of when Autumn had been admitted weeks before for low blood pressure, was overrun that night. It was nearly a full moon, which might have played a role. Didn't matter. This was the night that her honorary niece and nephew would make their debut into the world, and nothing could dampen her spirits. With an excited grin on her face, she made the drive with Isabel and Gia, who were overflowing with just as much energy as Hadley was. They were allowed to visit with Autumn prior to delivery and help her work through some of the harder parts of the process. She'd long ago okayed their presence right up until time to push.

"Where's the epidural guy?" they heard her say as they entered her hospital room, which appeared to be a rather spacious birthing suite. Labor and Delivery knew how to do it right! Across from Autumn's hospital bed was a long, comfortable-looking gray couch for friends and family. Oh, this was going to be lovely!

"Hi," Hadley said, as they approached Autumn's bed.

"You hanging in there?" Isabel asked.

Autumn grabbed Isabel's arm forcefully and squeezed. "I need the drugs. Do you know where the guy is who has them? You're the kind of girl who could find him, Iz. Do it! Find the guy."

"I don't know where the guy is." Isabel shook her head violently and looked to Gia. "Vise grip. Help!"

"On it," Gia said, and stepped forward. "Isabel doesn't know where the drugs are," she told Autumn, "but I might."

Autumn released Isabel and grabbed Gia, who winced at the force of her hold. "Find that person," she bit out. "Quickly."

Gia exchanged a quick glance with Kate, who smiled apologetically from the other side of Autumn's bed. "It's been a whirlwind of contractions since we've arrived. I think we're moving pretty fast."

"Not too fast for drugs, right?" Autumn said, breathless.

"Not yet," a friendly nurse said as she breezed past. "But if you don't slow down, we're gonna have babies in no time."

Hadley stared down at Autumn. "See? You're an overachiever!"

"No perkiness right now," Autumn said, through gritted teeth. "None at all allowed."

"Got it. I'll just be over here glaring," Hadley said, and fixed her face as she moved to the gray couch. She sat there and watched as Autumn's nurse brought her ice chips, her doctor popped in to say hello, and Kate counted through each contraction. Hadley counted along silently, too, holding Isabel's hand on one side and Gia's on the other, willing Autumn her extra strength but in not too perky a manner. She glanced out the window at the luminous moon, hanging bright and full over all of them. Keeping watch, she imagined, as a sense of calm washed over her.

An hour later, the epidural was administered and the Autumn much resembling Satan had been replaced with the Autumn they knew and loved. Her features relaxed and she laughed and joked with them all, fully enjoying the anticipation of what was to come and playing grateful hostess at the same time.

"Anyone need a drink or a snack?" she asked the room, sporting a serene smile.

"We're all good," Gia told her. "Vending machines are just down the hall there. They even have free coffee."

"I don't know that you want to drink that," Autumn-the-coffee-snob said.

"Any bets on time?" Kate asked the room, once the doctor took her leave.

"Five dollars says 2:34 in the morning," Autumn predicted, leaving her only another forty-five minutes to deliver. "Do you have five dollars?" she asked Kate quietly.

"I can spot you," Kate said, and placed a kiss on Autumn's forehead.

"No way," Gia said. "Too early. Going with 4:05."

Isabel looked over at her. "Going with 4:06 just because I've always wanted to be on *The Price Is Right* and kick your ass." Gia blew her the sweetest of kisses.

Kate typed their guesses into her phone. "Hadley?"

"Five minutes before five," she said calmly. Everyone nodded their approval and forked over their cash to Kate, who registered her own guess at 5:32 a.m.

Just then there was a commotion in the hallway and a loud clicking of high heels. "Wait, is it through here, sweetheart? What was your name? Kendra? Just point for me. This way? Great. I'm here! I didn't miss it, right?" Vicki yelled, rounding the corner into Autumn's room. "There's my baby girl!" Vicki yelled and kissed Autumn's cheek, leaving a noticeable fuchsia lip print. Kate handed a grateful Autumn a tissue. "Where are they?" Vicki asked, turning in a circle. Hadley and Gia exchanged a knowing look. Vicki, who lived a leisurely lifestyle with no job except the capturing of men, had clearly been drinking.

"I'll handle her," Hadley said under her breath to her friends.

"Vicki, why don't we walk down to the cafeteria and see if they have some water and something to eat?"

"I love you, Hadley," Vicki said, laying on the affection pretty thick. Yep, Vicki had slammed back at least three glasses of wine that night. Two prompted her to criticize. Three made her affectionate. She pulled Hadley into a lasting hug. Vicki's long acrylic nails scratched across the back of Hadley's neck while they embraced. "I could use a snack. Do they have Chardonnay?"

"Nope. The *hospital* we're in is fresh out." She did her best to keep her tone light and playful. This wasn't the time to make any kind of point to Vicki, though Hadley had been known to stand up to her on Autumn's behalf in the past and wouldn't hesitate if it came to that again.

"Damn. Oh, well. I guess the fun part of the evening is over, right?"

"Well, we are here for something pretty fun, if you think about it. Life changing, even."

"Well, yes. That, too."

Aghast at the afterthought status of her grandchildren, Hadley remembered her purpose, to keep Vicki in check. "All right, Vicki. Let's go. Back in a few, everybody. Don't go having any babies without us. I have my phone if anything happens."

"On it," Gia said with a grateful nod.

Hadley wrapped her arm around Vicki and passed Autumn an "I've got you" wink as they exited her hospital room. Autumn made the shape of a heart with her hands and passed it silently to Hadley.

She kept Vicki occupied for the next thirty minutes in the small portion of the cafeteria that was still open at such a late hour, listening intently to her detailed stories of how wonderful Taggart was. Taggart, whose name she'd heard about eight times already, was apparently Vicki's man du jour. Hadley didn't spend too much time memorizing the details Vicki dished out, as there'd be another guy next month. She could set her watch by it.

"He has the best shoulders, Hadley Bear, you should really see them," Vicki said, as she scarfed down a strawberry Pop-Tart.

"He sounds fabulous. He has shoulders," Hadley said, bored. "Very important."

Vicki closed her eyes, placed a hand on her heart, and swayed. "And the sex! The sex is simply delicious. Do you know that he can easily put my leg behind—"

"Is that Leonardo DiCaprio?" Hadley practically screamed. Anything to end that terrifying, impending sentence. Some things one cannot unhear.

Vicki squinted. "I think that's just a custodian, sweetheart. See his broom? Do you wear glasses?"

Hadley laughed it off, feigning a double take. "Oh, you're right! Might need to get my eyes checked. Not at all a Leo sighting. One day, though."

"No problem. I know a guy. Very handsome optometrist with the best hands. Trust me, he'd love you." Hadley closed her eyes at Vicki's hundredth attempt to set her up with a man, ignoring her sexuality yet again. For Vicki, the idea that everyone wasn't man crazy was incomprehensible.

On the slow and even walk back to Autumn's room, Hadley learned that Taggart took Vicki to all the best restaurants, and had multiple Swiss bank accounts, and leather shoes in both brown and black. Maybe even charcoal. Vicki wasn't sure but she could check. She'd not once mentioned her arriving grandchildren, however, which was really all Hadley could think about, but Taggart apparently loathed bleu cheese and demanded it be taken off his salad, so that was something to take note of.

"How are we doing in here?" Hadley asked, as they arrived back in the room.

"The doctor was just here. Getting ready to push in just a few minutes," Kate said, with a grin on her face. It wasn't her typical lazy smile, or even the reserved one Hadley had become so familiar with. No, Kate was glowing full on, which only tripled Hadley's excitement level. Autumn, however, looked nervous. She smiled up at Hadley briefly, faltered, and then smiled again. Yep, no doubt about it. She was scared, Hadley could tell, and Isabel and Gia must have sensed it, too, as they'd gathered around her bed. The three of them would be sidelined in the community waiting room when the pushing began, and this was their last chance to say goodbye to Autumn and leave her words of encouragement.

Isabel leaned close to Autumn's face and spoke quietly to her like a coach would to her team. "You're gonna fucking go out there and kick some delivery ass," Isabel said, with an intense smile on her face. "You will slay every step of the way. You are Ms. Pac-Man. You got me?"

"I think so," Autumn said. "Good advice, Iz."

"I'm so excited for you," Gia said, taking Isabel's spot. She was bubblier than her usual self, which spoke to how over-the-moon she was about meeting the babies.

"Thanks, Gia Pet. I'm so glad you guys are here."

Autumn nodded and squeezed both Gia and Isabel's hands. She turned to Hadley, her eyes searching, as if needing something. Hadley knew exactly what it was. She spoke sincerely from her heart. "It's okay to be scared," she told her calmly. "That's part of all of this. Embrace it. Listen to everything that the doctor says because she is not at all worried." Autumn seemed to latch onto the words, and nodded. "You're so close now, Autumn. You've wanted this for so long. I remember in the car on the way back from Tahoe when you first told me you wanted to be a mom. That's about to happen, and it's the most wonderful day ever."

Autumn's eyes filled and she smiled through the tears. "I remember. I can't believe they're almost here, Had."

"Think about that," Hadley said, and brushed a strand of red curls from Autumn's forehead. "You're about to make some amazing memories."

Autumn nodded, her eyes brightening. "Thank you, Hadley." It was clear she meant it.

Hadley kissed Autumn's cheek. "I love you."

"I love you, too," Autumn said. "I love all of you."

Hadley glanced up at her friends who, along with her, had encircled Autumn and Kate. "You let us know as soon as there are new people in this world, you hear me?"

Kate nodded. "Of course. I'll be out there as soon as I can be."

With a few final long looks, and happy tears, Hadley, Isabel, and Gia moved to the hospital waiting room. They gave Vicki a moment alone with Kate and Autumn, and Hadley prayed she wouldn't say anything to detract from the joy of the occasion. She joined them a few moments later, and the four of them waited. Time seemed to crawl by, and for Hadley the wait felt agonizing. She searched for anything to occupy her brain. While immensely happy, she was also a tight bundle of nerves, and her palms were sweaty. Talking generally helped. In fact, when she was nervous, she talked way too much.

"Who do you guys think looks good going into the preseason?" she asked her friends.

They exchanged a puzzled look.

"For what sport?" Isabel finally asked.

"I don't know," Hadley said. "Just thought that was something people said." She shook her head in defeat. "No?"

"Hey, they're gonna be fine," Gia told her, and hopped seats so they were sitting side by side.

"I know." Hadley took a deep breath. "It just feels like it's been a long time. How long has it been?"

"Thirty-two minutes," Gia said without missing a beat. Isabel and Hadley stared at her. "So maybe Had isn't the only one watching the clock. I just think—"

But Gia didn't get to finish. A singsong chime came over the loudspeaker, the one they'd been told about, Brahms's Lullaby! This was the public notification that a baby had just been born in the hospital. Passersby paused their conversations and smiled up at the ceiling in gentle recognition of the new life. For a moment, no one in their group moved, no one breathed.

"That's ours. It's gotta be," Isabel said, leaping to her feet.

"I'm a Gigi?" Vicki asked in disbelief, looking up from her phone. It was as if the gravity of the occasion had penetrated her self-involved bubble for the first time.

Hadley laughed and cried at the same time. "You are!" She pulled Vicki into a tight hug as the chime came to a conclusion. They traded people and did the hugging dance until everyone was sappy, crying, and smiling like idiots.

"It's a boy!" Kate said loudly, as she bounded into the waiting room with wide eyes and a happy smile. "He's beautiful and pink and already crying! One down, one to go!" With that, she bounded off again as they applauded her exit.

Hadley sat down, absorbing the joyful news, and then stood up again. She was lost in overwhelming emotion and unsure how to process it. She sat down once more. Then up. "Had?" Gia said, wrapping an arm around her shoulders. "You gonna make it? You're looking a little uneasy there."

"I'm fine," she said, wiping her cheeks. "Just really, really happy. He's finally here! And Autumn must be doing great, because Kate was glowing, so all is well, and we can just relax, everyone, and wait a little longer for more happy news. I just think maybe I should sit down again. Or stand."

"Good idea," Gia said, laughing. "I'll sit. You should join me."

"One more!" Isabel said, with a loud clap. She jumped around like a football player about to go into the game. "Let's do this. C'mon, Vicki!"

Not knowing what else to do with herself and her newfound sentimentality, Vicki joined Isabel hopping. Hadley stood up again. Then sat down. What a sight their group must have been. Twenty minutes passed and the second lullaby hadn't chimed.

"Didn't Autumn say that the average time between twin births is twelve minutes?" Hadley asked. "I'm pretty positive she said twelve minutes, and we're past that."

"Something like twelve," Isabel answered quietly. She'd settled back into her chair with the rest of them, hopping put on hold for now. In its place, concern seemed to have crept in, drawing her eyes pensively to the floor. Hadley felt it, too. The tension in the room was palpable and pressed down on her. She could feel it on her skin, causing her to rub her arm back and forth.

At the thirty-minute mark, Hadley took to walking the length of the waiting room, hoping for that darn chime. Surely any second. But nothing came.

"There are a ton of possible reasons for the delay. Maybe they're just giving her time to rest," Gia offered. "Delivering a baby is supposed to be exhausting."

"Maybe," Isabel said, and bit her thumbnail.

Vicki stood. "You know what? I'm the mom. I'll go back there and check. Let them try and keep me out!"

Gia caught her gently by the shoulders. "Maybe that's not the best idea. Let's give them some more time. I'm sure everything is okay." But from the look on her face, Gia didn't believe that any more than the rest of them did.

Forty minutes hit. Forty-five. Way too long. Hadley glanced down the hallway each time anyone with a badge walked through the automatic doors into Labor and Delivery, looking for any sign of Kate, the doctor, Kendra-the-nurse, anyone. The hallway remained eerily quiet. Too quiet.

Fifty minutes. "If the baby's in trouble, they won't leave her in there too long," Hadley said to the room. "That's what Autumn said, that twelve minutes was average but that an hour would be too long. We're close to an hour now."

"But we're not there *yet*," Gia said. She'd clearly emerged as the leader of their little group, keeping everyone calm, and under control. Hadley had no idea how she was able to speak in such a collected and measured tone, but then again, her job demanded nerves of steel.

"It's been fifty-seven minutes," Isabel said, with her hands laced behind her head. "Maybe it's time to be concerned. I'm thinking it is. You with me?"

"I'm already there," Hadley said just as the second chime began. She covered her mouth, as tears of relief hit. Isabel tossed both hands in the air in victory. Gia slung her arm around a very quiet Vicki, who now grinned proudly.

"Gooooooal!" Isabel hollered, and jogged in place, knees bouncing to her chest.

After a short wait, the nurse arrived in the waiting room and offered to bring the group back to meet the new little ones. Hadley hung back as they walked, wanting to take her time with this moment, to recover from the worry and shift to absorbing the happiness. Happiness was the best part, and she wanted to be ready for it. It's what she did in life, always seeking to savor the key moments so she could pull them back out and relive them later. She refused to take moments like this for granted, because they were what made life special.

Once she was ready, she peered around the doorframe like on Christmas morning. The sight she was met with, the new little family, was enough to warm Hadley from head to toe. Autumn held the tiniest baby wrapped in a pink blanket and Kate held a tiny baby, eyes wide open, wrapped in blue. Both Kate and Autumn peered up at their friends as they entered with looks of happiness and wonder on their faces as if to say, "look what happened while you were gone!"

Everyone oohed and ahhed at the new little ones while Hadley stood in the doorway looking on.

"Hadley?" Autumn said gently. "Want to meet her?"

Hadley nodded, the lump in her throat preventing her from saying any actual words. She walked slowly to Autumn's bedside and looked down at the perfect little face, all scrunched up and fresh.

"This is Caroline," Autumn said. "We think we might call her Carrie."

"Hi, Carrie," Hadley said. Big green eyes looked back up at her. Hadley gasped. "Look at her. She has your eyes!"

"Do you think? They could still change color over time."

"They won't," Hadley said. "I can already tell. They're just like yours."

"Want to hold her?"

She glanced up. The little guy across the room was already in Gia's arms. "Can I? Is that okay? I wouldn't want to overstep."

Autumn nodded and Hadley scooped up little Carrie, who blinked up at her curiously. "I'm your Aunt Hadley and I picked out your going-home outfit. I hope you like it. We can discuss it when you're older if you don't. It won't hurt my feelings."

Autumn laughed quietly. "You've told her that several times through my stomach, if I recall. I imagine she knows your voice pretty well."

Hadley beamed. "I hadn't thought of that!" Carrie yawned and shoved the back of her fist into her mouth in about the cutest motion Hadley had ever witnessed. Her stomach tightened. The little girl was warm and wrinkly and wonderful. Carrie's whole life was stretched out in front of her. She could be anyone she wanted to be.

Autumn shook her head in wonder. "I can't believe she's real. I just keep staring at her."

"She's real," Hadley said, and reluctantly handed her back to her mother. "How are you doing? The labor?"

"Was not so awful on the epidural. Mainly I'm just exhausted, but too thrilled to care."

"Congratulations, Autumn," Hadley said sincerely, and leaned down to hug her friend, who held her tightly. "Your family is amazing."

She pulled back and met Autumn's glistening eyes. "They really are, aren't they? I have a *family*, Had."

Hadley nodded. "And don't think I'm not borrowing these kids. You have built in babysitting, and don't you forget it."

"Holding you to it."

Hadley met William next, named after Kate's dad, whom she'd lost a few years back. They planned to call him Will, which seemed so fitting once she had him in her arms. "You look like a Will, don't you?" she whispered. He blinked in response. Will was the more curious of the two, taking in his surroundings with wide-eyed wonder. Hadley walked him to the window while the others doted on Carrie. "That's the great big world out there, little guy. Just look. You're going to take it by storm one day soon. And if you ever need anything, you or your little sister, you just give me a call. I'll be there." She placed a gentle kiss on his forehead.

"Want to hold him?" she asked Isabel, who immediately shoved her hands into her back pockets.

"I better not. He's breakable, and I'm a bulldozer. You've met me. A total klutz."

Hadley scoffed and approached Isabel with the baby. "Don't be afraid. Here, open your arms."

Isabel shook her head eight times. "No, bad idea. I'm serious, Hadley."

"Don't argue with me," Hadley said, employing her stern voice.

Isabel swallowed and allowed Hadley to place Will gently into her arms. In that moment, Isabel's entire face relaxed as she stared down at him. "Oh, wow," she whispered. She looked up at Hadley as if to say *are you seeing this?*

Hadley nodded.

"He's so small," she breathed.

"He says, 'nice to meet you, Aunt Isabel.'"

"He can talk, too," Isabel said reverently, with a smile on her face. Kate came up behind Isabel and wrapped an arm around her.

"Alert little guy."

"Right?" Hadley said. "He's a little investigator."

"Hey, who won the bet?" Gia asked, as she stood next to Vicki, who held Carrie.

"Oh, right!" Kate said, and pulled out her phone. "Will, the first baby, arrived at 4:55, so that means…Hadley was right on the nose."

Everyone turned to her in mystification.

"How'd you manage that?"

"I just had a feeling," she said, with a victorious shrug.

"Had's always had a close connection with these two," Autumn said, with a knowing look in her eye. "I'm not surprised."

"And I'm out five bucks," Gia said. "Dinner this weekend is on Hadley."

"Oh, we'll see about that," she said, with a scoff.

With a final kiss and wave, Hadley, Isabel, and Gia headed home to allow the new family some alone time. Plus, after everything she'd gone through, Autumn surely needed the rest. As they walked outside into the brisk morning air, the sun was peeking out over the horizon in a glorious glow of pinks, oranges, and yellows.

"Isn't that just the perfect ending to this whole thing?" Gia said, pausing a moment to take it in. "Damn."

Hadley linked her arm through Gia's and pulled Isabel to her. "To new beginnings," she said quietly. "This is a pretty monumental one."

"I can get behind that," Isabel said, giving Hadley a squeeze. "Even if those terrify me." Hadley picked up once again on Isabel's recent unease and made a mental note to check in on her more. She seemed to need it.

"You're gonna be just fine, Izzy," she said, kissing the side of her forehead. "I think there's a lot in store. For all of us."

Gia nodded. "There is. But can we go home and crash first? The future wants us rested."

They exchanged a fist bump and headed to Gia's Jeep on a sleepy, loopy, fantastic high from the historical night they'd just experienced.

When she arrived home, Hadley dropped into bed with a thump, falling asleep with a smile on her face almost instantly. When she woke up sometime close to lunch, there was a message on her phone from Spencer Adair, which sent a pleasant flutter to her stomach: *I've decided to revamp the line. And though this is hard to admit, I welcome your help. I probably need it.*

Hadley sat up and grinned at her phone.

To new beginnings indeed.

CHAPTER FOUR

Spencer hurried up Rodeo Drive on foot, carrying a series of garment bags on her shoulder. The paid parking lot where she'd left her car was a decent hike from Silhouette, and she was regretting the low heels she'd chosen to wear. Who was she trying to impress anyway? The store would be closed, and it would just be her and Hadley getting together for an initial work session. She checked out her reflection in the mirror, satisfied with her subtle makeup and the low twist she'd worked her hair into. And then swore at herself for being a stupid idiot.

She texted Hadley when she arrived outside the store, as they'd planned, and it was only a matter of moments before she arrived at the door, unlocked it with an energetic wave, and let Spencer inside.

"Hey there," Hadley said, beaming. "Come in! Come in! I hope you had a fantastic day."

"It was decent enough."

"Decent falls in the win column." She gestured behind her. "We can either work in my office, though it's sort of small, or on the second level around the couches, which are likely more comfortable."

"Couches and comfort sound good," Spencer said easily. She took in the boutique as they moved through the space, always intrigued when she got to step behind the scenes and see the inner workings of fashion. Silhouette, all closed up for the night, was dark and cozy, the clothes waiting patiently for the next day's wave of customers to look them over. There was a magical quality there that inspired a shiver to dance delicately across Spencer's skin. She smiled at the goose bumps.

"What's got that faraway look in your eye?" Hadley asked.

She hesitated, searching for a substitute answer, but changed her mind when she saw the warm expression on Hadley's face. She did something that she never did, and let Hadley in. "I get a kick out of stores after hours. Weird, maybe." She shrugged. "There's something mysterious and inspiring about them. Romanticism at work. Gets my fur up. It's dumb. Ignore me."

Hadley stared at her for an extra beat, as if something she'd said had struck a chord. "I don't know that I'll ever look at this place the same way again. I love that," she said softly, and Spencer allowed herself to take in how truly blue Hadley's eyes were. The fancy descriptors for blue eyes—azure, cobalt, sapphire—didn't work here, as Hadley's eyes were the truest form of blue she'd seen. To call them anything else would detract from their purity. "You have pretty eyes," she heard herself say. Apparently, Hadley conjured up extreme honesty.

"Me?" Hadley asked, her eyebrows shot up. Her cheeks showed a glimpse of pink.

"You," Spencer said calmly, wondering why she'd again felt the need to share her thoughts so openly. She settled on the fact that Hadley seemed so nonthreatening, so warm, that there was very little to guard against. The quality was refreshing and alarming at the same time. She made a promise to herself not to sign over her bank account or anything parallel during their time together.

"Thanks. That's really sweet of you to say." They stood there a moment, neither of them saying anything until it all felt awkward.

"Should we get started?" Spencer asked. "I figured we could use tonight for discussion. Go through each piece and toss around ideas, revamping for Silhouette and its needs."

"That sounds great. Can I interest you in some water or wine? We have both."

"Biblical," Spencer said with a laugh as she unzipped the first garment bag. She took out one of her favorite pieces, a boxy navy jacket that screamed of androgyny. "You really have wine?"

"We do." Hadley crossed to what appeared to be a refrigerator nestled around the corner. "Champagne, too, if you're feeling fancy. On hand for our important guests."

"What? And that's me?" Spencer asked, with a wry laugh.

"Of course. Red, white, or bubbly?"

"Always red. I'm too serious for anything else."

Hadley studied her. "You say that with conviction."

"Wine isn't something I take lightly."

Hadley laughed. "I'm learning more about you each time we meet."

"And?" Spencer raised a playful eyebrow. "What's the takeaway?

Do you find me at least a little bit fascinating?" She held her thumb and forefinger close together.

"I do. You're confident. Very confident."

"*Overly* confident." Spencer chuckled in recognition of her own Achilles' heel. "Often to my detriment. Just ask my design instructors who adjusted my As to Bs because I was hardheaded."

Hadley carried over a glass of Merlot for each of them. "What would they say if I asked them?"

Spencer reflected on those head-butting days in college. Back then, she thought she knew everything, was positive of that. These days, as she approached her thirty-first year on Earth, she was learning that perhaps that was not necessarily the case. Not that she didn't have more work to do on that front. In answer to Hadley's question, she adopted her best impersonation of the overly pretentious Professor Andrews from the Fashion Institute of Design and Merchandising. "Spencer comes with talent and passion and drive." She paused to toss her head around the way Andrews would have. "But she unfortunately gets in her own way, refusing constructive criticism and insisting she's always right, when in fact, she rarely is."

"Ouch." Hadley winced.

"I'm not saying she's wrong. You've been warned."

"Does that mean you're going to push back when I say that the jacket you just laid down could be tapered just a tad for a more flattering line?" Hadley winced in anticipation of Spencer's reaction, but it came off more adorable than apologetic. "The store is called Silhouette, after all. Maybe we should give one to the woman who wears this jacket."

Spencer stilled herself from too big a reaction. It was merely a suggestion. She was fiercely protective of her work, so this whole practice of "listening to another person's opinion" had her feeling defensive all over again and like a fish out of water. Hell, they'd barely even gotten started. "It's boxy on purpose," she said, with a forced smile on her face. "It's not supposed to be feminine, which is what you seem to be going for."

"Not necessarily." Hadley lifted the hanger and studied the jacket. "It's got a lot of personality. I love the epaulettes on the shoulders, but if you just pulled it in a touch at the waist, I think you'd have a worthy retail compromise." She sat back down. "It's not about femininity. But when a woman thinks she looks attractive, that translates to a sale. And some of the hottest male jackets on the market are tapered, while we're at it. Humor me. It's not even a major change. A few more stitches."

Spencer closed her eyes briefly, leaning into the skid, and pulled out the pad she'd brought with her to take notes. If high-end retail was what she was after, then listening to someone like Hadley, who'd worked successfully in that space, was likely wise. "Fine," she said curtly, jotting down the adjustment.

"Is this gonna be a long night, then?" Hadley asked, rolling her shoulders as if preparing for battle.

"It could be."

Hadley met her gaze. "Good thing we have a lot of wine."

"And good thing I already like you."

Hadley smiled. "Flatterer."

Spencer hadn't been wrong about the length of their work session. They had in-depth discussions (okay, debates) about each piece that were both frustrating and helpful. She hadn't settled on which emotion won out. She'd save that for later.

It was dark outside two and a half hours later when they came up for a break. The two floor lamps on the second level served as the only illumination in the store as Hadley stood and stretched, her top pulling and revealing a glimpse of her stomach. Spencer blinked, this time not lying to herself about the fact that she was checking Hadley out. She forced her gaze to the ground as an overwhelming heat moved through her from her toes to her forehead. She hadn't felt that kind of physical reaction since, well…ever.

"Can I get you a snack? Or we could order in if you're hungry for something heavier."

Spencer swallowed at the word "hungry" after the significant reaction she'd just had to a mere glimpse of Hadley's skin. She reached for her wine to cover the expression on her face. The one she couldn't seem to erase. Hadley waited while she drank and swallowed. "No, I'm good."

"You're sure you're okay?"

"Yes. Completely." She broke into what she hoped was a relaxed smile.

"I'll put out some fruit anyway," Hadley said, eying her suspiciously. "The peaches this time of year are juicy and delicious."

Spencer nearly spat her wine across the expensive beige upholstery. Her brain was a lecherous place. "Yeah? Cool. I bet they are. Those peaches."

Hadley headed into some sort of back room and Spencer used the time to become a normal person again, pep-talking herself into remaining on task and keeping her thoughts and wandering eye in check.

It worked, for the most part.

"The knife pleats, I love," Hadley said, pointing at the lime green skirt lying on the couch across from them. "I'd wear that tomorrow."

"Finally, something to green-light." Spencer decided to celebrate the small victory.

"Speaking of green. It's a tad bright. Can we tone down the color slightly?"

There went the victory. "Bright colors are part of who I am as a designer. We've been over this. I have a certain aesthetic that makes my work mine."

"Which," Hadley said, sliding down the couch so she was closer to Spencer, who sat in the adjoining arm chair, "is why we haven't touched the brights on some of the other pieces. I admire who you are as a designer very much or I never would have chased you down in the first place. But this skirt in particular is gorgeous and, in my opinion, is the linking agent of the line in its wholeness. What will make it more accessible for retail, however, is a slightly lesser value on that green." At least her eyes were kind when she said it. Hadley had a way of softening every blow simply in her style of delivery. "We're working on universal. Keep that in mind."

"I stand by the green." But she didn't entirely. She felt herself waffling, falling for Hadley's sweet girl charm.

"And you're not going to budge?" Hadley asked. "Even when you're incredibly complimentary advisor can see the forest for the trees, when perhaps you cannot, for purely understandable creative reasons?"

"What do you like to do when you have down time?" Spencer asked, as amazed at the question leaving her lips as she was by the disappearance of Amelia Earhart when she'd learned about it in the third grade. And why in the hell was she thinking about the third grade during a work session? Where had the hard-core, hardheaded version of herself gone, and how did she get her back? This was bullshit.

"Me?" Hadley asked, touching her chest. "Oh. Well, I'm a big crime novel enthusiast, but lately I've been into science fiction and fantasy."

"You like to read," Spencer said, happy to learn something new about Hadley and wanting to know even more, for reasons she would most certainly classify later as stupid and a distraction from her larger goals. Regardless, she couldn't stop herself. "What else?"

"I have a pretty tight-knit group of friends. We go to the beach, meet for coffee each morning. Oh! You know the place. It was the coffee shop where we met. Remember? The owner, Autumn, just had twins! They come home tomorrow morning, as a matter of fact, and I don't know if I'll sleep tonight for how excited I'll be." She grinned with the purest of joy.

"You seem to get excited by a lot of things. I don't think I'm wrong about that."

"You're not. I've heard that before, and I cannot deny the accuracy," Hadley said, her eyes sparkling as she shook her head in what seemed to be wonder. "But these babies are a whole new level of excitement. Surely you'd agree with that. You'd think these two were mine."

"I can definitely see you doing well with kids," Spencer said, reaching for an apple slice.

"And why is that?" Hadley looked intrigued. She reached for her wine as she waited on Spencer's response. She held it very close to her lips without taking a sip. The gesture was…something to behold. Spencer blinked as her body hummed in appreciation. How was someone so sunshiny sweet and also so incredibly sexy?

"I don't know. I suppose you present with a very definite warmth. It's not hard to feel comfortable around you, and trust me, I don't feel comfortable around too many people."

"I present with warmth," Hadley said, straightening in her chair. "I think I like that. Who doesn't strive to come across as warm?"

"I'm not sure I do." Spencer heard how that must sound and backpedaled. "I mean in the scheme of business, it works for *you*, the sweet manager thing, which is great, but it would just get me run the hell over. I'm not a blond, blue-eyed California girl. I have to be formidable out there to compete."

"You are certainly that," Hadley said, studying her as though she had definite opinions on the topic. "You don't give in easy, as I've certainly experienced tonight."

"Well, doesn't mean I'm that way in all areas of life." She said it with a smile and held Hadley's gaze. It was a mild form of flirting. Even she could see that. Hadley, who had ditched the heels hours ago, scrunched up her feet—her toes, to be specific.

"Long day?" Spencer asked, gesturing to Hadley's feet.

"What?" Hadley glanced down and turned the most impressive shade of red. Uh-oh. What in the world was that about? "No. Just a habit I have. A foot thing. It's stupid."

Spencer found the blushing to be not only attractive but amusing, which meant she couldn't stop now. Sometimes she was such a dog with a bone. She dipped her head playfully. "I feel like maybe I've hit a nerve, and we should explore that."

"Not at all," Hadley said, as if Spencer were insane. But the scoffing also brought on a glimpse of Hadley's dimples, which she'd been aware of before but hadn't seen fully showcased. Now that she had, she felt the heat hit her own cheeks, because life was certainly different after one saw them. There was "before Hadley's dimples" and after. She was finding that after was a nice place to be. "But less about me, why don't we get back to the skirt."

"The skirt?" Spencer asked, trying to remember the thread from earlier but failing miserably because what she had her mind on now was so much more satisfying. She sipped her wine.

"The knife pleats. The green. Remember?"

"Right. I'll think about it."

"You will? Just like that?"

Spencer made a note. "Consider your point made. Not that I like it, but I'm willing to at least mull over your advice."

Hadley sat back against the couch, enjoying the possibility of a victory. The dimples blossomed again and Spencer sucked in air. In that moment, she knew beyond a shadow of a doubt that she might be in a whole hell of a lot of trouble.

And wasn't at all prepared for it.

❖

The beige two-story with the white shutters that stood prominently at the end of Westmoreland Street was Spencer's. Well, technically it was her mother's, but she'd grown up there, which made it hers by proxy. That 2,300-square-foot house was busting at the seams with memories of Spencer racing in and out, hopping on her bike for a spin around the neighborhood or to sell lemonade on the corner. She'd apparently been an entrepreneur from the very beginning, spending extra time to make sure her lemonade was worthy of the extra fifty cents she charged.

She dashed up the three steps—the second one with the loose brick—that led to the quaint, covered porch suited for rainy day chatting and let herself in. The delicious aroma of something savory hit her instantly, and she took a deep, satisfying inhale. She located her mother in the recently redesigned all-white kitchen, still wearing her business suit from work as she flipped a chicken breast sautéing in the pan.

"Please tell me you're also making your famous white wine mushroom sauce."

Sonora Adair turned to Spencer with a hand on her hip. "There would be no other way. Now kiss your mama and grab some plates from the cabinet."

"Yes, ma'am. Hi, Pop," Spencer said, and tossed her father a smile.

Russell Adair sat comfortably at the kitchen table with his customary pile of magazines in front of him, likely chatting away with her mother about his day. It wasn't an unusual sight to see the two of them together, shooting the breeze. They weren't married anymore, and hadn't been since Spencer was thirteen, but remained steadfast friends. Her pop lived a few blocks over but spent a good chunk of his time doing odd jobs around her mother's house and eating as much of her food as she'd allow before kicking him out. They bickered and joked and carried on the way close relatives did, leaving her grateful for their evolved relationship. Some people just do better minus the romance over time. Her parents were the perfect example.

"How's the paper?" Spencer asked him absently, as she set the table the same way she had since she was five years old: knives on the inside, spoons on the out.

"Same as ever," her pop said. "Did you know Mr. Goodrich died? He was the assistant coach on your soccer team when you were about here." He held up a hand, indicating the height of a first grader.

"Oh yeah? I hadn't heard. I know his daughter, Mika, from school. I'll have to check in on her."

"Wrote his obituary today. Makes you see how precious life is. How precious the *people* in it are." He reached out and squeezed Spencer's hand, making her stop her progress and squeeze his back. "Life's too short, Sparky. Do all the things you want to do now. No waiting."

She smiled at his childhood nickname for her, originating from her precocious self-expression and refusal to follow rules simply because they were rules. She'd always been an independent thinker, quite often to her own detriment. She'd gotten better about holding her tongue. Well, mostly. "Working on it. In fact, last night I met with that assistant manager from that store I told you guys about on Rodeo Drive. I think she's gonna help me get my line in the door after all."

Her mother carried the plate of white wine chicken to the table and set it down alongside a fresh green salad hopping with ripe tomatoes from the garden out back. "If my child is designing clothes for Rodeo Drive, I might be taking out an ad in that paper myself, Russell. Get your pen and paper ready!"

He chuckled and served himself several forkfuls of salad. "I can get you a discount."

"No, no, no. We're not there yet," Spencer said, waving her hand. "But I think things are starting to happen. I just have that feeling you always talk about, Mama. Like when you know you're going to sell a house that day."

"Sometimes you just know. That's quite true. And this assistant manager? She knows what she's doing?"

"I think so. Her suggestions aren't...awful."

Her mother shot her father a knowing look. "Sounds like someone is feeling defensive about their artistic integrity again."

"Not a bad thing," her dad said. "You've always had a good eye there, Sparky. You know what you're doing."

"I do," Spencer said, digging into the chicken. "But she knows the space more than I do, so I'm trying to make mental accommodations for that. The clientele is different from those I usually sell to. Uppity, and opinionated. So I'm trying to be open and listen more."

"Is this my daughter?" her mother asked, glancing around the kitchen, her hand covering her heart. "I wish she'd been more open to listening when I raised her. One too many arguments about the paint colors in her room."

"We raised a knucklehead," her pop said fondly, nodding along. "But she's workin' it out, sounds like. Maybe she'll be less knuckleheadish soon."

"Call me a knucklehead all you want," Spencer said. "But I stand by that bright purple paint. All my friends were jealous of my room."

"Mm-hmm," her mother said, behind her glass of iced water. "That's why you painted over it a year later."

"Knock, knock," a voice called from the entryway.

"Kendra!" Spencer said, and leapt up. Her childhood best friend was still her mother's next-door neighbor after having inherited the house when her own mother had sadly passed on.

"I saw your car," Kendra said, walking in and making herself at home. Automatically, her mother added a fourth plate to the table. Kendra was just a second daughter as far as the Adairs were concerned. She and Spencer had gone back and forth between the two houses for the entirety of their childhood. No one knew Spencer the way Kendra did.

"I was about to call you."

"No need. I have presented myself on cue. What's for dinner?" she asked, with wide eyes. "Oh my God, did I come on white wine chicken night? I love that sauce."

"It's your lucky day," her mom said, making Kendra a heaping plate. She did love to feed people. "How are the babies? It's not fair that you get to see adorable children all day and I'm playing open house hostess to looky-loos."

Spencer suppressed an eye roll, because her mother loved her job and made a killing doing it. But the baby-snuggling life didn't sound so bad either.

"Adorable and fussy as always," Kendra said. "We had a delivery of twins earlier this week, though. A boy and a girl. Stole my heart. I swear the little boy was flirting with me." Kendra had worked as a labor and delivery nurse since graduating from nursing school and loved every minute of her job.

"He knows a pretty girl when he sees one," her father said.

"Kendra's taken," Spencer told him, referencing her new romance still in the hot and heavy stages. She'd had starry eyes for the past three months. While Spencer was happy for her, it was a lot to stomach.

"Not true." Kendra tucked a section of dark braids behind her ear. "I need to catch you up."

Spencer sat back in her chair with a whoosh. "Get out. You and Tucker broke up? Why didn't you call me?"

"More like he was also seeing the girl from his building, as well as the bartender at the same place he took me to on our first date."

"A dog," her father said. "A damn dog."

"You're too good for that man," her mother said, and placed a firm hand on Kendra's arm. "You will not go back to him no matter how much he apologizes or begs."

"I will not. My mother would turn over in her grave."

Her mother looked skyward. "Bless her, she would."

"Porch?" Spencer asked.

Kendra looked relieved. "Yeah, that'd be great."

"I'll be back to do the dishes after, Mama, okay? Don't touch them."

Her mother waved her off. "No need. I'll use it to take out my frustrations on that no good, lying ex-boyfriend of my Kendra's. Russell, bring the dishes to the sink so I can slam them around a little bit."

"Least I can do for the excellent meal."

"The least, indeed."

Spencer smiled at her parents' playful simpatico and followed Kendra to the steps of the front porch. It was in that very spot that the two of them sat, year after year, talking over the heavier subjects in life, hearing each other out when times got hard and serving as a shoulder to cry on whenever necessary. Kendra had been the one to teach Spencer how to braid her own hair on that porch when they were just eight years old. In turn, Spencer taught Kendra the right way to handle a bully on the playground (though wound up handling the bully for Kendra herself on more than one occasion). When they were teenagers, Kendra listened supportively as Spencer came out for the very first time to anyone. When they were twenty-two and Kendra's mother died, Spencer held her on the porch as she cried in Spencer's lap. Many a problem had been explored and solved on those steps, and if Kendra's heart was broken, there was no place better to talk it through.

"How'd you find out?" Spencer asked, as the neighbor kid flew by on his hoverboard.

"I did what I promised myself I would never do. I looked through his text messages. Just had this feeling that he was a player, and he is. The asshole. Played me the whole way."

Spencer laced an arm around Kendra. "You did the right thing. Always follow your instincts about a person."

"I know that now. Just still can't wrap my mind around the hurt. When you put a lot of stock in somebody and they let you down, it's a gut punch."

Spencer straightened. "Want me to slash his tires? I can find him."

That pulled a smile. "Don't you tempt me." A pause as they watched the quiet suburban street. "I honestly thought he might be the one, Spence."

Spencer sighed, dismissing the romanticized idea. "Yeah, well, now we know."

She felt Kendra studying her. "You still don't believe that there's someone for everyone, do you?"

She shrugged and stared up at the darkening sky. "I'm the pragmatist in this duo. You know that. People float into your life and they float away again. Just like Tucker, low as he is. Family like us? That's the only real constant. Love interests and romance? They come and go."

"Girl, that's the most unromantic of life views. One day we're going to change that."

She looked over at Kendra, dubious. "Not sure that's possible. Besides, there's a certain level of control that accompanies not letting yourself get too attached. Case in point, your heart is broken right now. Look at you. That wouldn't happen to me."

"Because you don't let people in. You keep 'em at arm's length. I don't want to be that. It's sad."

"It is not. It's the healthiest thing in the world."

"Right. Because you have it alllll figured out," Kendra said, playfully.

"No, no, no. I'm just capable of enjoying someone without making them the center of my life. When it doesn't work out, you pick up the pieces and move forward."

"Just move forward." Kendra shook her head. "Just you wait, one day when you least expect it, bam. Someone's gonna steal your heart when you're not looking. I hope they never give it back either."

"Have you met me?" Spencer scoffed. "Never gonna happen."

Kendra bumped her shoulder to Spencer's. "Famous last words, Spence. Famous last words."

"Not like I have a lot of time to date anyway." She grinned. "Not that I'm dead. Trust me on that."

"Oh yeah? So, you are still out there noticing people. Women," Kendra emphasized. "Tell me about who you've noticed lately. I'm all ears."

"No way. You'll wrap it up into some neat and perfect love package probably with hearts all over it. I'm not about that."

"Tell me who, or I'll tell your mama about the time you told her you were sleeping at my place but you'd secretly headed to San Diego to meet that college girl you were talking to on the internet."

The smile slid right off Spencer's face. "You wouldn't do that."

"Ms. Adair, you available?" Kendra yelled in the direction of the house.

"You're the fucking worst," Spencer said, just in time for her mother to appear.

"What do you all have going on out here?" she asked, wiping her hand on a dish towel.

"Fine," Spencer mouthed discreetly to Kendra, acquiescing.

Kendra smiled sweetly. "I just wanted to tell you how beautiful these hydrangeas came out this year. I can never get mine to look the way yours do. What's your secret?"

"Sunshine and extra love. I whisper sweet compliments to them daily when I leave for work. Tell them they're the best-looking flowers in California, and how far they're gonna go in life. That's the honest secret, too."

"Well, isn't that just the best advice?"

"Leave it to Mama," Spencer said blandly, still glaring halfheartedly at Kendra for the blackmail.

"I'm gonna make up some to-go plates for you two before I get started on my *Grey's Anatomy*. I'm up to season four, and don't even get me going on how doomed that hospital is." And with that, she fluttered back into the house.

Once they were alone, Kendra leapt from the porch and down three stairs and stood on the sidewalk smiling up at Spencer. "I'm ready. Who's floating your boat these days? If you're back on Corinne from high school, don't even tell me. I don't even want to know."

"What? No? That woman comes with more drama than the Trump White House." Stuck, and wishing she'd never so much as dropped a hint, she sighed, giving in to Kendra and her unrelenting enthusiasm. Her own fault for dropping the hint. "Remember the assistant manager from the boutique? She's a really nice person is all."

"Really *nice*?" Kendra said, as if there were a bad taste in her mouth. "Really. Nice. Well, that's a lot to write home about. I couldn't get my mind off of her, Kendra. I think of her hourly. She's really just so nice. Gets me all hot and bothered."

Spencer laughed. "Stop it already."

"No, no. When I'm into a guy, I know that's the first thing I daydream about. How polite he is. Not his tight ass or his luscious lips."

"That's superficial."

"That's human. Is she at least hot?" Kendra kicked her hip out.

Spencer scoffed, again refusing to pay Kendra much attention. "She's attractive, okay? Yes."

"Live a little, Spence. Pick a creative adjective and knock me out of my own socks over here."

"She's...white."

"Get the hell out. Spencer and a white girl. Okay, okay. I can get behind it. You're branching out."

She closed her eyes in offense. "I've dated white girls. I've dated Latin girls. What are you talking about?"

"Maybe for like two seconds."

"I'm about the person. Can I help it if we went to a largely black school?"

"See, now that's valid." Kendra returned to her spot on the step. "So, what's the plan? Now that I'm heartbroken and on my own love hiatus, I need to live vicariously through you, because I'm not ready to get back out there. Take me on this journey with you."

"Nope. There's nothing to live through. I've got an almost unattainable deadline to hit and have to practically undo half of my fall line. Lust is fun and all, but it doesn't help you get ahead."

"It sounded at dinner like the *really nice* assistant manager was helping with that."

"She is. Consulting is a good word for it."

"Perfect. Maybe things will boil over during an overly creative consultation." An idea seemed to take shape and Kendra's whole face transformed into a grin. "Hey, maybe we can call her ass manager for short, and she can handle your ass anytime."

Spencer stared at Kendra. "Sometimes I think you're still in high school. No, I'm confident that's the case."

"Don't hate me for my youthful disposition and body of an eighteen-year-old."

Spencer smiled. As crazy as Kendra was, she was pretty much the other half of Spencer and she loved her, ridiculous as she could sometimes be. They balanced each other out, which went a long way in life.

"To-go plates for my girls," her mother said, emerging from the house. She handed a tinfoil-wrapped plate to each of them and placed a kiss on each woman's head. "Gotta keep you both visiting me somehow."

"Thanks, Mama," Spencer said. "I'll stop by in a couple days."

"Good. I want to hit up that shoe sale. You in?"

"All about it," Spencer said.

"Thanks, Mama A!" Kendra echoed. Plate in hand, she stood. "I better get some sleep. Two inductions tomorrow morning and a nursery full of tiny babies in need of love and care."

Spencer stood and hugged Kendra goodbye, something they'd done every parting since the second grade. "See you soon, Kenny. You be good and stay away from that Tucker."

Kendra's face softened. "Good advice. Mine to you? Get to know that ass manager." With a final laugh, Kendra was off the porch and heading to her home next door.

Spencer chuckled quietly in spite of herself. She remained on the porch for a few extra minutes, taking in the sounds of summer crickets, the neighborhood as it grew still in preparation for evening, and the smoky aroma of one of the neighbors cooking out just a few houses down. Coming home once or twice a week helped center her and keep her on track for the days ahead. This was her comfort zone. These were her people. She nodded at the neighbor kid on the hoverboard, heading back home. He tossed her a wave. Everything was calm. Everything was as it should be. Just how Spencer preferred it.

CHAPTER FIVE

W hat do you think about the turquoise skirt? I feel it might be a tad long. No, it probably is. Just look at that. No, I can't do it. I'm not ready for matronly."

Mrs. Rossdale turned to the side and surveyed herself in the series of full-length mirrors on the second level of Silhouette. She held a hand against her stomach, a habit she had developed when trying on most anything. For Hadley, working with a client like Mrs. Rossdale (older, firm in what she wanted, and beyond rich) required a fine balance between honesty, so she'd likely return to the store for guidance, and flattery, which would make her shopping experience at Silhouette one she'd like to repeat. In this instance, the skirt was not at all long. In fact, it was too short for Mrs. Rossdale's age and stature, but Hadley was not in the business of saying such things. She refused to.

However, she moved easily into redirection. "The turquoise is nice, but it doesn't hold a candle to the way you looked in the red de la Renta. Stunning isn't the word. Not to mention red catches the eye, turns heads, which I hear you're known to do."

Mrs. Rossdale lit up and took a sip of her white wine. "This is exactly why I come to you, Hadley. I need direction! Done. Let's wrap up the de la Renta."

"Wonderful choice. What about the Gucci sunglasses from earlier? They'll likely be out of stock by next week. Still on your radar?"

"Should they be? Honestly, Hadley, you know better than I do." Mrs. Rossdale sighed with indecision. "What do you think about those?"

"When you put them on, it made me wonder about a pair for myself." It wasn't a lie. She had her eye on those glasses. They just weren't in her budget just yet.

"Then I guess we'll toss those in, too. Why not, right?"

"I think you'll be pleased you did." As she rang up the purchase with a bright smile, and did a quick calculation on her commission, Hadley slyly checked the clock. Mrs. Rossdale was the last appointment of the day, and the store would close to foot traffic in the next twenty minutes. She'd made it to the end of her workday at long last. She grinned, knowing she was scheduled to meet with Spencer an hour later, an appointment she'd been secretly waiting for all day. She scrunched her toes as she handed Mrs. Rossdale her receipt.

"You're a godsend, Hadley. You just know my tastes so well."

"Well, it helps when the taste is good." She patted herself on the back for that one. It wasn't that she was lying to Mrs. Rossdale, or sucking up, but she enjoyed steering her clients in the right direction while at the same time making them feel good about themselves. Nothing wrong with spreading a little joy while on the job. She carried the intricately packaged skirt-and-sunglasses combo to the door and waved fondly as Mrs. Rossdale's driver pulled to the curb to pick her up.

"Another satisfied customer," Hadley said to herself.

"Wait!" a voice yelled from the sidewalk behind her.

Hadley paused. "Iz?" she asked, peering around the door. Sure enough, there was Isabel, hustling up the walk to the store. Moving her arms like one of those intense speed walkers in the mall. "Wait!" she called again. "Don't lock me out. I know it's closing time! But I made it!"

Hadley beamed at her unexpected visitor. "You here for a fitting? A new wardrobe?"

"I wish," Isabel said, out of breath. "If you have anything black to go with my other black then we might be in business. But I'll need the heavy discount, Cooper. I can't be paying Beverly Hills prices." She dropped with her hands on her knees, hunched over, still huffing and puffing. "Just need a minute to catch up. Do you realize that the only reasonable parking in this area is that garage that feels a year away?"

"It's not like I would have locked you out, crazy pants. There was no need to race here. Send me a text."

"Crazy pants?" Isabel straightened. "Is that a legit crack at my pants? Because they came off the rack. I get it, and I'm feeling judged."

"No," Hadley said, leading them back inside the store. "Have I ever made fun of your clothes? No, and that's because you have your own style and it's very you, who I happen to adore. You'll find no criticism here." She glanced back at Isabel, who seemed to be a nervous ball of energy that had yet to settle. Hadley squinted. "Something is going on. Why are you here and acting strange?"

"I'm not acting strange." Isabel glanced furtively around the store. "Who's here with you?"

Hadley followed her gaze, intrigued. "No one. I sent the last two employees home an hour ago. I handled the final appointment personally."

"Okay, good. That's good," Isabel said, relaxing a little, moving among the mannequins. She waved at one of them for good measure. "I just wanted to chat for a moment, just us. You and me. Without the others participating. Or knowing."

"You mean Gia and Autumn?"

Isabel nodded solemnly. She showcased a vulnerability today that Hadley had rarely seen. Isabel had a delicate side, that part Hadley knew, but it was rare she let her guard down enough for anyone to glimpse it. "I just think you might be better for this is all. This conversation. People always go to you for advice when it comes to love, so I thought I'd give that a go."

"Okay." Hadley's heart swelled and squeezed. She was concerned about whatever it was that was on Isabel's mind but honored that Izzy had chosen to confide in *her* about it. "Do you want to sit down?" She gestured to the small staircase that led to the couches outside the fitting room.

"No, no. That seems too formal. Too official. We can just talk like fucking…I don't know…people."

Hadley kept her smile warm and gentle. "We can definitely do that. Let's start with what it is that has you seeking advice."

Isabel pointed at her as if impressed. "Yes, that would be the perfect place to start. Look at you. Already a pro. Okay, give me just a sec." She rolled her shoulders a few times and jogged in place. Her eyes now carried fear, which signaled to Hadley that they might very well be approaching an anxiety attack, and in Isabel those tended to be crippling. She needed to get in front of the symptoms if at all possible.

"You don't have to, but do you mind if I sit?" Hadley asked, stepping out of her heels and placing them on the counter. She knew if she could take the focus off Isabel and shift it to herself, they might sidestep any impending panic. "I've been on my feet for hours and just need to collapse."

"Oh!" Isabel said, her eyes wide. "I'm a total thoughtless asshole. Of course you should sit. Let's just hit up those couches up there."

"I'm also starving. What about some cheese and crackers from the back? I'm dying."

"Are we allowed to do that?" Isabel asked, following Hadley up the short staircase in the middle of the store.

"We are. Perk of the job. Free wine and cheese."

They sat on the floor in front of the couches, because Hadley was doing everything in her power to keep the conversation light and casual. As she spread a knife of brie across a cracker, feigning the utmost interest in the activity, Isabel went for it.

"I love Taylor more than any person or object in existence."

Hadley smiled, mid-cracker spread. "Aww, you're making me all warm and tingly. Of course you love her that much. You two are great together."

"We are. Right? I mean, *I* think so. She seems to agree, and the longer we're together, the more in love with her I am, Had." She paused and looked up at the ceiling. "She's so smart, and fucking creative, and don't even get me started on patient and loving and drop dead gorgeous."

"She's all of those things." Still attempting to keep things breezy for Isabel's benefit, Hadley bit into her cracker, making a big show of how wonderful and fortifying that particular bite was. Amazing! The cracker with delicious cheese was the real star of the show. Isabel was just supporting. It seemed to be working.

"I want to marry her," Isabel said simply. "And it's time, but I can't seem to do anything about it. I'm paralyzed, and not sure how to move out of that mode."

Hadley froze mid-chew. "Izzie," she said quietly.

"I know. It's good news, right?"

She nodded, trying her hardest not to mist up. "The very best."

A hint of a smile appeared on Isabel's face at the encouragement and slowly grew. "But I need help. I don't know how to propose. What to say. Where to do it. And when I think about it, I get all freaked out and clam up entirely. You'll find me sitting in a closet, wondering how the hell I got there."

"That's okay," Hadley said simply. "Don't beat yourself up about nerves." She handed Isabel a cracker with cheese, which she seemed excited to dive into. Talking in the midst of an activity was going well. Isabel hadn't shown further signs of anxiety at all.

"So, here's the thing," Isabel said, around bites. "I'm a great writer, and so my instinct is to do something amazing and grandiose, like you would see on a television show. But I'm not sure that's me. Or Taylor either, for that matter. She throws lavish parties for all of Hollywood, but when it comes to her personal life, she prefers things low-key. Everyday stuff is her jam."

"I don't think there's anything wrong with discreet and personal. Just be you. She chose *you* out of everyone for a reason, you know." Hadley considered some options, all the while tamping down the choir of angels singing in her head at this fantastic news. Isabel and Taylor were likely going to be married! "What about over a quiet dinner? Maybe take her somewhere secluded and romantic. Off the beaten path. Oh! What about that place that Elle raves about. The little inn with the restaurant that Gia took her to."

"Yeah, maybe so. What if I can't figure out what to say and utter something stupid like, 'Let's fucking get hitched.' That's so like me that it's terrifying. I don't want to disappoint her."

Hadley reached across the small coffee table between them and covered Isabel's hand. "I'm happy to report that I don't see that as a remote possibility. She loves everything about you, Iz. You should see the way she stares at you when you're not looking. It takes up all the air in the room."

Isabel's cheeks were dusty with an adorable rose color. "Really?"

"I've seen it more times than I can count. And I know you feel the same way. So here's my advice. Speak to her from your heart. No script required."

Isabel ruminated on the idea, finally, blossoming into a grin. "I think I can do that."

"And put way less pressure on yourself. It's just another way of telling her that you love her, isn't it? That's all you're doing, and you're a pro at that."

"I am. Hadn't thought of it that way."

"Well, now you have." Hadley wrapped her arms around herself in a cozy hug. "You two and what you have is everything. Do you realize that? I'm so envious that I could devour this entire tray of brie just to console myself." And then because the lines of communication were so wide open, she decided to go for it. "Can I confess something to you now?"

"Hell yeah," Isabel said, sitting taller, brimming with anticipation. "That never happens. What do ya got?"

"The woman I'm supposed to meet with in a half hour? The designer?"

"Yeah, Spencer someone."

Hadley nodded. "I think I have a crush on her."

With her hands, Isabel impersonated a bomb dropping. "I've been waiting for this moment. For our sweet Hadley Bear to catch the love bug and fall under its spell."

Hadley shrugged in an effort to minimize the news. "I'm not sure it has any staying power. Just a temporary distraction I can't seem to shake." A pause. Hadley lowered her voice, as if there were others who might overhear, which was ridiculous. "Iz, my toes wiggle when she's around."

"Really? The toes specifically?"

Hadley nodded solemnly.

"Huh, that's a new one."

"What do you think that means?"

"I think it means she's under your skin. Can I borrow that? My main character is about to meet someone special. Could work to incorporate the toe wiggling and her confession of it to a friend."

"All yours," Hadley said, picking up the platter of cheese and crackers.

"You going to ask her out?"

Hadley's face felt hot. "No. No, that would be outlandish. She's creative and successful and driven and determined."

"Those are *bad* things?"

Hadley's eyes went wide. "I didn't mean it that way. No, of course they're not bad. They're wonderful! To be admired, even. It's just, what would she want with someone like me? I'm just regular."

Isabel covered her eyes with her hand. "When are you going to stop undervaluing who you are? I'm going to have to murder you with a sledgehammer. We've been over this time and time again. Everywhere I take you, people check you out. Men and women, by the way. I've seen both. You're a fucking knockout, a head turner, and everyone knows it but you."

Hadley opened her mouth to speak, but Isabel silenced her, holding up a hand.

"Not to mention you have the kindest heart of anybody I've ever encountered. You're also funny, carefree, and have a killer eye for color and design. Do you know how jealous I am of your apartment? Don't answer that. Very jealous. You just refuse to see yourself the way we all do, you lunatic." She lowered her hand. "Talk now."

"That was nice," Hadley said, elevated by the words Isabel had just spoken, trying to hold on to them as a confidence booster. "Even the lunatic part."

"And true. Don't forget goddamned true."

Hadley tilted her head from side to side in consideration. "I'll work on remembering that. Minus the goddamn."

"I suggest you work on it with Spencer. Ask her out. Tonight."

"Absolutely not." Hadley's jaw fell open at the suggestion. "Do you even know me? I can't ask someone out. I just…can't. No."

"You're confident in every other area of your life, and as we've seen here tonight, you offer fantastic advice on the subject of love and all things connected. Time to put your money where your mouth is, blondie."

Hadley nodded, and sucked in air. "Maybe."

"Aha! A semi-commitment, I can accept," Isabel said, as she led them down to the first floor. Hadley allowed herself to trail behind her a bit to catch her breath. For whatever reason, talking about her stupid little crush left her more nervous than ever. That didn't seem fair! Talking about things was supposed to help alleviate them. She placed a hand on her fluttering stomach and checked the clock. Spencer would arrive soon, and they would work. She would not wiggle her toes, or allow herself to acknowledge how attractive Spencer was or how her determination really got Hadley going in…all of the important ways. This was her job, and she would remain professional and on topic. "Well, it's now time for me to hike my way to the parking garage for real people who don't actually shop in Beverly Hills."

Hadley brightened. "I'm so glad you came. And you know what? This is only the beginning of what's going to be a fantastic life with Taylor. You're so lucky."

The comment seemed to land and Isabel grew an inch or two taller. "I think so, too. Bouncing things off you really helped, Had, you superstar of all things mushy. Now go fluff your hair for your meeting. And do what you told me to do. Don't overthink it." But before she left, Isabel thrust her arms around Hadley's neck for an unexpected hug. For a minute, the two of them just stood there as all the wonderful things Isabel had brought into her life since arriving in LA flooded Hadley's memory: the laughs, the sarcastic wit, and the never-ending friendship. She could safely say that Isabel would be her friend for the rest of her life. She would have it no other way. "Getting out of your hair now," Isabel said, with a sheepish smile. "Thanks for the Dr. Phil sesh."

"Anytime," Hadley called, from the doorway of Silhouette.

Once she was alone, she turned back to the deserted store and did something she never saw coming, she fluffed her hair. "Oh, dear goodness," she muttered, shaking her head. Who exactly was she becoming?

"Knock, knock," Spencer called from the entryway twenty minutes later. "You didn't lock the door," she said, with a sly look on her face. "I thought this place was always bolted up tight after hours." She wore blue and green camo capris and a short-sleeve lace-up green top that she paired with army green heels. Stunning. Her dark hair had been styled so that it framed her face, brushing her shoulders, which was new.

"Hi," Hadley said, realizing she was thrilled to see Spencer, to spend the evening talking to her, or arguing with her, depending on the direction they took. Either was welcome.

"I brought clothes," she said, glancing over her shoulder toward the thick garment bag. "But I was thinking maybe we could ditch that plan and talk sketches over drinks. Would you be game for that?"

"For drinks? With you?" Hadley was hopeful she hadn't squeaked the response.

Spencer glanced around the store lightheartedly. "You would be the one I'm asking. Correct."

"A working-drinks-get-together is what you're proposing?"

"Kind of."

Oh, that wasn't enough. Hadley, in her newly jumbled nervous disposition, needed more details than that. A girl needed clarification when crushing on another girl who then went and asked her to a public place. With alcohol. "Not entirely business?" Hadley asked.

Spencer took a few steps into the store, taking her time deciding what she would say next, apparently. She came with such a confident swagger, which was sexy for days. Whether she was choosing words or just drawing out saying them wasn't clear. Hadley felt the seconds tick. "I really want to show you some ideas that have popped into my head since we last spoke, and I'd also like to just talk. With you. About anything." She leveled that stare on Hadley, and damn it all, her toes took over.

"That could be fun," she heard herself say. "Let me just turn off a few lights and grab my bag. I'll drop these in my car and meet you out front in a few?"

"I'll be there."

"Perfect. It's a date," Hadley said, and then covered her mouth at the utterance.

Spencer didn't seem fazed. In fact, she grinned, nodded, and left.

"Oh, my dear goodness," she whispered to the empty store. "Here goes nothing." She walked from Silhouette with a self-assured strut she was only just beginning to feel. Look out, LA. Maybe little Hadley Cooper was about to embrace the saucy side of life.

CHAPTER SIX

The quiet little jazz club Spencer suggested was sultry, dimly lit, and surprisingly not that far from Silhouette. The sign out front blazed red with the club's name, Notes, in a lazy script. Though outside was nondescript, the inside came with a lot of personality. Small tables dotted the main floor, flanked by an elevated perimeter of additional tables looking down on the main floor. A lantern-like candle sat on each of the white tablecloths, and attentive waitstaff carried trays of drinks. Sophisticated ones.

She and Spencer nestled themselves at a quiet table near the back where they could still hear the music but converse easily enough. The place was about three-quarters full, but night had just fallen. Hadley imagined it'd be overflowing within the next two hours. She very much enjoyed the vibe.

"Where did you hear about this place?" Hadley asked.

"Spencer, where have you been?" a glamorous-looking woman in her fifties asked as she approached their table. Spencer stood and embraced the woman who kissed her cheek. "We thought you'd taken off for Europe or someplace, never to be heard from again."

"One can only dream," Spencer said with a wink, and took her seat. "Just been busy is all. You know how that grind can be." She turned to Hadley. "Hadley Cooper, meet Mabel Van Muir. She's one of the club's owners and a very impressive vocalist. Also, a friend of my mother's."

"Now you're just tossin' flattery. So very nice to meet you, Hadley. What can I send over for you two from the bar?"

Spencer gestured to Hadley to order first. "I'll take a glass of the house white."

Mabel nodded.

"Old Fashioned for me," Spencer said. "Extra cherry tossed in, if you don't mind."

"As usual," Mabel said, with a wink. "I'll send Ted over with the drinks and a snack on the house. You two enjoy yourself. We got the Miller Trio up next and Fred's on the keys."

"Then we arrived at the right time," Spencer said. "Thanks, Mabel."

"You must come here a lot," Hadley said, once they were alone.

"Once in a while. It's a nice place to escape to. Clear my head, have a drink, and listen to some good music. I can still sketch in the low light, and the music undoes the world for me. Just don't know much about it is all, so don't expect me to expound on it."

"Well, you know that you enjoy it. That's enough."

They stared at each other for a weighted moment. Nothing could have made Hadley look away. Spencer, she was beginning to understand, was able to cast a spell. One that she didn't mind at all.

"You make a valid point. I think I just like chasing the melody. With jazz, you never know where it's going to go."

"Reminds me of real life."

Spencer pointed at her. "I get that." Another pause. "We should get to work."

"Yes," Hadley said, her focus still on Spencer, who had the most expressive eyes and perfect mouth. Her eyebrows had been delicately sculpted, Hadley decided. The results were subtle but effective, as was her hint of rose lipstick. Enough to make a difference but never stealing the show. Spencer Adair was all balanced style and certainty wrapped up together. Two qualities Hadley admired very much. Neither one of them had moved. "We're not working," she said, finally, leaning back in her leather club chair.

"We're not." Spencer blinked, dipped her head, and smiled. "But I'm glad we're doing this."

"And what is this, exactly?" Hadley asked, still on uneven footing and searching for a way to right herself. She could fly by the seat of her pants in a lot of circumstances. This wasn't one of them.

"*You* called it a date. I'm just following your lead."

"I'm not to be relied upon for diagnostics," Hadley said. "There's a top half of a groundhog costume on a mannequin in my closet, and I'm not even making that up."

Spencer nearly spat her water back into the glass. "That is an entirely random statement. And why the display? Fan of the groundhog?"

"A fan of anything celebratory. I head up a theme night each month for my friends and neighbors. You probably think that's lame, but that's who you're dealing with. I need you to know now. Someone who likes frivolous parties, and anything warm and fuzzy. Is that someone you'd want to date?" Hadley blinked, awaiting Spencer's response.

Spencer sat taller. "Well, this is getting interesting. Are you trying to talk me out of it?"

"I don't know," Hadley said. It was a truthful answer. "I also tend to believe whatever people tell me. That might make me naïve, but I like to think it's my attempt to see the good in everyone. I don't think that's a bad thing, either. I'm keeping it."

"It's not a bad thing," Spencer said, intrigued. "But it's helpful that you're laying out all your quirks so early." She seemed to make a decision. "I can't stand roller coasters. They're impractical."

Hadley nodded, and reciprocated. "I make up songs about my friends' pets. They don't always rhyme and I'm fine with that. It's about the effort you put in."

"I'm a fantastic soccer player, but can't stand running. The internal conflict is rough."

"I'm not so great at *Ms. Pac-Man*. Or any video game, for that matter."

Spencer squinted. "I burn Rice-A-Roni. Every. Damn. Time. Even when I have the best of intentions. San Francisco must detest me and has sent its treat to sabotage my kitchen."

"I adore Barry Manilow in any possible incarnation. I will fight for him." Hadley placed a hand on her heart. "'Mandy' makes me cry. She gave without taking."

"I don't cry often, but when I do, it's because I'm deeply affected. And it's not pretty either. I ugly cry for the record books."

"I love to roller-skate even though I'm an adult. Once in a while I'll do so in the courtyard of my apartment complex. My neighbor, Stephanie, calls me Starlight Express and rolls her eyes in disgust. She hates most things and people."

"Last year, I lied a little on my taxes about how many business dinners I'd had. I don't feel bad about that."

Hadley held up her hand in guilt. "I'm obsessed with chunky peanut butter and *Days of Our Lives*. Mainly in combination. One isn't the same without the other."

"I've always wanted to go to Paris. I turned down an internship there once and have always regretted it."

"Me, too." Hadley leaned forward at the mere mention and placed a hand over her heart to show her abiding love. "About Paris, I've always dreamed of going. I've traveled close but never made it to the city itself. One day."

They paused. "Would you look at that?" Spencer said. "Unexpected common ground. That wasn't so bad, was it?"

"You don't want to run screaming yet?" Hadley asked, with a smile. "Even about the Barry Manilow thing?"

Spencer shook her head. "I can deal with Manilow. Does make you extra white, though."

Hadley nodded solemnly. "I've heard that before."

Their drinks arrived and they enjoyed them while listening to the music. At one point, several songs in, Spencer slid her chair around the round table so she was sitting next to Hadley, which allowed them to watch together. The band transitioned into a mellow slow song, and Spencer slipped her hand into Hadley's. It was so natural, so discreet, and so wonderful that Hadley couldn't seem to wipe the smile off her face and play it cool. Who was she kidding? She would never be that kind of cool. She was Hadley Cooper, and she wore her emotions on her sleeve. And with Spencer this close to her, she could detect the scent that always seemed to follow Spencer into every room, strawberries and cream. Her shampoo? A lotion? She wasn't sure, but it reminded her of summers growing up and movie nights outside. She loved strawberries and cream. She secretly wondered what Spencer's lips tasted like. Would strawberries come through in a stolen kiss? And that did it. "Is it warm in here?" she whispered, fanning herself ineffectively with the limp cloth napkin.

Spencer nodded, downed her drink, and leaned into Hadley's ear. "Want to get out of here?"

Hadley didn't even hesitate. "Sure." They walked the streets that surrounded the club, looking in closed-for-the-night store windows, pointing out fascinating trinkets, restaurants they'd like to come back and try, and nodding to the occasional fellow pedestrian. Hadley took a deep inhale and let the warmer summer air fill her lungs. She'd long ditched the white jacket she'd worn over black pants, leaving her in a sleeveless charcoal blouse that let her body breathe.

"You seemed to like the club," Spencer pointed out, as they continued their circling of the block.

"The guy on the piano!" Hadley marveled. "He has so much talent, and it looks so effortless up there, as if he wasn't even thinking that hard about what he was doing. That right there is an honest to God *gift*." She looked over at Spencer. "Reminds me of you, actually."

Spencer balked. "In what way am I like Freddy, whiz of the keys?"

"Your talent. It amazes me. The minute I looked you up and saw how many people were talking about your designs, I was impressed. When I saw the line itself? Blown away. That's when I knew I had to meet you. You're going to be the next big thing. Only a matter of time."

They walked in silence for a moment. Spencer looked over at her. "Ever since you called me that first day, I've felt..." She shook her head as if searching for the word. "Empowered. That someone like you, with ties to the high end, the best of the best, sees promise in my work. In fact"—she glanced over at Hadley—"I've never felt more inspired in my whole life. You, for whatever reason, bring that out in me."

"I had no idea," Hadley said, floored.

"I've been sketching nonstop, and part of that comes from you challenging me the other night. Forcing me to look at things I know in a whole new light and toss my stubborn opinion out the damn window."

Hadley laughed. "Does that mean we're toning down the lime green?"

"It does." They arrived at their cars that were parked on the street, one in front of the other. This was where they would say good night, and what a nice evening it had been. "Before you go, I want to send this with you." Spencer pulled a sketch pad from her bag. "Some of the redesigns, and a couple new ideas to go with them. No rush. I thought maybe you could take a look and tell me what you think."

Hadley accepted the pad. "I'd be happy to. And, Spencer?"

"Yes?"

"Thanks for tonight. I needed this, I think. Best time I've had in a really long time." And then she did something awful. She took a step back, clearly breaking their connection, and offered Spencer a wave. A wave? Why? "See you soon." And without so much as waiting for a reply wave, she hastily headed to her own car, a nice safe distance away from the heat she'd felt bouncing between them all night. She already missed it. "No," she said out loud, with hand on the handle of her car door. "Not like this." She tapped the hood and turned, looking over at Spencer, who still stood in front of her own car door. She looked back in mystification. Channeling Kate's confidence or Gia's or Wonder Woman's herself, Hadley decided to act. She walked herself back to Spencer's car and paused briefly in front of her before doing the one thing she'd wanted to do for over a week now. She cradled Spencer's face in her hands momentarily, and holy goodness, she kissed her, losing herself then and there in front of that car in the warmth of those amazing lips. The soft, surprised murmur that escaped Spencer went right through Hadley, escalating the confidence she didn't have just two minutes ago. She slanted her mouth over Spencer's and deepened the kiss, surprised by Spencer's eager participation. Hadley had allowed herself to secretly wonder if the reality would be as good as her imagination. It was better. Spencer tasted every bit as sweet as she'd hoped, and she pressed her incredible body up against Hadley's in welcome connection. She could feel Spencer's heart beating along with her own. The intoxicating rhythm swept her away to places wonderful and foreign…and very, very sexy. She no longer remembered where they were, or what brought them to this amazing moment in time, but she didn't want it to end.

When she reluctantly pulled back, Spencer seemed softer than ever before. Her gaze held a new quality: innocence. But also vulnerability, and that had Hadley's heart hammering for her all the more. Her world was rocked, forever affected, and all she could do was blink back at Spencer in surprise at what she'd just done and subsequently experienced.

Not only had Spencer allowed Hadley to kiss her, but she'd melted right there in her arms. Now what? Was she supposed to just turn and go back to her car, her life, as originally scheduled? They'd see each other again for a work meeting in a few days? Before she had a moment to answer those questions, Spencer leaned back against the car, caught Hadley around the waist, and pulled her back in. As hard as it was for Hadley to believe that the second kiss was more scorching than the first, it most certainly was. Spencer held her close, their weight against the car, as her mouth angled and opened wider across Hadley's. Her tongue explored skillfully, deliciously. Right on cue, Hadley scrunched her toes as arousal hit hot and fast. She took everything Spencer gave and craved so much more.

Distantly there was the sound of a car honking and voices approaching. Spencer released her, and Hadley remembered that they were right there on a public street. How easy it had been to lose track. Still dazed, she managed a foggy smile and gestured to her car. "I should get going."

Spencer nodded, her gaze intently trained on Hadley's. They were both breathing erratically. "Can I call you? About work. And other things."

"Yes. I hope you will."

Spencer straightened, looking alluring as could be with swollen lips and a satisfied smile. "Good night, then."

"Good night," Hadley said, though there were five hundred other words ready to gush from her lips at any moment. Play it cool, she reminded herself, and headed to her car.

Hadley drove home with the windows down and the soft, romantic station that took requests playing quietly from her radio. What an unexpected night it had been! She hit her steering wheel in happy disbelief. She'd been kissed. No! Even more shocking, she'd done the kissing, and loved how empowered it made her feel to take what she wanted. Spencer brought out a new and exciting side of Hadley and she, for one, was more than okay with that. And don't even get her started on the explosive chemistry they had. She'd never experienced anything like it. Unable to help herself, she dialed Isabel and put her on speakerphone in the car.

"I kissed her," Hadley said, the second Isabel answered.

"Fuck me. You did?"

"Yes! I'm not even making it up. Best kiss of my life, and I just missed my turn because I was thinking about that kiss. Gotta go!"

"You owe me more tomorrow. Proud of you, you little crafty minx!"

"Thanks, Iz. Bye!"

As Hadley made her way back to Seven Shores, a million and nine thoughts buzzed through her overcrowded brain. She did her best to remain levelheaded and optimistic, which she'd deemed long ago was the best version of herself. All the same, she smiled at the winding road as she drove, and vowed to take each moment as it came. No need to overanalyze anything at this point.

But for the first time in a long time, she felt the stirrings of something important. She would tuck that feeling away and take it out when she needed it. It was exciting to realize that someone like Spencer was out there. That Spencer herself was.

She turned up Manilow and sang along loudly. Oh, the possibilities.

❖

Spencer woke up thinking about her date with Hadley, as she'd done each of the three mornings since they'd kissed against her car. Not an awful way to wake up. Lying in her bed and staring up at the ceiling,

Minnie upside down on the floor next to her, she allowed herself to relive the tantalizing moment that Hadley, who seemed so unassuming and sweet, had taken Spencer's damn face in her hands and kissed her into next Tuesday. "Damn," she muttered, shaking her head. She didn't let herself live in the clouds on a regular basis, and today would be no different. A little reveling never hurt, though. She and Hadley would see each other soon and maybe pick up where they'd left off. Spencer wasn't someone who romanticized love and dreamt of butterflies and happily ever after, but she wasn't opposed to her and Hadley getting to know each other better and enjoying each other's company for however long they chose.

As she showered, she ruminated further despite her own protestations. She liked Hadley. Hell, that was a lie, she more than liked her. She thought she was beautiful, and kind, and quirky enough to be fun and not scary. Not to mention knowledgeable about fashion, with a keen eye for detail. Spencer couldn't quite wrap her mind around her ability to kiss, because it was off any chart she could have constructed. She shook her head to clear it. While thoughts of Hadley were fun, she had to focus on the day ahead of her.

An hour and a half later, she arrived at her meeting with Dez McBride, who'd been such an early champion of her work that he'd invested in her brand and now owned 15 percent of her business. As part of that deal, he handled and financed all manufacturing, which had turned out to be a godsend. Dez was a wheeling, dealing businessman with plenty of high-up connections. He also happened to know a lot about the textile industry, and she was lucky to have fallen in with him.

"Dezzy Mac," she said, accepting a hug and kiss on the cheek. He was roughly twenty years older than Spencer and well-dressed, always in a shirt and tie. Did she mention he was smart as hell? He was. "Thanks for working me in. Your assistant said your day was booked."

"I can always make time for my favorite partner," he said, taking a seat behind his incredibly messy desk. She didn't let that worry her. Dez always had a million balls in the air, and they always seemed to land, safe and sound. She trusted him immensely with her business in spite of the clutter. "How's the spring line coming?"

"That's actually what I stopped by to talk with you about. Do you know Silhouette on Rodeo?"

"Everyone knows Silhouette on Rodeo."

"Right. Of course. They want to place an order. The first of what they hope will be many, but have requested some minor changes."

His eyebrows rose and he sat up, fully attentive now. "Impressive that you've attracted their interest. A store with their visibility can get your name in the high-end retail market. How do you feel about the changes they're asking for?"

"I'm coming around with time. You know how I can be."

"Unbending, like a guard dog standing in front of your designs, ready to rip anyone to shreds who speaks ill of them?"

"Yes, that," she said with a laugh. "But I've developed a decent working relationship with one of the managers, who's been placed in charge of scouting new buys. Apparently, they're working toward a revamp."

"Trudy Day has agreed to a revamp? Well, call me Tulita Pepsi. Leopards can change their spots. What do you need from me? You have controlling interest. You call the shots."

"Expedited manufacturing once we're a go. They want samples in three weeks and inventory not long after."

He whistled and stared at her. "You realize what you're asking?"

"For a huge favor, yes. But I genuinely think if this deal goes through that it could be a game changer for us, Dez. I'm only sitting here because I want to make you very, very rich." She smiled, knowing she'd tapped into his weakness.

He didn't so much as twitch an eyebrow. "And what about the inventory we already have queued for production on the original designs?"

"Pull it if we're not too late. If we are, I can still sell the pieces online and make us a killing. You know me. I'll put in the work and make it happen. I can slog all day and night. It's what I do."

He nodded and jotted a few notes on his iPad. "Understand that at some point, Spencer, we're going to have start outsourcing the shipping. Your brand is getting too big for this format. Let me start putting some numbers together and see what's feasible."

"If that means I'd get my living room back without having to fork over too much cash, I'm in."

"I also want you to meet with a friend of mine who'll be in town next month. I think she'd be a great connection for developing an overseas strategy. Let's do lunch."

She shrugged. "Yeah, sure. I'd love to."

"I'll have my assistant set it up. We need to get going on those samples for me to make this happen."

She stood and offered a salute. "Let me get finished up, then."

"Don't let me stop you."

She tapped on the doorframe a couple times. "You're a keeper, Dezzy. I'm sending you a gift basket."

He straightened his tie. "Make sure it's full of high-end booze."

She laughed. "Way ahead of you."

Walking victoriously through the office building, Spencer marveled at how all the difficult pieces of the puzzle were falling into place. She didn't hesitate when the instinct hit to call Hadley, who answered after only two rings.

"Spencer?" she said.

"I'm an idiot for calling because no one calls anyone anymore, but I wanted to tell you that my manufacturing guy thinks he can make Trudy's deadline. We're a go!" She couldn't smother her smile at the good news, and Hadley was the first person she wanted to share it with.

"Do you know how amazing that is?" Hadley asked, almost yelling into the phone. Her excitement was contagious. "Sorry, ma'am. Just heard some big news from a friend. I'll send Daisy over to help you with that shapewear."

Spencer laughed.

A moment later, "How are you not freaking out right now?"

"I am. I just freak out on a lower key than most people. Minimal movement, a little bit of grinning. Some blinking."

"Well, forget that. We need to celebrate. Are you free later?"

She had plans with Kendra and a handful of their friends. They'd generally get together at someone's house and head out on the town from there. But she'd make herself available if it meant she'd get to see Hadley who, let's be honest, took up a lot of her brain space lately in the most unexpected way. "Yes. I'm most assuredly free. I'll pick you up. Venice, near the beach, right?"

"The complex next to the coffee shop. Meet me in the courtyard at seven?"

"Where are we going?"

"I thought we'd figure it out together. Somewhere carefree where you can do more than blink."

Spencer chuckled. "Sounds intriguing. I'm in."

"Ohhh! I've never been called intriguing before." She imagined Hadley smoldering playfully as she'd done before. "I accept that descriptor and will attempt to do it justice tonight."

"Well, now you're just teasing me." Spencer shook her head at how frivolous she felt lately. Who was she exactly? Didn't matter. She was enjoying herself, and the last time she looked, that wasn't a crime. "See you at seven."

"Wait! Don't outdress me. You're always more stylish. Never mind. I happen to love that. Do your thing. See you tonight!"

"Goodbye, Hadley."

"Bye, Spence."

She exhaled where she stood on the corner of Sunset and Doheny, already thrumming with anticipation of the evening ahead. Where would they go? What might they discuss? Would she kiss Hadley again? Whatever they did, she was confident they'd have fun together. Seeing the world through Hadley's eyes, as she had the other night, was an entirely new and addictive venture. But first, she had a mountain of work waiting for her back home. Her online shop had hit a new sales record and she and Minnie had more than a few orders to fill.

Those damn blue eyes would have to wait until later.

CHAPTER SEVEN

Hadley dashed inside Autumn and Kate's apartment mere milliseconds after Autumn opened the door. "Don't mind me!" Hadley said. "Just got home from work, and I need a quick fix before my plans tonight. Are they up?"

"They are," Autumn said, laughing. "They were wondering why they hadn't laid eyes on you yet this afternoon. This morning was so long ago in baby time."

"It feels like an eternity has passed," Hadley said, desperately. Per Autumn's rules, she quickly washed her hands before handling the babies. "Are they talking yet? Have they said Auntie Hadley is our best friend? If not, we can keep working on it."

"Shockingly, no. They did, however, master crying in tandem for forty-five minutes and then staring in amazement at the light show the mobile puts on. Will, in particular, makes eyes at it. He's learning to flirt."

"Because my William notices everything! It's his gift. Hi, Care-Bear," Hadley said, scooping tiny Carrie up from where she lay in her Rock 'n Play. She was swaddled snugly and the cutest baby in all the world as she blinked up at Hadley. Her hair was starting to show red highlights in the blond, maybe signaling that she would take after her mother's red locks in the end.

"Have you noticed that Izzie seems quieter than usual lately?" Autumn asked, as Hadley made her goofiest of faces. Of their group of friends, Autumn was the consummate mother hen, eagerly observant and watching over the others. "She nodded along at Breakfast Club this morning, but it was clear she was distracted. Her head is somewhere. I just hope it's somewhere good."

Hadley was torn between putting Autumn's fears to rest and

holding on to Isabel's confidence. She trusted her gut and went with the latter. "I think she's just tired, you know? They pull some crazy hours at the studio and she probably needs a break."

Autumn tapped her chin. "I don't know. It feels like more."

"I'm sure if it is, we'll hear about it soon enough. You're such a sweetheart, though, always looking out for us."

"Well, someone has to. Speaking of looking after people, my new hire quit yesterday. I have an interview this afternoon with their potential replacement."

"Is this moonwalking-barista we're talking about? Or smells-way-too-much-like-mint girl?"

"Mint girl," Autumn said. "She thinks coffee just isn't in her blood, to which I scoffed and politely accepted her resignation, because what kind of person is she anyway? A lunatic. That's what kind. I mean, seriously, she should go find a mint farm somewhere and live out her days chewing gum and wearing coats."

"I'm sure she would leap at that suggestion." Hadley smiled at Autumn's fiercely loyal stance when it came to coffee and its importance in the scheme of life. She would go toe-to-toe with anyone who argued differently. While she was still checking in daily on the happenings at the Cat's Pajamas, she'd left Steve in charge so she could spend the twins' first few weeks at home with them before slowly rotating herself back onto the schedule. She and Kate had secured a nanny they liked very much, who would help watch the kiddos when both parents were at work. Luckily, with Autumn just next door, she could peek in on them and kiss their tiny cheeks whenever she wanted.

"So, what's new with you?" Autumn asked.

"I have a date tonight," Hadley said. "A real one. Not just one with my television."

"Get out of my apartment. You do? I miss the outside world. What does it look like? Who is your date? Will you go to a restaurant with a menu and not a drive-thru? What kind?" Autumn rested her chin in her hand and looked up at Hadley, who'd swapped out Carrie for Will, like she held the keys to the kingdom.

"You know, I'm thinking we need to work on a night out for you and Kate soon. You've been cooped up in here too long."

"Are you serious?"

"Very."

"You're like a blond Mother Teresa," Autumn said, nearly moved to tears. Sleep deprivation tended to bring Autumn's emotions to the surface, Hadley had learned, and then stirred them up like a big stew.

"Wouldn't be the first time I've heard that," Hadley said, with a proud smile.

"Tell me about your date so I can live vicariously through you. Tell me. Tell me."

"It's with Spencer. Remember, we had the business meeting at Pajamas a couple weeks back?"

Autumn reached for Carrie, who'd begun to whimper. "I knew it. You were so into her that day, like a little hummingbird to her nectar."

Hadley felt the familiar tingle move through her. "Well, the hummingbird's wings are still a-flapping."

"This story just keeps giving. Don't slow down."

Hadley could oblige. "We went to a jazz club the other night, so maybe this is date two."

"We're counting it," Autumn said vehemently. "Two it is."

Hadley shook her head. "I'm the opposite of a pro at this, though, Autumn, and really feeling the learning curve. The last time I went on a date was the woman from the online dating site who talked for hours about the insects on her patio and the factions they'd formed. That I could handle. This has me all wobbly. We don't even have a destination tonight."

"Wobbly is a good sign, though. Embrace it. Oh! There's a whiskey tasting at that cute little new age shop not far from here."

"Really?" Hadley nodded a few times, considering the option. Imagining it playing out.

"Someone posted a flyer on the bulletin board in Pajamas."

"That could be something fun to do together. I don't know much about whiskey, but Spencer ordered something boozy at the jazz club the other night, so she might like that. I'd be playing to my audience!" she said with exuberance, really finding her momentum now. Her papa had always instilled in her the importance of playing to her audience whenever possible. It had paid off so far in life. "Do you realize you and these babies might have saved me? I feel so much better with a direction to head in."

Autumn held up a finger. "Let's not go crazy with credit placement. These munchkins stared in awe as I solved your destination dilemma. Me. Do not give this goofy twosome points for being handsome and beautiful."

"Too late!" Hadley said, kissing little Will's cheek. "This guy is looking sleepy."

"That's because he blew off his nap two hours ago. Almost time to try again, isn't it, little guy?" Autumn asked, taking him from Hadley, who missed his cuddly warmth almost instantly.

"I guess that's my cue to get out of your hair and let them sleep."

"But you better be around tomorrow with an update." Autumn set the baby into his Rock 'n Play and took Hadley firmly by the shoulders. "I'm isolated here with people who do not speak and rarely allow me to sleep. I need this. Do you understand?"

Hadley, caught a little off guard by Autumn's uncharacteristic intensity, nodded back like an agreeable soldier.

"Good," Autumn said, releasing her, though her stare remained unrelenting. "I'll be waiting."

Hadley passed Gia in the courtyard on the way back to her own apartment. "Hey, G. I'm a tad worried about Autumn. I think we may need to give her a break from the twins at some point soon."

Gia nodded, her eyes full of fear. "Did she grab you and look at you like she could see right to your soul?"

"She did."

"She did that to me yesterday, and I haven't forgotten it. What do we do?"

"I'll see if we can schedule an outing for the two of them this weekend. I think Kate has Saturday off from the station. Want to help me watch them?"

Gia looked like a tiny animal caught in a trap. "I'm not sure I'm qualified."

Hadley punched her arm. "We got this. Besides, you'll have me."

"If you say so," Gia said. "In the meantime, I need to work out harder than Elle is. She's ridiculous and lapping me. Cannot happen."

Hadley winced. "Best of luck. I've seen her in action." Gia and Elle often battled it out on the Women's Pro Surf Tour. After Elle finished the previous season ranked second in the world, and Gia fourth, they were training with a new kind of vengeance that seemed to be paying off. They'd learned how to juggle love in the face of competition quite effectively over the last few months. Both had their eye on number one by season's end. While they loved each other relentlessly, they also stoked the fires of competition.

"You think I haven't?" Gia asked. "Her stamina is terrifying. Her abs alone should make me quit the sport altogether."

"Who has great abs and terrifying stamina? I need to meet this woman," Elle called down from the second-floor exterior railing. Caught! Gia and Hadley exchanged a wide-eyed OMG stare. Gia glanced up. "No one you know," she said, in the worst display of lying ever. She was simply awful at it, which made her awesome. Hadley covered her smile.

"Is this because I kicked your ass on that last sprint this morning?" Elle said playfully.

"You took off early and you know it," Gia said.

"Did not. And if I remember correctly, the winner was supposed to receive a victory massage. I secured that vanilla lotion and everything. I've just been up here, all by myself, waiting for the hands that would take me places. Still waiting."

Gia relaxed into a lazy grin. That had done it. Competition spell broken. "Yeah, you probably won fair and square."

Hadley decided to get out of their way, noticing the moment seemed to be shifting to the private variety. She took the stairs to her own apartment quickly, high-fiving Elle as she passed and then waving at Stephanie down below, her stoic neighbor who dressed daily in all black. Stephanie, all eyelinered up, just stared back at Hadley as if she were invisible. Nothing new. Didn't mean Hadley would stop greeting her in the future. It simply wasn't in her DNA to be unfriendly.

She dressed quickly in white capris and a royal blue off-the-shoulder top she knew would bring out her eyes. A small silver necklace would accentuate her neckline and a pair of tan slingbacks with a small heel would elongate the lines of her legs. If there was one thing Hadley found confidence in, it was putting together the right outfit for a given physique, and she was intimately familiar with her own. She bolstered her perceived strengths and minimized her weaknesses. All in a day's work.

She spent the remainder of the early evening going over Spencer's sketches, making notes along the way. Most everything she had to say was complimentary, however, as Spencer had taken her notes from their last session and run wild with them, adding touches, details, and textures Hadley would have never dreamed up—yet all in the right direction for high-end retail. "Gorgeous," she muttered to herself, and dropped the sketch pad into her bag to meet Spencer below.

She'd only been waiting in the courtyard for a few minutes when the woman she couldn't stop thinking about appeared. Right on cue, every part of her sighed dreamily and she stood, bag on her shoulder. As their eyes met, Spencer broke into a million-watt smile.

"You look amazing," she said. "Not that there's a world in which you couldn't."

Hadley let the compliment land and spread out. "Hi," she said happily. "And thank you." Spencer's own outfit was in the vein of her designs. Sophisticated, with a side of rebellious tossed in. Her short-sleeve black top had small rips down the side, offering only a fleeting glimpse of skin. She had a scarf with a faded leopard print around her neck, and her slim-legged jeans had Hadley's mouth watering. It was a really good look for Spencer.

"Where should we go?" Spencer asked.

"Hear me out, and understand that you can totally say no."

"The suspense is killing me."

"I'm told there's a spirits tasting tonight at this great little shop down the street. What do you think?"

"I'd be one hundred percent down with that," Spencer said, easing her hair behind her ear. "But I've only ever seen you drink wine. You'd be up for something a little heavier?"

"Pshhh," Hadley said, as if she did spirit tastings on the daily. "I can hang with the big girls, Spencer. You don't give me enough credit."

"Okay," Spencer said, as if still not quite able to picture Hadley tossing back whiskey neats. But then again, this would only be a tasting. They would sip, and see where the night led them. And really, who knew where that might be? Hadley was nervous and excited to find out.

"Follow me."

Spencer smiled. "Anywhere."

❖

The night was definitely going places. Spencer realized she was doing that thing where her feet weren't touching the ground, and called herself on it. As much as she enjoyed Hadley and felt reeled in by her contagious, bubbly charm, feet-on-the-ground realism was where Spencer preferred to live.

Before they'd met, she didn't have any intention of getting tangled up with a woman, but Hadley made her laugh and go weak in the knees. Plus, the whimsical aspect of Hadley's personality coaxed something lighter into her disposition. While she couldn't quite imagine herself roller-skating through Hadley's courtyard, she could damn sure smile at the reality of Hadley doing so. Hell, maybe she could even cheerlead. As a kid, she'd rejected dolls, stuffed kittens, and anything sparkly. She'd just never been a fan of cute things, feeling that they'd signal something weak in her. Hadley had tossed the entire notion on its head. She was the definition of cute, and Spencer couldn't get enough. Toss in her alluring appearance, and Spencer had trouble remembering her own name.

They hopped an Uber to Chadwick's, the little shop Hadley had mentioned, just as the sun began to set. The store was just as quaint as Hadley described, selling liquor and incense and candles of all soothing scents. A classical guitarist had set up in the corner and had his case open for tips. Spencer tossed in a five as they approached the tables that had been set up in parallel rows for tastings.

"Have you done one of these before?" Hadley asked. Her small silver earrings caught the light, as the guitarist began to play "Hotel California."

"A handful."

"Tell me, what's your favorite?"

She thought on the question, distracted by the way Hadley pursed her lips as she waited for the answer. She had really good lips. "I'm a rum devotee, but I try not to discriminate."

"An open mind. I like that."

There were so many other things Spencer was feeling open to, but she focused on the task ahead of them and enjoyed merely being in Hadley's presence, all optimistic and eager.

Two small glasses with intricate silver designs were placed in front of them. Hadley's glass was pelican themed, and Spencer's a series of fishing hooks. Chadwick's was certainly eclectic, as nothing else about the shop said ocean. Their server was named Jeremiah, and he briefly explained that there would be six tastings provided, to which she made mental note to take it slow.

"Where are you from?" Hadley asked Jeremiah.

He was close to their age with sandy brown hair and a pointy goatee Spencer thought he should lose. She imagined all the ways she would style him, given the opportunity. Gray and light blue would be a killer combination on him. Occupational hazard. Sometimes she just couldn't turn off that portion of her brain.

"Calabasas originally. I live in the city now."

"Oh, wow! Me, too," Hadley said beaming. "My dads still live out that way. I visit them a couple of times a month. They just remodeled the whole house. It was quite the project. You don't want the details."

"Who handled the work?" he asked.

She thought a moment. "Um…a company called Mandalay Brothers. They were great, but it took close to a year for everything to go in. The end result was stunning."

He extended his hand. "Jeremiah Mandalay. My two older brothers own that company."

"Get out!" Hadley turned to Spencer with a look that said, "Can you even believe this?" Back to Jeremiah. "You get out of here right now! Turn around and leave this instant."

Jeremiah held up his hands, smiling right back at her. "Honest to goodness truth. I didn't get the construction gene, so I stick to alcohol. Learning about it, not just drinking." He laughed.

Hadley joined him. "Can you imagine?"

Spencer listened as the two chatted animatedly about Venice, the cooler weather, and how often they visited Calabasas and its little-known ice cream shop. It turned out she wasn't the only one who found Hadley easy to talk to. It was becoming clear that she made friends wherever she went, like an inescapable ray of sunshine. Where in the world had this woman come from? Nice people didn't work on Rodeo Drive: a cosmic rule.

"And this is Spencer. My date," Hadley told Jeremiah, after their first tasting, a shot of tequila that Spencer made sure to sip and discard. Hadley, on the other hand, drank and talked, and drank and talked until her shot glass was empty.

"Nice to officially meet you," Spencer told Jeremiah. "I feel like I already know so much about you."

He shook his head, a giant grin spread across his face. "The world is a small place, and it's nice to meet a kindred spirit like Hadley."

"We should exchange information after," Hadley said. "Two Calabasas kids and all."

"Definitely," he said, and poured them a sample of vanilla rum. "My girlfriend would love you guys. We could make it a foursome some night for dinner. Either here or in Calabasas."

"You're on." Hadley turned to Spencer after downing the small glass. "My lips are numb," she said, touching them. "Do you think it's okay that my lips are numb? Where did they go?"

Spencer grinned. "Might mean that you want to slow down."

"Good call," Hadley said. "I'd love my lips to come back." Her cheeks were flushed and she seemed a tad tipsy. Spencer decided to keep an eye on her intake, just in case.

After they progressed to a mellow vodka, Hadley was talking kind of fast. "The thing about Venice," Hadley said, speaking with an alcohol-fueled conviction, "is that it's so darn expensive. I just can't get away from it though. The people, the culture. They speak to me, ya know?" The alcohol was also speaking to her. It was cute, but Spencer thought maybe they should pause the tasting.

"Hey, Hadley?" she asked. "You know what I've always wanted to do in Venice?"

"What's that?"

"See the canals. Maybe we can skip the rest of the tasting and check them out. What do you think?"

"Yeah. Yes. Definitely," she turned to Jeremiah. "Do you mind if we skip the rest? My lips never returned."

"Not at all," he said warmly, and passed Hadley his card. "I'm glad you two stopped in."

Hadley took his hand and shook it. "You've done an amazing job tonight. You're going to go far."

Jeremiah and Spencer exchanged an amused smile. "Thanks," Spencer mouthed back at him and then walked a very tipsy, quite possibly drunk Hadley, out of the store. "So, that was fun," she said,

"Wow!" Hadley exclaimed once they hit the streets. "That stuff hits you out of nowhere." She touched her forehead. "I apologize. I'm not used to straight alcohol all on its own. Oh! Look at the birds up there, flying free!"

"It's nice when they're able to do that," Spencer said. "Can I tell you something? You're a different kind of fun when you're drinking. Like regular Hadley times six."

"Can I tell *you* something right on back? You're really sexy when I'm drinking." She closed her eyes. "That's ridiculous. You're really sexy all the time. I just said that out loud and it's fine."

"It is." Spencer smiled. "Nothing wrong with that."

Hadley held up one finger. "Time to cut me off, ma'am."

"I'll fight off any potential barkeeps who may approach us."

"You would do that for me?" Hadley asked, exponentially touched. Spencer laughed at her drunken sincerity. "Come on. Show me these famous canals I've heard so much about, and then you can tell me how sexy I am again." She handed Hadley one of the bottles of water she'd picked up in the store.

"Don't tempt me," Hadley said, gesturing with the water. "C'mon. It's a nice night out. We can walk. Maybe the air will help sober me up so I stop complimenting you like an idiot."

"Maybe there's a compromise in there somewhere," Spencer said. "We could negotiate."

Spencer liked the idea and took Hadley's hand in hers. The stroll to Washington Boulevard and Pacific Avenue was a short one, but something about walking the streets together hand in hand had Spencer warm and comfortable and feeling close to Hadley.

"Wow," she said, taking in the view before them once they arrived. The last bit of daylight was barely hanging on, illuminating the canals with a tiny sliver of sunlight. A family of ducklings paddled along in the water, parallel to the sidewalk.

"Hey, little gentlemen," Hadley said, sweetly. "Hope you're enjoying your night." She turned to Spencer. "I don't know why I imagine that they're boys, but I do. I insert little top hats onto their heads as I look down at them."

"Well, who doesn't?" Spencer said, and then passed Hadley a you're-a-weirdo look.

"Apparently, everyone." Hadley knocked Spencer's ribs slightly with her elbow.

The ducks pressed on and so did she and Hadley. A series of walkways took them past a variety of interesting-looking houses, most with a paddleboat or rowboat tied up in front.

"I love coming out here," Hadley said, surveying their surroundings. "I don't do it enough."

"Why do you like it?"

"It's so peaceful. Don't you think?"

"I was just going to say so." This time, no weirdo look. Spencer meant it.

They nodded to an older couple passing on their left. The woman had her arm linked through the man's. Hadley looked back at them. "That right there is what life's all about."

"Sharing a nice evening out?" Spencer asked.

"No." Hadley led them up onto one of the overarching pedestrian bridges that looked down on the canal. "Finding your person. Your one."

"Huh," Spencer said. She leaned her arms on the railing and looked out. It was getting dark now. The light from the nearby lampposts glistened on the water's surface as the soft sound of it lapping against the bank underscored their conversation.

"What?" Hadley asked. She mirrored Spencer's stance over the railing and looked over at her.

"I'm just not sure I can get behind that philosophy. I think we're drawn to a number of different people throughout our lives for different reasons."

Hadley frowned. "True. Until you find the one you're meant to be with."

"See, I'm not sure I agree with that. Why would one be the most important? I can imagine that you might meet two or three people over the course of your life that significantly change it. Maybe at different points."

Hadley frowned. "Wait. What about marriage?"

"I think it screws things up, so I don't believe in it. Take my parents. Divorced when I was younger. These are two people who get along great now but failed miserably within the confines of marriage. They were better without it. I think we all probably are."

Hadley straightened. "I think if I wasn't sufficiently sober, then I am now." She took a defeated step back from the railing.

"What? It upsets you that I don't believe in forever?"

Hadley took a moment before raising her gaze to Spencer's. "The problem is that I do. In fact, if I were to make a list of all of the things I want most in life, falling in love and getting married and growing old with one person is at the top of my list. It's all I've ever wanted, and I very much believe it's possible."

"You're a hopeless romantic," Spencer said. "Not an awful thing at all."

"But naïve."

"Maybe a little."

"Well, I don't have any plans on changing. In fact, I like who I am. You can call me unrealistic or starry-eyed all you want. Some people do. But happily ever after can be real."

"People like to *think* it's real. It's a comforting idea, I admit. But if you think about it, so is Santa Claus."

"I can't believe you just said that!" Hadley shook her head. The metaphorical distance between them seemed to be growing by the second, but Spencer wasn't sure there was much she could do to change that short of lying about her values, who she was.

"Then prove me wrong," she said good-naturedly.

"Well, think about it. It's more than an idea or figment of someone's imagination," Hadley said. "It's who we are as humans."

"Not most of us," Spencer said. "Have you seen the recent divorce rate?"

Hadley's gaze fell in dejection to the ground and Spencer hated that she'd caused such a look.

She took a breath and attempted to regroup, softening. "Hey, wait a sec." She placed her hand gently under Hadley's chin and raised her face so she could see her eyes. "I think the world of you, Hadley. Please believe that. This doesn't have to change anything between us."

"Doesn't it?" Hadley asked, sadly. "I feel like it changes everything. We're looking for different things, so what's the point?"

"Let's not get ahead of ourselves. This is only a second date."

"Up until this moment, it was an outstanding one. And if we go on a third, or a fourth? Then what?" Hadley dropped her hand from the railing. "What you may not know about me, Spencer, is that while I may be outgoing and confident on the outside, I have a tender heart and a lot of feelings."

Spencer nodded, already understanding the truth of that statement. She was seeing so firsthand. "I wouldn't ever want to hurt you, Hadley, and I'm a big believer in meaningful relationships. Don't mistake me. Marriage and all of that? Might not be for me. But that doesn't mean I sleep around and it doesn't mean I don't feel things just as deeply as the next person."

Hadley seemed confused. "But if you don't believe in the possibility of forever, then what would we be working toward? Fun for a little while?" She sighed and tucked a strand of hair behind her ear. She was grappling. "It sounds like a whole lot of heartbreak waiting to happen. At least for me. At the end of the day, I'm looking for the *one*, not a good time. I don't think I'm made that way."

"I would never think of you as a good time."

"I appreciate that, because there's a lot more to me than the physical."

Regret twisted in Spencer's stomach, uncomfortable and sharp. She wanted badly to just enjoy their time together, complications be damned. She liked Hadley. What was so wrong with focusing on only that for now and seeing where it led? "Hey," she said, moving to Hadley. "Let's not get hung up on this one detail." But it was clear from the desolate look on Hadley's face that the mood had been shattered irreparably. There was nothing Spencer could do.

"I think we need to take a step back from this part of us."

It was like a punch in the stomach. Spencer closed her eyes and took a moment. "Okay." She understood where Hadley was coming from, but she didn't have to like it. "So, what now?"

"We take those designs of yours and get them on the retail map, and that starts with Silhouette." Hadley attempted a smile, but Spencer didn't buy it. Her eyes didn't shine, and when Hadley smiled genuinely, her eyes shone brighter than any she'd ever seen. She hated that something she'd said had inspired the change in that beautiful smile.

"Fair enough."

They stared at each other. They were on new, uncomfortable ground now.

"I love what you've done in the new sketches." Hadley reached into her bag, pulled out the pad, and returned it to Spencer. "My notes are in the front, but honestly, I'm not sure I contributed anything to this round. Consider me your cheerleader."

"What you said before, your suggestions, inspired all of it. You set me in a new direction."

"Oh," Hadley said. "I'm happy to hear I helped. What's next to make it all happen?"

"We go to manufacturing and wait. I was also hoping you'd take a look at some ideas I have coming up for the summer. It's still early and the designs are rudimentary, but there's enough there for you to get an idea of where I'm heading."

"I'd love to," Hadley said. Something in the water caught her eye and she turned. Her whole face lit up and she laughed, melodious and free. "I think the duck and that fish are having a fight over what looks to be a piece of bread." Spencer followed Hadley's gaze to the water, but her eyes moved back to Hadley almost immediately. Much more to watch there. The sparkle was back, brought on by something so common as some splashing in the water. "Oh, and one for the duck," Hadley said, shaking her head. Hadley took enjoyment in the little things life had to offer. If they all took a page from her book, the world would be a much happier place.

They made the loop around the canal and finished their walk mostly in silence. The sounds of nature took over, edging to the forefront. The rustling of palm trees, the quiet ribbits of the frogs, and the easy lapping of the water. All would have been like music to her ears any other evening. Tonight, they couldn't pull her from the melancholy that had settled like a heavy drape over everything.

"Listen, I don't want you to have the wrong impression of me," Spencer said finally, once they approached the sidewalk in front of Seven Shores. They stood outside the complex between two streetlights, where Spencer's car was parked along the curb. "I'm not some callous, unfeeling person who discards one woman for another like tissue. I'm capable of maintaining and valuing a meaningful relationship."

"For the foreseeable future," Hadley stated delicately.

"Or longer. It depends on the woman, on the relationship." She wasn't making herself as clear as she could. "I am just very much aware of the fact that life is about chapters, and sometimes a chapter ends and that's okay. There are more to come."

Hadley smiled. "Are you offering me a chapter, Spencer?"

"It could be a *really great* chapter. Life changing. We don't know. Are you willing to walk away from that possibility? Tell me goodbye forever and miss out on what could be?" She held her arms wide open.

Hadley sighed, as uncertainty crisscrossed her features. "Why did you have to use a book analogy? I love books."

"I know." Spencer took Hadley's hand and gently pulled her in. "Neither of us knows where this might lead. Fair?"

Hadley nodded. "I suppose that's fair." A pause as Spencer moved even closer. "You smell like strawberries."

Spencer laughed quietly. "That's a new one."

"It's true. I can't get enough of it."

"I'm going to kiss you now, and take my time doing it, unless you tell me not to."

Hadley offered the slightest of nods. She held Spencer's gaze but said nothing.

"You understand? This is your out."

Hadley only blinked at her in response.

The anticipation was almost too much. Spencer moved in slowly, hovering just beyond Hadley's mouth in case she had any change of heart, and then all bets were off. The magnetism of the other night returned instantaneously as soon as her lips met Hadley's in an unpredictable dance. Like some kind of lightning bolt had descended and zapped them into the most tantalizing connection that washed over Spencer from her head to her toes. When she kissed Hadley, it was so much more than just a kiss. She'd kissed a lot of girls in her life. Some were even quite excellent kissers. This was different. With Hadley, Spencer felt her everywhere: in her thoughts, her body, her being, which was a new and unnerving experience. *More* was the only word on her mind. Hadley's mouth moved over hers expertly, matching her rhythm. Her hands slid into Hadley's hair, holding her in place as she kissed the lips that had captivated her all evening, that slayed her now and had her questioning everything she thought she knew. Damn it, if Hadley said the world was triangular, she'd be inclined to agree in this moment. Why the hell couldn't it be? She sank further into the kiss, pressing against Hadley, melding their bodies together, and savoring that friction. She felt Hadley's breasts pressed into hers, and the unexpected arousal that snaked down her spine and took up residence between her legs had her deliriously shaken. She wanted her hands beneath that shirt. She wanted to touch those breasts, kiss them. What in the world was this intoxicating dance? Finally, it was Hadley who took a step back with one extended hand on Spencer's shoulder, leaving her cold and grappling.

"Whoa" was the only word Hadley spoke. Yep. She'd felt the lightning bolt, too. They stared at each other, recovering, becoming reacquainted with oxygen and equilibrium. She pointed at Spencer, touched her lips, and pointed at Spencer again. "Did you feel that?"

Spencer nodded back, her hand finding its way on top of her head. "How could I not? It's...we're...yeah." Her most eloquent of moments.

"We might be approaching big bang." Hadley's eyes closed momentarily before her gaze landed on Spencer's. "You don't know what big bang is, but this is feeling close. I think that we need to—"

"Well, hey there!" a petite brunette woman called happily, coming up the walk. No. More like strutting. She beamed at Hadley and then at Spencer with her hands on her hips like a proud mom on picture day. "You must be Spencer."

"Oh. Yes. I am." She extended her hand and was met with a firm shake from the woman, who studied her with interest. Way too much interest.

Hadley looked on with hesitation. "Spencer Adair, meet one of my best friends, Isabel Chase, who was probably just heading into her apartment back there. Where she *lives and is heading*. We're also neighbors."

"And super close," Isabel said, rocking back on her heels and smiling at Spencer, still seeming to be in research mode. "Hadley tells me, like, fucking everything. It's amazing how much I know." She tapped a finger to the side of her head.

Spencer's eyebrows rose. "Is that so?"

"So much knowledge right here." Another tap.

"Okay!" Hadley said, clapping once and shooting Isabel daggers with her eyes, all the while smiling. A true feat to accomplish all three. Spencer was impressed. "Isabel probably has her cat to feed. Yessiree Bob. He's the hungriest cat. Always counting the minutes until she walks in the door."

Isabel nodded. "Fat Tony. He's a mess but means well. Hopefully, you can meet him sometime soon. Provided you'll be around. You think you might be, Spencer? Around."

Hadley pinched the bridge of her nose.

Because Spencer wasn't sure what else to say, she went for the common ground angle. "I have a cat, too. And yeah, that'd be great. I hope to see you."

"Perfect!" Isabel said happily, clapping Spencer on the back. Hard. "I better get outta here so you two can spend some time alone." She wiggled her fingers at them like a ghost. "Don't let me get in the way if you have more kissing to do."

"Izzie."

Spencer shook her head. "You don't have to—"

"Yes, I do," Isabel said, and made a circular gesture between the three of them. "In the way here. I sense it." She pointed at Hadley. "I'll see you in the morning at breakfast, unless you'll be otherwise engaged?" She pulled a face that said, "am I on the right track?"

"I'll be there," Hadley said, through a tight lip.

"Aces," Isabel said. She shot finger guns at them and headed into the courtyard of the complex.

What a weird individual.

Hadley passed Spencer an apologetic look. "I swear to you that I've never seen her do that. The fishing for information, flashy game show host routine. I think she's in a mode lately. She has a lot on her plate."

"She's heard of me?"

Hadley looked like a person surrendering in embarrassment. "She has."

She chalked it up to a small victory. "I won't ask for any more details. What I would like to know is what you were about to say before we were interrupted." But now it felt a little like the magic bubble had been popped.

Hadley nodded, and attempted to take them back there. "I don't have the answers, Spencer, okay? But I know that we seem pretty far apart in terms of what we want in life. That's scary for me. The kissing? Not so scary at all. That part is full on amazing. No complaints there."

"I agree on both counts." She kicked at a rock on the sidewalk. "What about this? I can try and keep an open mind if you can. No one has to compromise anything at this point." Spencer had never been one to gravitate toward intimate confessions, but this moment felt like a necessary exception. She geared up, softening as a wall came down. This part wasn't easy. "When I'm with you, a lot of what I thought I knew dissipates. I'm willing to admit that. So, who am I to make any sort of grandstand on what my future may or may not be when it comes to us? I'm feeling things that, quite frankly, have me shocked. Maybe there's more shocking ahead. I don't know." She held out her hands in surrender and let them drop. "I only know that I'd like to find out."

The smile took shape slowly on Hadley's face, and its maturation sent a chill right through Spencer. Hadley was an angel, through and through. Just look at her, standing there, haloed by the street lamp, looking more stunning than any woman on the planet.

"So, you're saying you're open to the chance that this could blossom into something…lasting?"

Spencer hesitated. She didn't want to give Hadley false hope, but in that moment, she was open to the sliver of a possibility that there could be a forever waiting. With the right person. Hell, who knew? "I'm saying I can try to be."

"I'm thirty years old and not looking for another good time. You should know that straight off. No surprises."

Spencer's entire body relaxed. "You could never be just that, Hadley. Never."

In response, Hadley placed her hands on the lapels of Spencer's shirt and pulled her in for one more wild kiss. Spencer heard herself moan quietly as their mouths clashed. She caught Hadley's tongue lightly with her teeth, encouraged when Hadley murmured back, her arms around Spencer's neck. She kissed Hadley long and slow, realizing that she could do this for hours, days. She rested her forehead against Hadley's and enjoyed breathing in the same air. Even that got her going. Nope, chemistry would not be a problem. Not even a small one.

"I need you to be honest with me as we go," Hadley said, her mouth still inches from Spencer's, "and if you ever get to a point where you think 'This is nice, but maybe only in the temporary,' that you'll say so."

"I will," Spencer said. "You, too."

Hadley nodded. "That will be our plan. We'll just be, you know, honest. No hard feelings."

"No hard feelings," Spencer said, and stole another kiss. It was time to say good night, that much she knew, but she liked where this was heading. They'd constructed a straightforward strategy, eliminating invisible strings, and were proceeding with reasonable expectations. "Can I see you soon?"

"I was hoping you'd say so." Hadley's blue eyes sparkled once again with hope. Spencer didn't ever want to be the one to dash it from those eyes, but they'd have to take things one step at a time. She was willing to try if Hadley was. They'd come together in a rush all over the course of a short time period, but what they had between them wasn't something Spencer could minimize. Hell, after two dates, Hadley Cooper had her world standing on its side as she struggled to hang on one finger at a time. That's the kind of power this unsuspecting woman wielded.

"I guess it's good night for now," Spencer said.

"For now," Hadley repeated. She brushed her lips over Spencer's softly, sending every nerve ending Spencer had into high alert. Hadley stood on the curb and watched as Spencer drove away. She glanced one last time in her rearview mirror, awestruck at Hadley and her windblown blond hair, what she made Spencer feel, and the concession she was able to pull from her, a concession Spencer never thought she'd make.

When it came to Hadley, she wanted to push her own boundaries. Well, she was at least willing to try. Time would tell if she was truly capable, and she did have her concerns. She didn't want to angle her way through it, or play any kind of games, because Hadley deserved much more. Now all she had to do was figure out how to undo years of intellectual conditioning. Shouldn't be too hard. She flipped on the radio to drown out the murmurings of self-doubt that whispered loudly in her ear.

CHAPTER EIGHT

When Hadley pushed open the door to the Cat's Pajamas the next day, she saw three large pairs of eyes staring back at her in eager expectation. Autumn rocked Will in her arms and Gia gently pushed Carrie back and forth in her stroller. Isabel stirred her coffee in time. They were primed and ready, a chorus demanding their pound of gossip.

"So, I take it you heard," Hadley said, approaching their table and making eye contact with Isabel, who was no doubt the town crier in this case.

"Did we ever," Autumn said, shifting a sleeping Will. "We've gathered, we've waited, and now we're ready for the hot and heavy details, and don't you dare balk, because you'd demand them of any one of us."

"Every step of the way," Gia said, pointedly. "Sit and talk."

Isabel slid Hadley's waiting caffè mocha her way and pulled her hands away slowly as if to not disturb the force. "And go."

Her three friends relaxed into matching smiles and Hadley knew better than to protest, because Autumn was right. She would have never let the others off with anything less than a full debriefing. When it came to romantic stories, or sexy stories, or kissing stories, she was a maniac for details, and the juicer the better. It just felt different when they were *her* details. "Spencer and I had a nice night last night," she said conservatively, and took a dainty sip of her mocha.

Isabel made a loud buzzer sound. "Wrong. That was so much more than a nice night." She turned to the others full of energy, gesturing wildly. "When I pulled up, they didn't see me. They were climbing each other like animals."

"Oh," Gia said, nodding along, entranced.

"It was hot and bothered and like nothing I've ever fucking witnessed. I'm getting heated just thinking about it."

"Well, well, well," Autumn said, entirely scandalized. "Little Miss Hadley, I do declare."

Hadley shrugged. "I'm a human being, you know. Not all daisies and cupcakes like you guys seem to think."

Isabel fanned herself. "Not anymore. Not after what I saw last night."

"I knew there was a tiger in there," Gia said. "She just needed the right woman to bring it out in her."

"I have needs, too," Hadley said. "I just don't express them all the time. I actually enjoy sex a lot."

Gia touched her coffee mug to Hadley's, who nodded back at her in appreciation, because she wasn't a shrinking violet. It was true that she'd never been a go-getter and hadn't exactly taken the dating scene by the horns in the past, but that was because she was a *romantic* and it was important to wait for someone she truly connected with. She felt that connection with Spencer, ideal or not.

"So, you enjoy sex. You're an unleashed tiger, but you still whisper swear words. How does that work?"

Hadley shrugged, because that answer was easy. "Swear words are entirely different from sex. They're forbidden and crass. At least when I say them. Sex is natural and amazing and sensual."

Isabel pointed at her. "You are the most foreign creature."

"Tell us more," Autumn said.

"Well, she's a really good kisser. The best, actually. Not at all shy or timid about it."

"She wasn't," Isabel said seriously. "I love it when they just grab you and go for it, and you walk away wondering what the hell just happened to you, ya know?"

Autumn and Gia nodded in hearty agreement.

"That was last night."

Isabel grinned. "Trust me. I know."

"What else?" Autumn asked. "Give us more. We need it. This is lifeblood for a cooped-up mom."

"Well, Hadley had Spencer up against the car in one of those moves." Isabel stood to demonstrate.

"Oh, that's lovely," Autumn said, sighing.

"But Spencer had a hold of Had's waist and then her neck and then face." Isabel swapped out positions to demonstrate Spencer's portion, like the cover of a torrid romance. "I have to say that they were a very evenly matched pair."

"Wow," Gia said, blinking hard. "Then what?"

Isabel straightened out of her pose. "They talked for a minute and then more kissing."

Hadley smiled and nodded at her friends. "That's true. There was definitely more."

"More passion this time," Isabel said dramatically, leaning across the table like a leopard. "Lips were parted. Tongues clashed. The sidewalk was on fire."

Autumn and Gia smoldered, and for the first time, Hadley could nod along with them, because she got it now. The romance novels had not invented moments like last night. They weren't unicorns in the mist. Unbridled passion existed! And there could quite possibly be more of those moments in her future. But then she remembered the rest.

"It's not all great, though," Hadley said, deflating their very full balloons. Three crushed faces turned to her in accusation. She was killing their fantasies of romantic grandeur, and as much as she hated to do that, she needed advice.

"No. Really?" Isabel asked, in disbelief. "What's gone wrong already? This was mere hours ago."

"Spencer doesn't believe in marriage or forever."

Her friends stared at her. "Okay," Autumn said, holding up a cautionary hand. "That doesn't have to be awful. What *does* she believe in?"

"That people find each other for a reason and drift in and eventually out of each other's lives, making way for a new chapter. That's how she put it. Life is about chapters."

"Chapters," Gia said. "Nope. I don't get it."

"I'm as cynical as they come, and even I'm not that dark," added Isabel.

Hadley shrugged, not sure she could explain something she didn't fully understand herself but gave it a try. "She's an artist, so she has her own take on the world. I also think her parents' divorce might be an influencing factor."

Autumn handed Will to Gia and picked up Carrie, who was beginning to fuss. "Uh-uh. That doesn't work for me. My mother was a walking bad example as far as relationships went, and I still believed the one was out there for me somewhere. Spoiler alert, she was!"

Hadley smiled at the memory of Autumn and Kate's story. "Trust me. I get it. I want that for myself."

"What are you going to do?" Gia asked. "Do you think you're up for changing her mind?"

Hadley shrugged. "Maybe?"

"It's definitely possible," Gia continued. "I used to think that surfing mattered to me more than anything, more than the person I was in love with. I don't believe that for a second anymore. People can change."

"Good point," Isabel said. "I vote for hanging in there for a bit. See what happens."

"And if I fall for her, and she breaks my heart into millions of tiny pieces, which could fully happen, what then?"

"Then we break her kneecaps," Gia said, smoothly as if it were the simplest solution in the world. They looked at her in horror. "It's an expression. I'm joking." A pause, and then quieter, "But only kind of."

"Here's what I think," Autumn said, seeming to settle on something important. "Love is love. It can be temporary or it can be long lasting, but it's never a bad thing. If you think there's a chance at love here, Had, you have to follow your heart and sort the rest out as you go."

Hadley knew that underneath it all, but hearing the words out loud made her face the facts. Spencer was placed in her path for a reason, and she needed to see this thing through, wherever it took her. Big bang candidates didn't show up every day. "I think you're right."

Isabel squinted. "The bonus is there will likely be more up-against-the-car kissing."

Hadley sighed dreamily. "It would be hard to turn that down."

"Just look out for yourself as you go," Gia said. "And if there's trouble, kneecaps."

"Kneecaps," Autumn and Isabel echoed. "Now drink that mocha," Autumn said, "and think up some new details from last night. I have fifteen minutes before I have to take these two back for a nap and I need to bask in decadent details."

Hadley launched into the remaining tidbits from the night prior as her friends leaned in. "Well, to start with, she smells like strawberries…"

❖

"I need you to tell me how to make Cornish Game hens, and fast," Spencer said, from the floor of her living room. This was serious. She wasn't messing around. She hadn't seen Hadley in four days, and she was coming over to Spencer's place that night for dinner, and she needed everything to be perfect.

Kendra set down the latest issue of *Cosmo* and regarded her from where she lay on Spencer's couch. "Girl, you don't cook."

"Not usually, no. Tonight, I need to."

"Nope. Not enough information."

"Fine," Spencer said, dropping the shipping box in her hand. "I have a date, and I need dinner to be good."

"Then you should order in."

"No! Not with this woman. She's better than just ordering in. She deserves home cooked."

"Not from you. No one deserves that."

"Are you going to help me or not?"

Kendra sighed, dropping the magazine entirely. "Is this the woman from the fancy store?"

"Yes."

"And you're still really into her?"

"Yes."

"Lord. We're going to need some paper and a lot of patience."

Two hours later, once she was on her own, Spencer couldn't decide whether to go with a tablecloth on her small dining room table or not. She rarely ate there herself, preferring either the counter or the couch for meals, but for the two of them? They should definitely eat at the table.

She'd hit the grocery store earlier with the list Kendra had provided her, and with a quick call to her mom for her vinaigrette salad dressing recipe, she felt like she was making real progress. She placed her hands on her head and made the decision. Tablecloth was the way to go!

She dashed back to the kitchen. The hens were in the oven. She'd peeled the potatoes, and now she just needed something to wear. Not too dressy, but not too casual. Tonight was important. Tonight was date three, and who knew what date three would bring? She didn't want to be presumptuous, but she couldn't help but wonder and hope. It was still summer, so she settled on white capris and a maroon tunic. Should be fine.

"Oh, you're getting some tonight," Kendra said, after returning to the apartment to check in on Spencer's progress. "Everyone knows what date three means."

"It doesn't have to mean sex," Spencer scoffed. "That's a myth and way too assumptive for my taste."

"It doesn't have to mean sex, but it does and every adult is aware. Plus, it's not like you're off to a night at the movies. She's coming to your apartment, Spence."

"I get it."

"But if you want to help matters along, change that top."

She glanced down at the tunic, the one she had designed and sold thousands of. "Why? This is one of my best sellers." She turned to the side. "Are you missing the detail over here? Look at this stitching. It's badass."

"Who cares about stitching on a date?" Kendra pointed at Spencer's chest. "No cleavage at all. What are you trying to do? Teach a yoga class or entice a female to want you so badly she can barely concentrate on dinner? You've got choices to make."

She paused. "That second part sounds nice." Kendra stalked to Spencer's bedroom, and Spencer followed.

"This one," Kendra said, selecting a blue tight-fitting top. "It hugs and it dips in the front. You need the dip."

"Really?"

Kendra squinted in disbelief. "You're better at this than you seem, right? I mean, you've never had trouble getting women that I've noticed. How do you not know this stuff?"

"The question is, how do *you* know this stuff?" Spencer asked, as she shrugged out of her tunic and replaced it with Kendra's suggestion. "You're *straight*. How would you know what a woman wants in another woman?"

She shrugged. "I watch television. Plus, I've been to enough of the gay clubs with you to see who gets the most action, and it's not the girl in the flowy shirt. You feel me?"

"Yeah."

"I think your hens are burning."

"What?" Spencer raced to the kitchen and threw open the oven door. "They look okay." She turned to Kendra with her please-help-me face. "Do they look okay to you?"

"Ladle some more butter over the top and turn the oven down. I gotta head out. Got plans of my own on this fine evening."

"Please tell me it's not with that loser Tucker."

"I can't. Bye, Spence. Date three! You got this."

"I don't. I feel weird and vulnerable and I think I need you to stay and help me with the prep."

"Nah. You just need to enjoy this little ride you're on, because I am. Can't say I've seen you this rattled before." She took out her phone and snapped a photo of Spencer. "Now I can always remember it. Ta ta."

"But how do I keep the hens from drying out?" Spencer called to the closing door. In defeat, she raced back to the kitchen and read over the instructions Kendra had left, reiterating them to herself one more time. She surveyed the living room, now clear of shipping supplies, fabric, and mannequins. But the throw pillows on the couch looked lopsided. She fluffed them, wondering who the hell she was to care so much about couch pillows impressing a date. She shuffled back to the kitchen to make sure the potatoes were soft enough, only to run into a sticky note on her refrigerator that said, "Light candles before she arrives." She snatched the note, crumpled it, and shoved it into her back pocket. But light the damn candles, she did. She really did owe Kendra. She put on some mellow background music and waited. And waited some more. Her hands tingled in anticipation. Hadley was due in ten minutes. The time ticked by ever so slowly until, at last, a knock at the door.

"Hey," Spencer said, stepping aside so that Hadley could enter. "You look amazing."

"So do you. What smells so fantastic?" Hadley asked, turning in a circle. "Wow. What is that?"

"Cornish game hens. Is that okay? I also have red-skinned potatoes and a green salad with homemade dressing."

Hadley truly did look impressed, which was a victory for Spencer. "I had no idea you were a chef as well as a soon-to-be-famous designer."

Spencer's cheeks heated, which prompted her to turn away, leading them into the kitchen. "I'm not a chef. I had to have help from a friend. I did do the cooking, but she offered some instruction."

"I don't care," Hadley said.

"You don't?"

She smiled lazily. "Not in the slightest. You went to a lot of effort. For me." She placed a hand over her heart. "That means a lot." Hadley's gaze dropped from Spencer's eyes to her neckline. "Oh," she said. "You look really sexy." Hadley covered her mouth. "I shouldn't have said sexy. It just flew right out of my mouth. You look...lovely. Pretty."

"Let's stick with sexy," Spencer said, holding eye contact. And hello to the heat she felt once their gazes settled. She owed Kendra big-time for the top suggestion. Big-time. She would send her on an all-expense paid vacation if this evening worked out.

"Sexy it is." Hadley glanced around, moving them out of the charged exchange. "I love your apartment. The framed sketches on the wall. Very you. Are those yours?"

Spencer glanced behind her. "No. I wish. Gerard DeVoux, one of my favorite French designers and someone who's inspired me a great deal over the years." She studied the sketches. "He takes risks and they always pay off. But not the kind of risks that make you attend one of his shows and think 'that was cool, but I'd never wear that.' His stuff is risky but practical, which I want for my own brand."

She felt Hadley's hand on the small of her back as she stared at the closest sketch. "I think you're more than on your way to that very combination. Also, I have good news for you."

Spencer turned. "And what's that?"

"I showed Trudy the final sketches, and even without the samples in hand, she's in. She's putting together a round one order now. Get ready for paperwork in a matter of days."

Spencer covered her mouth as the information sank in. "I'm going to be on Rodeo Drive?"

"And not just any part of it. One of the most highly acclaimed stores you could land. You should be really proud of yourself, Spencer." Hadley beamed at her, which made the celebration that much sweeter.

"This is all because of you," Spencer said, meaning every word. She kissed Hadley, because she needed to. She was not only beautiful and kind, but she'd gone out of her way for Spencer at every turn.

Hadley laughed. "Was that a thank you?" she asked, softly touching her lips.

"It's many things." They smiled at each other. Spencer felt ridiculous, but there was just one thing she had to do. "Do you mind if I call my mom? Just a real quick call."

Hadley softened. "Please do."

Her mother picked up on the third ring. "Baby girl? Everything okay?"

"Mama, why do you always think there's something wrong when I call you? You have to stop this."

"Because you text more these days. I'm a worrier, so when the phone rings, I worry. Does that mean nothing is wrong?"

"Everything's fine." She walked farther into her small kitchen to not completely embarrass herself in front of Hadley, but she couldn't wait until later to share the news or it would be cold and stale. This was the moment she wanted to share with her mother. "Better than fine. I got the Rodeo Drive order!" Because she was no dummy, she held the phone far from her ear just in time to dodge the ridiculous scream that came through the ear piece. Hadley laughed and Spencer pointed at the phone, shaking her head. "Sorry," she mouthed. Hadley waved her off as if it were the most natural thing in the world for screaming mothers to show up on dates.

"My baby!" her mother crowed when she came back on. "You're famous now. Oh, I gotta call your grandma, and Susanne from across the street, Aunt Gladys. Her daughter works at the bowling alley part-time, and mine designs clothes on Rodeo Drive!"

"Don't give Aunt Gladys a hard time. You two are way too competitive." Her mother and Aunt Gladys were now competing LA real estate agents who had been rivals since childhood.

"Just let me gloat a little. She deserves it."

Spencer closed her eyes and smiled. "A tad, then ease up. You know she's sensitive about Denise."

"The girl has no ambition. Wants to watch soap operas all day in a housecoat and chat up bowlers all night in a miniskirt. Do you know what she said to Gladys the last time she tried to talk sense into her?"

"Mom, I do want to know, but can we talk about Denise later? I have to go now. I'm on a date."

Her mother's voice dropped to a whisper. "Is she pretty?"

Spencer turned to Hadley and nodded. "Very."

"Is she nice?" her mother whispered.

"Way nicer than me."

"She have a job?"

Spencer laughed. "A promising one."

"Oh, I'll let you go then. This one sounds good."

"I think that's the case."

"Bye, baby. I love you and am so proud! I need to make those calls now." Another squeal.

"Thanks, Mama. Bye." She clicked off the call and took a deep breath before turning back to Hadley. "Thank you for indulging me. We have this thing where we tell each other stuff as soon as it happens. Ignore me."

"You two sound close."

Spencer tossed her phone into her bag on the counter. "We are. Always have been."

"I'm close with my parents, too. Though I never had a mom. I used to wonder what that would be like." She leaned back against the counter and held up a hand. "Don't get me wrong, I had an amazing childhood and wouldn't change a minute of it."

"Raised by your father then, or…"

"Both of them actually. Gay dads. They were the best parents I could have. Warm, funny, and thoughtful. Well, Papa is definitely funnier than Dad, but I try not to point that out or it becomes a whole thing."

"And they're still together?"

"They are," Hadley said with a smug smirk.

Spencer let it go. "How was your Saturday today?"

"Long. I worked for most of it, but we pulled in some relatively high numbers for this time of year, so I chalk it up to a win in the sales column."

"I bet the clients love you."

Hadley ran a hand along the edge of the counter. "I do okay."

"You're wearing heels."

She glanced down and lifted one heel-clad foot. Gray strappy Jimmy Choos. A nice choice. "I am. I wanted to look nice. For you. For tonight."

"Your poor feet must be feeling it."

Hadley winced. "Minor compromise, but yes."

Spencer shook her head. "Why would you ever do that to yourself?"

"Because I adore fashion and all things related to it and am willing to suffer for the cause. That simple." Spencer couldn't argue with the logic, and in fact, Hadley looked fantastic as always in a pale blue belted sundress, and the gray heels that made her legs look like they went on for centuries. No one could accuse Hadley of anything other than fantastic legs. Tonight, she'd styled her hair partially back, with soft curls that hit just past her shoulders.

"Yeah, here's the thing. Fashion be damned. I'm going to have to insist you take those things off." Hadley raised an eyebrow and a bolt of heat hit Spencer at the sound of the words. Asking Hadley to take anything off had her mind overheating. She ordered it to quell and focused on Hadley and what she needed in the moment, which was a break from discomfort. She glanced at the timer. "In fact, we have some time before dinner." She pointed at her dark leather couch with all the wonderfully soft, broken-in wrinkles. Code for worn and comfy. "Sit. That's an order."

Hadley, who regarded her with a suspicious smile, walked silently to the couch, slipped out of her heels, which trimmed a good three inches off her height, and took a seat. "Is this where you want me, Ms. Adair?"

"That's perfect," Spencer said and took a seat down the couch. "Now give me those." She pointed at Hadley's feet. Without hesitation, Hadley lifted both feet and placed them into Spencer's waiting lap, her eyes dancing in amusement.

"Are you really about to do this for me?" she asked, in excitement.

"I really am."

Spencer got to work, starting with the right foot, pushing her thumbs along the bottom, back and forth.

"Oh, my dear goodness," Hadley said, which pulled a chuckle from Spencer.

She was expecting some sort of reaction, but "Oh, my dear goodness" had not been it. "That's a new phrase."

"It's mine. You can't have it. Well, maybe I'd share if you keep doing that. Lord help us all. Sweet mercy in heaven above. Yes. I approve. Right there is amazing." Spencer pushed firmly on what she knew were the sensitive pressure points on the ball of the foot, which prompted a loud moan from Hadley. At the sound, every part of Spencer went into hyperalert. Blood rushed from her head, her limbs, to…other parts. But the sounds didn't stop there. As Spencer massaged her feet, her ankles, her calves, Hadley continued to gift her with little noises of pleasure that did powerful things to Spencer's mind and body. Wicked things. And they made her want to do a few corrupt things to Hadley in return. She reached the top of Hadley's calf with its expanse of smooth skin while the soft music played and her blood pressure climbed. Her fingers itched for more, and not in any capacity to resist, she slid her hand beneath the fabric of the blue dress and boldly caressed Hadley's lower thigh. Their eyes connected as the massage continued. Hadley's lips parted and she drew in a shaky breath, making Spencer aware of the fact that she wasn't alone in her growing arousal. They were off the rails now, and Spencer was okay with that. Keeping her eyes on Hadley, she slid her hands up another inch. Hadley's eyes fluttered closed just in time for the loud beeping of the egg timer.

"Dinner is ready," Spencer said quietly, withdrawing her hands from Hadley's leg reluctantly.

Hadley nodded wordlessly, as if back from a dream, and accepted Spencer's offered hand to help her up from the couch. When they stood face-to-face, a hint of a smile hit. "That was quite a massage."

"Wasn't it?" Spencer said, still shocked at herself for having gone there, but a little proud at the same time.

Hadley nodded. "I can't say I've had one like that. Disneyland on fire, that was good."

"Glad to hear it. Why is Disneyland on fire?"

"It's an expression."

Spencer laughed. "Can't say I've heard it."

"That's because I made it up. Just something you wouldn't expect. Disneyland is a happy place. There would be no fire. Why would there be?" Hadley pointed at the couch. "That massage was just as rare."

"Okay," Spencer said, smiling at the random parallel. "Maybe we can do it again sometime soon. I've been told I have good hands."

Hadley swallowed noticeably.

"Let me guess? Tiny oceans of wonder? Is that a relevant phrase here?"

"More like kittens marching into battle."

Spencer chuckled. "There's so much to learn. In the meantime, how about dinner?" Spencer headed to the kitchen and took stock. What she found there deflated her recent confidence. The hens looked dry and a tad overcooked. The potatoes had lost their shape and perhaps she'd taken the salad out too early because the leaves had a slight wilt. "Damn it."

"What's wrong?" Hadley said, coming up behind her. She placed her hand on the small of Spencer's back again, which helped almost immediately. She softened into the touch like magic. She could use a Hadley with her at all times. What an incredibly useful skill.

"Apparently, I'm no Rachael Ray. I clung to that delusion earlier as I made dinner preparations. It's proven false."

Hadley scoffed. "I'm sure what you've made for us will be wonderful. The fact that you went to the trouble at all goes a long way in my book." She glanced around suspiciously. "Music, candles, a massage, and a home-cooked meal. Hmm. Am I being romanced right now?"

Spencer considered her answer and went for it. "Yes. Yes, you most certainly are. Is it working?"

"Uh-huh," Hadley said, then scooped up the serving bowl of potatoes and carried it to the table. Spencer dimmed the lights to better accentuate the candles and carried the rest of the food to her small dining area, now clad with a tablecloth, of all things.

"Wine?"

"Yes, please!"

Spencer took a look at the options she'd picked up at Kendra's suggestion. "White or red?"

"Always white. It's just so much more fun. Wouldn't you say? I feel like it has more friends, too. It gets along with so many of the foods."

"Interesting. All right. All right. Fun and friendly wine coming up." She poured two glasses of a moderately priced Sauvignon Blanc into a pair of wineglasses and carried them to the table.

"To keeping an open mind," Spencer said, holding out her glass in a toast.

"And to changing the minds of others," Hadley said, with a triumphant smile.

Spencer shook her head and sipped her wine, which was surprisingly refreshing. Maybe white really did have some fun points on red.

As they ate, she had trouble keeping her eyes off Hadley, who, whether it was good or not, seemed to be enjoying her food. She really was an easy person to please, and you didn't run into too many people with that descriptor in Spencer's line of work.

"What attracted you to fashion?" Spencer asked, dabbing her mouth with her napkin. "I can't believe we haven't covered that."

"I can tell you that easily." Hadley didn't hesitate. In fact, her whole face lit up at the subject matter. "I love the effect the right combination of clothes can have on someone. It gives me the biggest rush when people find their meant-to-be clothes. I leave at the end of the day thrilled with my job." She sat taller in her chair. "Have you ever noticed? I'm not talking about how they look either. That part is sheer cherry-on-top-of-the-sundae. It's more about how the clothing makes them feel. When a woman, or anyone for that matter, wears something she feels attractive in, it can change her whole outlook on life, or more importantly, on herself. Make her day better. I love helping with that process."

Spencer was intrigued by that answer, because in her years in school, it was always about the designer. Their vision, their perspective, their art, and the stamp they wanted to leave on the fashion world. She'd embraced that ideology but hadn't really considered the end result and the effect her designs might have on a customer. On how they'd *feel*.

"We're so different," she marveled, though it was more of a confession. Because Hadley left her humbled. Not at all a bad thing, just…eye-opening. Like the fun aspect of white wine.

Hadley took a bite of chicken and considered the statement. "How so? You disagree?"

"I don't. I'm just a selfish asshole, apparently. I see my job and evaluate my success based on my role in the process. It's all about me. You're looking at it through the lens of how others feel. The result that fashion has on the world, which is a much more noble stance. I suck."

"You don't either. It's your job to focus on your designs, making you not at all selfish. Stop that. As someone who handles the *retail* side of things, I'm customer focused. More salad, please. This dressing is from the angels."

"Also known as my mother. Her recipe." Spencer passed the salad bowl.

"Don't lose it. It's a keeper. You'll want to pass it down to your own children one day." Hadley paused. "Do you want children?"

"Yes," Spencer said. "Does that surprise you?"

Hadley poured a good amount of dressing onto her salad and then added some more. And then a little more. Spencer smothered a smile at her pile of dressing with a little bit of salad. "It does, actually, given what I know."

"I mean, I don't want them *today*. But in the scheme of life, I would definitely like one, maybe two rugrats if we're talking about best case scenario."

"So, you're not afraid of long-term commitment when it comes to children?" Hadley ate a forkful of salad.

Touché. "I'm not afraid of long-term commitment, Hadley." She gestured with her fork in a circle. "I'm just not going to stress out about forcing it with one person my entire life when I'm not sure humans are made for it."

Hadley leaned in, dipped her head, and caught Spencer's gaze. "Trust me. They are."

Spencer laughed. She should have seen that coming. "Your thoughts are noted for the record. But let's say it doesn't work out after ten, fifteen wonderful years with someone. Without the messy piece of paper binding two people together, they can disentangle their lives and move forward."

"That is the most unromantic sentiment, Spencer. Does your mother know you feel this way?"

"I think so."

"You should make sure she does. If not, maybe she'll give you a talkin'-to."

Spencer nearly spat out her food. "A talkin'-to?"

"Yes, a stern one. You need it." Hadley stood and placed a hand on Spencer's shoulder. "You sit and finish your wine and let me get these dishes."

"Absolutely not. You're my guest. I'll do the dishes."

"You prepared a wonderful meal for me and I'm doing them and that's final. If you say no again, I'm going to throw a fit and leave. Do you want me to leave?"

Spencer stared at her wide-eyed, unable to tell if Hadley was bluffing or not. "I mean, no, I don't."

"Good, then sip that wine, and I'll be with you shortly." Luckily for Spencer, she had a dishwasher, which only required Hadley to load and not scrub. As she rinsed the dishes under the faucet and moved them to the dishwasher, she hummed softly to the music and swayed her hips. At one point, she pulled her hair out from the clasp that held it partially back, letting the strands of blond tumble down fully. If washing dishes had ever looked better, Spencer wouldn't have believed it.

"You sure I can't help?"

"Only if you want to see me break down, tears cascading from my face in failure." Hadley passed her a preview of what that might look like.

Spencer held up her hands. "All you, then." As she watched a calm, cool, and collected Hadley putting the finishing touches on her now clean kitchen, she couldn't help imagining the kind of life where they'd trade off on those kinds of chores or take quiet dinners together. Way too early to be envisioning those kinds of evenings, but she found herself doing it anyway.

"What are you daydreaming about over there? Whatever it is, it looks pretty wonderful," Hadley said. "I detect you're a million miles from here." She dried her hands on a dish towel and tucked a strand of hair behind her ear.

"No, I was actually much closer." She stood and walked slowly to Hadley. "Thank you for doing that."

"I might have earned a little something," Hadley said, looking skyward and pointing at her lips.

"More food?" Spencer asked playfully. "I have an apple pie we can pop in the oven for later, and it has the most interesting lattice design on the crust. I think you'll like it. I didn't make it, though. It's one you buy and heat."

"No. That's not it," Hadley said, holding her pose. There was nothing cuter, or hotter, than this woman standing in her kitchen.

"Lip gloss?" Spencer asked, loving the delayed gratification, and turned the hell on by it. "I could grab you some if—"

Hadley gasped in mock indignation, snapped her focus to Spencer just in time to be kissed. "Oh," Hadley murmured. And kissed some more. Spencer could taste the sweetness of the wine still on her lips, and for good measure licked the bottom one. They were up against the counter, and then the refrigerator as their mouths danced and their hands explored. Both spots were good, but not enough. Yes, it was date three, but there was no way she was going to be presumptuous or expect anything beyond what they had going. Three was technically really early, and she was a practical-minded person. If anything, making out with Hadley would be blissful and torturous but she could handle—

"Where's your bedroom?" Hadley asked in her ear, her hands tugging at the hem of Spencer's top.

Kittens marching into battle.

"Down the hall. But fair warning, Minnie Mouse is in the bathroom. Door is open. She just prefers the tub when I have company, so I let her chill there and take everything in."

"Pause. You have a cat named after a Disney character?"

"I do. Minnie for short."

Hadley's lips found hers again instantly and worked wonders the Magic Kingdom couldn't keep up with. All hail Walt Disney. Hadley slid her hands into the backs of Spencer's pockets as they walked, and kissed, and walked and kissed. She paused and pulled something from Spencer's jeans. The crumpled Post-It from the fridge. Spencer rolled her lips in. Wonderful.

"What is this?" Hadley asked and unrumpled the paper. "Light candles before she arrives," she read out loud. She shifted her gaze to Spencer, eyebrow arched like Sherlock Holmes hot on the trail.

No point trying to finesse her way around this one. "My best friend, Kendra, had a hand in helping me plan the details for tonight.

She's better at all of this than I am. A good portion of credit goes to her."

"And what else did Kendra say you should do?" Hadley asked. She undid the top button of Spencer's capris. Spencer's eyes fluttered closed and she swallowed. How in the world was she supposed to answer a question like that when Hadley, the wide-eyed innocent, was slowly starting to undress her? How?

"She said something about the hens. Cook them, I think."

Hadley tugged on Spencer's open pants and pulled her into the bedroom. "What else?" She began kissing her neck slowly, seductively.

Spencer tried to think. "Um, she said I should probably play music."

Hadley lifted her head and looked at Spencer with those perfect blue eyes. "You did an excellent job of that."

"Thank you." Her responses were slow because her brain was deprived. All the blood had gone elsewhere, and the dampness in her underwear had just graduated. How had that happened so quickly? The effect of Hadley. That's how.

"Any other advice from Kendra?"

Spencer blinked. There had been so much, and now it all rolled together in a jumble, because she really just wanted to kiss Hadley some more, get her on that bed and...oh, that's right. "She said date three could be an important date."

Hadley nodded calmly. "Why is that, do you think?"

Spencer couldn't make herself say the words. "It just meant that we were...progressing."

"To right here in your bedroom?" Hadley asked, and lowered Spencer's zipper.

"Something like that."

She stroked the soft skin just above Spencer's bikini line. "Kendra told you that if you played your cards right, you'd get lucky tonight?"

Spencer nodded. "But I'm not Kendra. I didn't invite you over expecting anything other than dinner and—what do you call it? Fun wine?"

"It was fun. It might also be fun if you touched me now."

Spencer nodded. She eased her hands under the back of Hadley's top and slid them upward, reveling in the warmth of her skin, how soft it was beneath her fingertips. Hadley inhaled at her touch, and even that slight reaction sent Spencer places. The music from the living room drifted in, and she wondered if the significance of Hadley's desire mirrored her own. They kissed and walked their way toward the bed. The room was almost dark. In a few more minutes, the sun would be down entirely.

When Hadley began to unbutton her blouse, Spencer interjected, "Let me. I want to undress you."

Hadley stared at her, and slowly dropped her hands, a sultry smile on her lips. Spencer put the lights to low so they'd have something to see by, and returned to Hadley. She unzipped her dress slowly, taking in each tiny glimpse of skin revealed to her. *God, this body.* The gentle curve of Hadley's breasts came into view as she turned, accentuated by a dark purple bra. She swallowed at the bolt of arousal. She'd hardly touched Hadley, yet her center, her thighs, her knees shook and ached. She wanted nothing more than to lick her way across that bra line and beneath. She'd take her time and acquaint herself with every inch of Hadley. She'd hoped to keep tonight light and playful, but this was feeling anything but. The tight gathering of lust that she'd carried with her the past few weeks had melted and spread to every part of her. She wanted Hadley so badly that it was hard to maintain control. She tried to take a breath to settle herself, but there was simply no air.

Hadley stepped into her space, and with one easy motion of her shoulders, her dress slid down her arms to the floor, leaving her standing there in the purple bra and matching bikinis. "My turn," Hadley said. She slowly lifted Spencer's shirt up and over her head. "Look at you," she breathed, staring down at the expanse of cleavage now on display. Spencer's breasts were fuller than Hadley's. She'd never been hugely confident of them…until now, that is. The way Hadley stared down left Spencer breathless and aching for them to be touched. How quickly the tables had turned. As if reading her thoughts, Hadley traced along the top of her bra line, watching Spencer's reaction with interest. "You're so beautiful, Spencer," she whispered, reaching behind Spencer with one hand and adeptly unclasping her bra. With gentle ease, she leaned down and captured a nipple in her mouth in a manner that could be described as anything but timid. *Fuck.* Pinpoints of pleasure hit hard and Spencer threaded her fingers into Hadley's hair as Hadley pulled her in by her waist. If Spencer had any delusions about taking charge, she let them fly right out the window as Hadley angled her topless and hazy onto the bed. In a matter of seconds, her pants and thong had been removed from her body and discarded on the floor. "Oh wow," Hadley said, running a hand from Spencer's stomach down to her thigh, while Spencer concentrated on simply obtaining air.

"I love these sheets," Hadley said, pulling back a fistful. Spencer couldn't have told you where she'd purchased them or even what color they were in that moment, but leave it to Hadley to not miss the year they were made and the thread count. She was a details girl.

"I'll send you a set."

Hadley laughed and Spencer was topped before she knew it, and staring up into big, blue eyes that now carried a touch of fire. "I'm going to do things to you now," Hadley said in her ear, "that I've wanted to do for a long time, if you'll let me."

Spencer nodded and pulled Hadley down for a heat-laden kiss.

Hadley spent the next few minutes bathing Spencer's breasts with an amount of attention they'd never received, and just when Spencer thought she was done, Hadley pinned her hands above her head to start again. She heard herself making soft humming sounds of pleasure, which would apparently serve as their soundtrack because every kiss, lick, or suck brought her closer to the brink. Her body quaked noticeably beneath Hadley's fingertips, her mouth. She was distantly aware of her rolling hips, pushing against Hadley for friction, anything, and coming up empty. It was torment, but the memorable kind, and worth every second.

"Your bra," Spencer whispered. She so badly wanted to see Hadley's breasts. Without a word, Hadley adjusted to a seated position and removed her bra slowly. With her hands now free, Spencer was able to reach up and cup the breasts she'd been dying to greet, perfect in every way, just like the rest of Hadley. She sat up and, with Hadley straddling her lap, went to work with her mouth, showing Hadley's perfect breasts the same kind of attention, sucking a nipple, biting it softly.

In response, Hadley dropped her head back, exposing the long column of her neck. Spencer didn't hesitate to lick her way up from Hadley's collarbone to just below her chin, holding her tight, lost in the warmth of her skin. It was Hadley's turn to rock her hips, and Spencer was certainly willing to help her with the endeavor. In a quick move, she deposited Hadley onto her back on the bed. Spencer parted her legs and kissed her thighs one at a time, making her way slowly to Hadley's center, eager to taste her, but also wanting to take her time. Both were achievable goals. The matching purple underwear shouldn't go unappreciated, so she kissed Hadley through them thoroughly, loving the way it made her squirm and whimper. She slipped the rectangular piece of fabric to the side and tasted her full on. Holding her legs in place, she kissed her open mouthed as Hadley moaned above. It wasn't enough. She slipped her tongue inside and then out again, repeating the action until the sounds Hadley made reached a fantastic crescendo. Her hips bucked, increasing rhythm, begging Spencer for more. Slow and steady, she removed the bikinis altogether. "Thank God," Hadley said, to a smile from Spencer. That's when she went to work with her tongue, tracing one intricate pattern after another, never giving too much attention to any one spot. Hadley shook her head as the attention continued. "Please, Spencer," she breathed, clenching the sheets with her fist. She raised her gaze to study Hadley who looked down at her with flushed cheeks and parted lips. Gorgeous. With a final well-placed kiss, followed by direct pressure from her tongue, she simultaneously pushed inside Hadley with her fingers, slow and deep. She wasn't prepared for the immediate reaction. With an inarticulate moan, Hadley threw her head back as she rode Spencer's hand, legs trembling. She murmured Spencer's name over and over again, grasping Spencer's head gently to hold her right where she needed it. Then, with a twist and a cry, Hadley was gone. She arched into Spencer and shattered, clenching around her hand gloriously.

That did it. Spencer, in an uncharacteristic turn, felt her own orgasm approach. Desperately, she straddled Hadley's thigh and pressed against it. Hadley was too quick. Before Spencer knew what happened, she was on her back with Hadley's tongue intimately swirling her center. Her eyes slammed closed and she gasped in shock as the pressure, accompanied by hits of pleasure, steadily grew until she thought Hadley would drive her out of her ever-loving mind. Damn, this woman knew how to use her mouth. Hadley sucked and nibbled until there was nothing but light behind her eyes. A cry tore from Spencer's lips, unexpected and loud. She swore in the midst of it all because what should have been merely a physical act had stirred up a myriad of emotions that bubbled to the surface. The physical payout was never-ending as it washed over her, sweet and insistent. The emotional one was nearly as powerful. She held Hadley to her as she struggled to right herself. She couldn't quite wrap her mind around the very powerful event. She knew for sure there was something different about what she'd experienced tonight. She also knew that she was likely in a lot of trouble.

"I love seeing you let go like that," Hadley mused, snuggling into

Spencer's side. "You are easily the sexiest human alive when you're turned on. Do you know that?"

Spencer chuckled and kissed Hadley's lips as she looked up at her. "Impossible. You're here."

"We have to get you to let go more often."

Spencer smiled. "When you're around, I'm not thinking that's going to be a problem. I've never…" She trailed off and laughed instead, covering her eyes with her forearm.

"What?" Hadley asked, laughing along with her, pulling her forearm away. "Tell me. You've never what?"

She met Hadley's gaze. "Come that fast before. It hit me out of nowhere. I promise I'm not a lightweight usually."

"I happen to love how into it you were. It was hot."

Spencer raised her head. "Yeah?"

"Definitely."

She dropped back onto the pillow. "I'm not sure I have any brain capacity left after that."

"Good thing I don't need your brain," Hadley said with a grin and crawled down Spencer's body, sending every nerve ending into high alert.

They fell asleep wrapped in each other somewhere after three a.m. At least, that was the last time Spencer caught sight of the clock. Her mind was scrambled with the best sex she'd ever had and the emergence of powerful feelings she didn't know how to categorize or what to do with.

When it came to Hadley Cooper and the newfound hold she had on Spencer's heart, all bets were off. Tonight had been a game changer. It would easily go down as the best damn date she'd ever been on. It was becoming clear to Spencer that she was simply along for the ride, hoping against hope that they weren't careening for heartbreak.

Making love to Hadley should have been simple, basic even. This kind of thing happened all the time in life: Two people who were attracted to each other enjoyed a night in each other's company. Only it wasn't basic. It came with layers of sensations, and feelings, and complexities that Spencer hadn't planned on. It would take some time and processing for her to fully understand what was happening between them. For now, she planned to simply bask in the enjoyment, and there was a lot of that.

"I think we're good at this together," Hadley said, an arm thrown over her head as she stared up at the ceiling.

Spencer laughed. If it had been any better they'd have gone up in flames. "I thought we might be. We crushed those expectations, though."

"I like to be naked," Hadley said, turning onto her side to better see Spencer. "You should know that about me. Not many people do."

"I can definitely find a way to cope if you plan to strip down in the middle of a conversation." Spencer mirrored Hadley's position and faced her. "You're loud in bed. I love that."

"Too loud?" Hadley asked, blinking at her with concern.

"Not in the slightest. You're so…"

"What?" Hadley asked, enjoying this now. She propped the side of her head on her hand and waited for more details. "What am I? I need to know what you're thinking."

She circled before finding the right descriptor. "Free. That's the word. In everything you do, you know how to let go. I need to work on that."

"Well, listen," Hadley said, inching closer. "You were pretty free just a few minutes ago. I have nothing but compliments for that kind of freedom and think you should embrace it any time you feel compelled."

Spencer closed one eye and admitted something to herself and to Hadley. "You coax it out of me. Lately, I'm appreciating details more, and I think it's your influence."

Hadley didn't say anything. Instead she grinned a beautiful, luminous smile that made Spencer long for a camera to capture it forever.

"Why are you smiling? Not that I mind a bit." She brushed a strand of hair back from Hadley's face. "Tell me."

"Because you just paid me the highest form of compliment. If I make the world seem more beautiful to you, then I've done a good thing."

"A very good thing," Spencer said, with a nod. "I've never met anyone like you, Hadley."

"Well, there can't be two of us! I'd have to look her up, have it out." She raised a finger. "With words, of course. I'm strictly anti-violence. Another thing to know about me."

"Naked and passive. Got it." Spencer chuckled. "Now I'm imagining two Hadleys battling it out for the sweetest person award. Hurling compliments and cupcakes at the other."

Hadley looked so wistful. "I'd work so hard to win if that were real."

Spencer pulled Hadley on top of her. "You wouldn't have to."

"Ohhh," Hadley said, as they came together, skin on skin. Hadley rolled her hips against Spencer, almost as if testing the waters of her interest. Spencer reached between them and touched her intimately, watching as Hadley's eyes darkened. A ripple of excitement shimmered through her. "Spencer, I'm not feeling exactly tired. You tired? Because I seem to have energy."

"Do you know what I say to that?" Spencer asked. "Who needs sleep? Not me."

Hadley laughed. The night was young and full of so much opportunity.

Spencer smiled just as her mouth took Hadley's.

CHAPTER NINE

Spencer arrived at the hospital cafeteria and immediately spotted Kendra wearing her pink scrubs with the kittens on them at a booth in the back. She dodged the traditional scene of doctors and nurses and hospital staff all crisscrossing the space with their varied lunch trays. "Excuse me. Excuse me, sir. Oops, sorry about that. Excuse me." Kendra only had forty-five minutes for lunch, so Spencer had no problem coming to her for their occasional lunch date to capitalize on their one-on-one time. Plus, for cafeteria food, this place had it together. She slid into the booth and didn't even wait for a hello, accepting the cheeseburger and fries that Kendra slid her way.

She tossed her bag into the seat next to her and leveled Kendra with a desperate stare. "Thank God you were free today."

Kendra slowly bit into a fry and studied her. "You're moving at a different pace today, Adair. There's a buzzing to your energy. What's with that? I'm unsettled."

"You noticed that, too?" Spencer nodded, realizing she was vibrating as she sat there. "You aren't wrong. I'm feeling…" She didn't have the word. Instead, with her palms she made large circles around the sides of her head, hoping that the chaotic gesture would communicate it all.

"Mm-hmm," Kendra said, squinting. "I see we're going the charades route. Princess Leia!" she said pointing, as if a lightbulb had shot to life above her head.

"No."

"Princess Leia got lucky last night," she said, with a wider smile and danced to a groove in her head.

"Yes. Yes, she did." Spencer sighed, and took the bun off her cheeseburger for proper ketchup application.

"Spence, time's ticking. The babies upstairs need me, and I need them. We had two born just this morning. Spill your guts and stop being a weird-ass."

Spencer nodded, and found her footing. "Fine. I'm sounding an alert. That's what's up. She's not who she claims to be, Ken."

"Who? Hadley? She's not an assistant manager white lady who works on Rodeo Drive?"

"No, that part is true. But she's sweet and nice and unassuming. You think *that's* who you're dealing with and you can handle it. But then, *then*, you find out she's a total tiger in the bedroom. It's mind blowing."

"Well, well, well," Kendra said and laughed, stealing back the ketchup. She lowered her voice. "Sounds like you might have stumbled onto the jackpot with this one. A lot of people would kill for that combo, Spence. Stop the stressin'."

"I can't even wrap my mind around it," Spencer said, slapping her palm across half her face and holding it there. "She's so many things. And I have everyone figured out. You know this about me. It's my gift." She shook her finger. "But I didn't see her coming. I still don't and now I'm in my head about it. My concentration is at fifty percent, and I'm falling behind on my work."

"Oh, my effing stars." Kendra fanned herself in amusement. "Spencer Adair is on her heels at long last. She's met her match, ladies and gentleman." The tables around them nodded in amusement and went back to their meals. "Lord Jesus. Oh, yes. I'm loving every second of this. For once, I'm not the lovestruck idiot in this duo." She did another shoulder dance to celebrate.

Spencer scoffed. "No one said anything about lovestruck, all right? I'm just…intrigued and now preoccupied. Let's not get crazy."

"Sure. You're not mooning over this woman and I'm not a sucker for Idris Elba with his shirt off, and oiled up, and caressing a woman's face, preferably mine, and—"

"You're stealing from my crisis with a straight girl fantasy."

"I'm using it as a stepping stool to Idris."

Spencer smiled at Kendra being Kendra but moved beyond it. "Maybe I should stop seeing her."

Kendra pulled her face back and studied the tables around them as if to say "did you just hear this woman?"

"I'm serious, Ken. I don't like feeling like my brain is all over the place, and besides that, we have very different beliefs about love and marriage and the grand scheme. I'd probably be a letdown for her in the long run. Those are big issues one shouldn't ignore."

"Oh, are we back on your fear of marriage because your parents' didn't work? That old chestnut?" She rolled her eyes as if the subject was a tired one.

"You're minimizing my whole ideology, but yes, it's a factor."

"Let me help you unfactor that nonsense, because I work with families bringing little ones into the world every day, and that love is purer than anything you can toss forth in an argument. So, you need to check yourself, Spencer, before you blow something that could, in the end, be your mother-effing everything."

"I always know you're serious when you almost swear."

"Good, because that's now. Eat your burger. We're not just here for Dr. Phil time, Lil Miss. You need nourishment or your mama would kill me."

Obediently, Spencer took a bite of her burger and then a couple more, because hospital food had never been this good. Seriously? Where did they hire their chefs? "What about you?" she asked around three fries. "Staying away from Tucker, right?"

"Away is such a general definition."

Spencer shook her head. "You're going out with his ass again? Speaking of mamas killing their kids, it's my job to stand in for yours since she can't be here. Don't be an idiot. Don't."

Kendra shrugged and pulled a pathetic face. "He says he's sorry and only wants to be with me from now on."

"Are you stupid? Were you dropped on your head? Those are the only explanations I can summon in this moment."

Kendra waved her off. "Don't go getting all worked up. I get it, okay?" She tapped her chest several times with force. "I know he's a player now, and what to watch out for. Knowledge is power."

"What a pair we are, sitting here," Spencer said. "You running around with a no-good dog, and me chasing a—"

"A starry-eyed white woman with moves," Kendra said, laughing.

"What am I gonna do with you?" Spencer asked.

"More like what am I gonna do with *you*? Eat your burger, Spencer Spice, and don't forget the tomato. It's good for you." A pause. "When do you see her again?"

"As soon as humanly possible," Spencer said, with a very guilty smile.

❖

Janika and her co-captain, Roger Raines, were running out of air. They'd managed to cram themselves into a small pod before the spaceship lost all power, careening to Earth where it would undoubtedly burst into flames. Gah! Hadley swallowed and turned the page, her heart rate out of control, and why wouldn't it be? This mission was crazy! The move had been a risky one, but somehow Janika and Roger had made it out of there in time. Now it was a matter of finding the space station before the pod itself became a death chamber from which they'd never escape!

"Hurry, Janika," Hadley murmured. She was tempted to look ahead to be sure they made it out in one piece, but that would be cheating and Hadley wouldn't be able to live with herself if that's who she became. A knock at the door. She glanced up but couldn't stop reading. Not yet. She flipped the page. Roger suggested they take turns breathing, to which Hadley wanted to scream, "That's not practical, Roger. Hurry! *That's* what you need to do!" Another knock. "Oh, dear goodness," Hadley said, closing the book and scurrying to her front door. She found Larry Herman there, their interesting and sometimes tightly wound landlord. She happened to have a soft spot for him.

"Hey, Larry," Hadley said, smiling. "What can I do for you?"

"I'm here to report that Gia Malone is officially sick. I'm filling in tonight."

Hadley watched him shuffle nervously, and push his plastic-framed glasses farther up on his nose. "You're filling in for *babysitting*? With *me*?"

"Well, she certainly shouldn't be around children with the multiplicity factor of germs. Consider the likely outcomes, Ms. Cooper."

Hadley glanced outside and to the right for any sign of Gia near her own apartment. Nothing. "Are you…certain she's not well?"

"Do I look certain?" He seemed to make a show of pursing his lips and tightening his eyebrows, which really just reminded Hadley of Bert from *Sesame Street*, but she let it go, deciding to seek out Gia instead. Larry followed, hot on her heels, to Gia's apartment door, which was opened promptly before she could knock.

"Hey," Gia said, brightening. "Was just coming to see what time we're scheduled for at Autumn's tonight." But something was different about Gia. Her voice was lower and her nose looked red. Her normally bright brown eyes carried a dull, dim quality. Oh, no! Poor Gia.

"I'm filling in for you, remember?" Larry Herman said. "We decided. The young lady you carry on with decided along with me."

"Elle's just being overly cautious. I told you guys I could do it."

"Elle thinks you shouldn't babysit?" Hadley asked. "She might be right. Look at you. Do you have a fever?" Hadley ushered Gia back inside and Larry followed them in. "Sit," she instructed, and placed the back of her hand on Gia's forehead. "You do. You have a slight elevation."

"That decides it!" Larry crowed. "I'm in and you're out."

Gia stared at him. "You just want to spend time with Hadley, and you know it." It was true that Larry did seem to carry a bit of a torch for her. While she tried not to encourage the crush, she couldn't help but be nice to him. He tried so hard, and always came up so...awkward.

"What I'm most interested in doing is making sure that the Carpenter infants are cared for and not exposed to the plague." He scowled at Gia.

"I don't have the plague," Gia said. But it sounded a lot more like "I don hab the plague" due to her very noticeable cold.

"It's okay, G," Hadley said, rounding the kitchen island and pouring Gia a glass of orange juice from the fridge. She also grabbed a couple Tylenol for good measure. "I want you to rest right here on this couch tonight. Here." She dropped the Tylenol into Gia's hand and smoothed her hair back affectionately. "Take those and drink every drop of that juice, you poor sick person. Where's Elle?"

"She had a meeting with her sponsor rep tonight. A dinner thing."

"Gotcha. In that case, I will check on you soon. You need someone to say things like 'Poor baby, Gia' around every ninety minutes or so. It's part of the healing process."

"I'm probably okay without that."

"You are not. Accept your fate." She turned to Larry. "It looks like it's you and me tonight, Larry. You sure you're up for it?"

He rubbed his hands together with an intensity that said he meant business. "I've already googled the multitude of swaddling techniques and practiced in my car with my revolutionary flag. I'm more than prepared."

"War reenactment this week?"

"Tomorrow morning. I've been cast as colonial militia, probably for being too ambitious in past battles where I was featured. I tend to steal focus."

"Well, you have star quality." She patted him on the back of his shoulder. "Let's head over to Chez Carpenter. Go, team!"

They made their way down the stairs and across the courtyard in duty mode. Hadley prepared to make this night work if it killed her. She paused mid-thought because she spotted Spencer entering through the wrought iron gate. Well, then. Things had certainly taken a *turn*. Hadley couldn't hold back the grin if she wanted to. They hadn't seen each other in three days due to their conflicting schedules, yet here she stood, all sleek and shiny and sigh-worthy, which Hadley executed on cue. "What in the world?" Hadley said, abandoning Larry and making her way to Spencer.

"I'm sorry to just show up," she said, dipping her head and catching Hadley's gaze. "I was in the mood for some killer coffee, and since I was so close, I thought I might pop over and see if you were around."

"Killer coffee can make a person drive."

"That's a total and complete lie I just told," Spencer said. "I love the coffee next door, but I made that up just to see you. I can't stop thinking about you, us, the other night. It's an ongoing battle and I've now surrendered."

Hadley warmed from her hairline down and gave her toes a good wiggle. "You don't have to make up an excuse to see me, ya know."

"I do now, and I will never forget it again. You free?"

Hadley glanced behind her. "Not exactly. But how do you feel about babies?"

Spencer shrugged. "I'm a fan. My best friend's pretty much a baby whisperer and has taught me a few tricks to use on my little cousins here and there."

Hadley turned around. "Larry, I think you just might be off the hook."

"I am not," he said staunchly, and stood at attention. "I have a duty to sit with the children so the Carpenters can go out in the world. I do not shirk my duties."

Hadley laughed at what she should have expected to be his response and walked Spencer over to Larry. "Spencer, meet my landlord and friend, Larry Herman. He agreed to babysit the twins with me tonight when Gia caught a cold. But since you've been so kind to offer, I'm sure he has preparations to tend to for the Battle of Monmouth."

"Sorry?" Spencer asked, looking confused. She held out her hand anyway. "Nice to meet you."

Larry didn't budge. Instead he eyed Spencer like one would a pesky fly. "I certainly do not need to make preparations. I did that last week and the week prior to that."

"Okay," Hadley said, doing her best to pacify him and still capitalize on this opportunity to spend time with Spencer, even if it was in between diaper changes and feedings. "Spencer can back us up, then." She turned to Spencer for approval.

"I'm an excellent backup babysitter."

"I've never heard of a backup babysitter," Larry said suspiciously. "It feels made up."

"It is made up," Stephanie, their all-black-wearing neighbor said, as she crossed behind them through the courtyard.

Hadley ignored her. "We're all constantly learning, aren't we, Larry? Just today I learned that escape pods shouldn't accommodate more than one person, as the air supply will grow dangerously low. Shall we?"

With Hadley leading the way, the three of them made their way to Autumn and Kate's doorstep. When Kate answered, she studied their three faces. "Hi, Had. Larry." She paused when she came to Spencer. "I don't think we've met. Kate Carpenter."

"Spencer Adair. I'm the babysitting backup."

"Great. Nice to meet you," Kate said, with mild hesitation, because of course she'd be wary of leaving her children with a complete stranger.

"I can vouch for Spencer," Hadley said. "She's to be trusted."

Kate relaxed. "The more the merrier, then. These babies could use the backup, if you ask me. They take turns wreaking havoc. Currently, Will's up to bat."

"You just hand that little numbskull over to me," Hadley said, eager to get her hands on him. "Did you get the newsboy cap I had shipped?"

"He wore it all day yesterday," Kate said. "You're spoiling them rotten."

"Did I hear the name Spencer?" Autumn's voice said excitedly, from somewhere in the apartment.

"You guys should come in," Kate said, as if forgetting herself.

Moments later Autumn appeared in the living room looking as happy as a bride on her wedding day. She was going out on an actual date and getting to lay eyes on the much-talked-about Spencer, something she'd been asking to do for days now. It was like her version of Christmas morning, and she glowed. "Hi, Spencer! I'm Autumn from the coffee shop next door."

"Big fan of yours, then," Spencer said. "Killer brew."

Autumn studied her. "Oh, yes. You're very cute. Just as I remembered."

"Autumn," Hadley said, quietly and gave her head a subtle shake.

"I'm sorry, but she is. You *are*," she said, turning back to Spencer.

"Ms. Primm-Carpenter, we're here to babysit the little ones," Larry said, in an authoritative voice—surely his way of getting them back on track and off the subject of Spencer's good looks.

"So, no Gia-Pet tonight?" Autumn asked.

"She's down for the count with a cold/flu thing. I'll check on her later, but I thought it best she not be around the babies. Larry volunteered to sub in and we ran into Spencer unexpectedly in the courtyard."

Spencer winced. "I'm crashing."

"You are most certainly not," Autumn said, forcefully, taking Spencer by the arm and ushering her to the couch. "Please make yourself at home and eat all the food you find. Oh!" She scooped up Carrie from the baby swing and handed her to Spencer. "Meet Carrie. She's our favorite this hour. It rotates."

Spencer smiled down at tiny Carrie, who stared up at her with sleepy eyes. The image of the two of them about melted Hadley's heart into a pile of wonderful goo.

"Hi, baby girl," Spencer said in a low voice, and rocked her softly.

"You know where everything is, yes?" Autumn asked Hadley.

"I do! We got this. You two crazy kids get outta here and have a much-needed fun night out."

Kate and Autumn exchanged a flirtatious glance that prompted Hadley to roll her shoulders for all the cute in the room.

"We'll be home in a couple of hours," Kate said, and nodded gratefully.

"No reason to hurry," Larry told them. "Ms. Cooper and I have this under control. Where is the boy child?"

Kate pointed to the playpen. "Under the mobile, there. He seems to be calming down, which is good news for you all."

Larry nodded and offered a small salute as he headed in Will's direction.

Autumn looked from Spencer to Larry and back to Spencer. "This is going to be quite the evening."

She wasn't wrong.

Spencer took custody of Carrie and occupied her with funny faces, while Larry spent the better part of an hour explaining to Will that there had been many complications on America's growth to becoming the country we know today.

Hadley ran back and forth between the parties, offering burp cloths, warmed bottles and soft, soothing words as needed. "I think she's really taken to you," Hadley told Spencer.

"Well, Carrie and I have gotten to know each other a bit. She prefers a quiet voice and only the gentlest of rocking. Anything more sets her off and she gives you what for."

"What for?" Hadley asked.

"It's a technical term."

Carrie, who'd fussed a bit when her mommies left, seemed to have found her rhythm in Spencer's arms. Her eyes drifted closed and Spencer leaned back so Carrie could sleep uninterrupted on the warmth of her chest, a spot Hadley knew from personal experience was a great place for sleeping.

"Hey," Spencer said quietly over Carrie. "I'm not sure your friend Larry likes me very much."

Hadley wasn't sure where to begin in order to explain Larry and all of his idiosyncrasies, including his affinity for her. "I think he's just a little wary of you stealing his thunder tonight."

"He has thunder?" She glanced over at him surreptitiously. "I'm not seeing the thunder on that dude."

Hadley considered how she might explain it another way. "He likes to spend time with me."

A pause. "He has the hots for you?" Spencer asked, and grinned. "Okay, got it. Guy after my own heart. Can't fault him at all."

"I wouldn't go that far. But yes, he carries a unique torch for me."

"And I've totally blocked him tonight. That's what's going on here. Now I feel bad for the man."

Hadley tossed a glance over her shoulder to make sure Larry was occupied before continuing the conversation. "Don't. I've been waiting to see you again."

Spencer closed her eyes and smiled. "On the drive over, I changed my mind about twelve times before forcing myself to just bite the bullet and show up. That's not like me."

"No. You're not the tentative type," Hadley said.

"Until you."

A beat as they stared at each other over the sleeping baby. "Are you free after babysitting, per chance?" Hadley asked.

Spencer opened her mouth to answer but was beaten to the punch by Larry, who stood over them, holding a crying Will as far from his body as possible. All down the front of his shirt and pants was an orangey-looking spit-up. "I'm in need of assistance," Larry said. "Backup person, would you mind doing your job instead of fraternizing?"

"I got him," Hadley said, scooping up Will and holding him close. "Someone had a little too much to eat." She studied Larry. Honestly, his entire outfit was ruined. Completely unwearable. "Tell you what, Larry. Why don't we see if Autumn has anything you can change into?" The only problem was that Larry was over six feet tall with large limbs and Autumn and Kate's clothes were not likely to fit. Oh! Unless...

"Perfect!" Hadley said five minutes later when Larry emerged in black leggings that were too short to extend beyond his mid-calves and a purple maternity shirt with bright yellow flowers all over it. "Maternity clothes rock and stretch in fantastic ways. I think we've solved our problem."

"I'm uncomfortable with this," he said stoically.

"Well, you shouldn't be," Hadley told him. "You look great, and Autumn won't mind at all. I've got your clothes already going in the washing machine."

"Dear Lord in heaven," Spencer murmured, studying him. "He's like the Incredible Pregnant-Hulk."

"Actually, that's not a bad comparison," Hadley said, smothering a smile. "Just trying to keep him happy."

"You're a smart woman. And about later?" Spencer asked, once Larry excused himself to check on his clothes. "I do happen to be free."

"Great. Me, too. Well, I have a few things I need to take care of, and then I'm all yours." Spencer's eyes darkened and Hadley felt the warmth gather in her stomach. "Don't look at me like that until later. There are children in the room."

"As if I can control it. Have you seen yourself?" Spencer asked. She dropped her voice to a whisper. "And now that I've seen you naked, it's just worse."

Hadley felt the blush hit her cheeks and warmth prickle up her spine and settle behind her neck. Oh, dear goodness. Yep, blatant and undeniable lust had arrived right on schedule. "Later," she said, with what she hoped was an effective smolder. She knew it probably wasn't.

She wasn't the smoldering type. Spencer's amused laughter only confirmed her status as smolder impaired. She'd work on it.

"You're adorable," Spencer whispered. "And ridiculously hot. I don't know that I can wait for you."

Hadley's eyes widened. "There are childlike ears about."

Spencer glanced down at Carrie. "This little mama is my wing woman and an exceptional one at that. Skills beyond her years. You have no idea." Will fussed in Hadley's arms. "Boys are always a little slower to mature," Spencer said with a wink. "Why don't we switch?"

Hadley pulled her face back and let her mouth fall open. "Is that a challenge? You think he'll calm down for you?"

Spencer grinned. "I know he will. Let me show you."

Hadley obliged and handed Will to Spencer, placing him in her free hand, and scooped up Caroline gently, so as not to disturb her peaceful slumber. The little girl stirred for a moment, opened her eyes, and peered up at Hadley. Realizing all was well, she sighed and went back to sleep with the back of her fist to her mouth, stealing Hadley's heart for the eighty billionth time. When she glanced up, she was shocked to see that not only had Will ceased his fussing but was enamored of Spencer's face looming over him. The twins were old enough now where they were capable of authentic smiles and she was pretty sure Will was showing off that skill now. "I think he has a girlfriend," Hadley said, mystified. "Look at that."

"He just needs a slower vibe is all."

"That's what you've done? You've slowed your vibe? How do I do that?" Hadley offered her smolder of earlier as an attempt. "Like this?"

"Are you doing Elvis? I don't think Will knows him." Spencer stared down at the little guy and talked to him in that soothing low voice, the same voice that had struck Hadley as so melodic the day she'd met Spencer. "He just needs to know that he can relax. Isn't that right, little Will? We'll take care of all the rest. You just take some chill time."

He blinked back at her heavily, clearly not long for the land of the conscious.

"Wow," Hadley said. "I'm not kidding when I say that you're the baby whisperer. You talk to him in your sexy voice, and he's done for."

"My sexy voice?" Spencer said, emphasizing the smooth quality. "That's what you call it?"

"Is there another term for it?" Hadley asked. "I'm going to have you read me the phone book each night now if that's how quickly you snag results."

Spencer laughed quietly as she rocked Will. "Putting you to sleep is not always going to be in my best interests."

Hadley shimmied her shoulders. "There you go again with the perfect saucy line."

"Where's William?" Larry asked, stalking through the living room in his maternity shirt and short leggings.

"Shhh," Hadley said. "Spencer got him to sleep."

Larry glared at her suspiciously. "How did you do that?"

"Just my own little brand of mojo."

"You're the backup babysitter." It was a firm reminder, which Spencer took in stride.

"And I won't ever forget that, Lar. Can I call you Lar?"

"No."

"Okay." They stared at each other.

"Hey, why don't you take Carrie," Hadley said to Larry. He seemed to soften as Hadley approached him.

"No, no. You have her content and cry-free. I'll just sit over there until there's a crisis." On that last word, he shot daggers in Spencer's direction, making it very clear where said crisis would likely emerge.

An hour later and the door to the apartment opened slowly and two very smiley mothers entered the space, holding hands. "How's everything in here?" Autumn asked quietly, glancing around the room. She took in Carrie sleeping against Hadley's chest, Will curled up in Spencer's arms, and Larry working a crossword puzzle in the *Wall Street Journal* he'd brought with him. "What in hell happened to Larry? That's my shirt!"

"Your shirt is unharmed," Hadley said calmly, with a we-did-what-had-to-be-done look. "Larry is taking good care of it."

"The boy child vomited." He glanced down at his ensemble. "Emergency measures were called for." He stood. "You're home now. I'll take my leave. Ms. Cooper," he said, nodding politely to Hadley as he passed. "Backup," he bit out to Spencer. "Good night, both Mrs. Carpenters."

Kate knocked him on the shoulder. "Thanks for your help, Larry. Because of you, Autumn and I got to have a nice dinner out. I think we needed it."

"Yeah, thanks, Larry," Autumn said with a warm smile.

Larry's entire demeanor shifted, inspiring him to soften and appear sheepish and sweet. You didn't see that side of Larry too often, but Hadley had always understood that's who he really was underneath all the odd, intense bravado. "Just wanted to do the noble thing."

"Well, we couldn't have done it without you," Hadley said. "I mean that."

He nodded to her chivalrously and now seemed embarrassed and beet red. "Good night, all."

"Wait, Larry," Autumn called after him. "Your clothes."

But he was already around the corner and on his way, escaping the perceived limelight. They looked at each other.

"Well…it is Venice," Hadley offered. "He'll blend."

"So how about ten dollars an hour?" Kate asked, thumbing through her cash.

Hadley placed her free hand over her wounded heart. "How dare you offer me money for the care of my honorary niece and nephew, even if you're coming from a very good place because you're Kate. I refuse any and all monetary gestures!"

"Are you sure?" Kate asked. She gestured with the money to Spencer, who shook her head and held up a hand.

Autumn waved off Hadley's theatrics. "Free labor. Don't argue." She turned her attention to the babies, racing over to Carrie and pulling her gently into her arms. "It was so strange to be out in the world and not here with them. It's like some sort of parallel universe out there. How did they do?"

"Luckily, we had Spencer the baby whisperer along for the ride. They've been asleep for the past hour."

Autumn's eyebrows rose and she turned in appreciation to Spencer. "What are you doing tomorrow? I don't know what very successful designers make by way of salary, but I'm willing to try and match it."

"Don't you try and poach her from me!" Hadley stepped between them. "We have big plans for Spencer at Silhouette, and she can't moonlight as a babysitter and keep a clear head."

"It's not awful to be fought over," Spencer said quietly, to Will.

"Let me steal him from you," Kate said, gently taking the sleeping boy in her arms. "You're off the clock. Big plans tonight?"

Hadley exchanged a look with Spencer. "Not sure yet."

Autumn shook her head vehemently as if that answer were not at all acceptable. "It's still early. Get out there and cause trouble, dammit. Dance on tables and wave your shirts over your heads. You have no children. Live, for God's sake." She looked from Hadley to Spencer in desperation. "Promise me."

"We promise," Spencer said solemnly. It's possible she was afraid.

"Already on it," Hadley said, pulling Autumn into a hug. This was a transitional time in Autumn's life and she needed all the support she could get. "Did you have fun tonight?" she asked her quietly.

The undisputable smile that hit and grew did all the talking for Autumn. "The best time. It was like we were dating all over again. We kissed at the car. For a really long time, too. I owe you one, Had."

"Anytime. And I mean that." She gave Autumn's hand a squeeze, pulled Kate into a hug, and then with Spencer at her side, left the new little family to the rest of their evening.

"That was fun," Spencer said, once they hit the courtyard. "But I don't think Larry and I will be reprising our partnership."

Hadley scrunched an eye in apology. "He's jealous."

"I can completely see why," Spencer said, taking her hand. "And because I just promised a woman that I would live, for God's sake, I have to do this." Hadley grinned as Spencer closed the distance between them and caught Hadley's mouth with hers. She'd been longing to kiss Spencer all night and the reality was every bit as gratifying as she'd hoped. In fact, it knocked her out of the socks she wasn't wearing. The crackle, the sizzle, the chemistry did not let her down. Her spirits soared even as she tried to maintain control. It wasn't just the kiss itself that had shepherded her to this inarguable high. It was everything leading up to it, their give and take, the fashion overlap that left them so much to talk about, the amazing night they'd spent together, and the domesticity of the last two hours. She was losing custody of her own heart and it was thrilling and terrifying like a roller coaster you didn't want to get off. She was on a path to something big.

"We're more than a big bang kiss," she murmured when they came up for air. She hadn't intended to say it out loud, but it was as if the words flew from her lips, refusing to be suppressed.

"Is that good?" Spencer asked, dreamy-eyed and gorgeous. Hadley would never tire of looking at her, kissing her, or talking to her.

Hadley nodded, too trepidatious to explain any further. Spencer didn't buy into forever, so how would she possibly understand Hadley's childhood fantasy come to life? And how was Hadley supposed to reconcile the fact that Spencer might never share in the sentiment, no matter how strong her feelings for Hadley might grow? Nope. She

wasn't doing this tonight. They'd agreed to keep open minds, and that
was exactly the plan she would stick to. Plus, she wasn't willing to
do anything that would put a damper on her big bang realization. She
would tuck it away and keep it safe.

Spencer took her hand. "What now?"

"Chicken soup," Hadley blurted.

"You're hungry?" Spencer asked. "If you're hungry, girl, I will
happily feed you."

Hadley laughed, and gave Spencer's arm a tug. "No. I need to
pick up some chicken soup for Gia at this little deli. They're known for
miles for their delicious, not to mention comfort-inspiring soup, and
Gia isn't feeling so great, so she needs the best soup possible, posthaste.
She needs to be comfort inspired."

"Posthaste sounds important." Spencer tugged back. "So, let me
get this straight. You just spent two hours babysitting infants for one
friend, and now you want to head out into the night for soup for another
without so much as being asked?"

"Well, yeah. I can't let Gia feel awful without a helpful remedy.
Soup will make her feel better, at least temporarily while she's eating
it. We should probably pick up some Nyquil, too. I don't know if she
has any."

Spencer went soft. "You put nuns to shame. Do you realize that?"

Hadley grinned. "I like nuns, so I'm going to embrace that
comparison. I just feel it's important to look out for the people I care
about. I always make sure I do that. Always."

"That's an honorable trait. Don't ever change it."

"You're on, because I'm not sure I'm capable."

Spencer stole another kiss. "All right, then. I'm in. Take me to the
soup," Spencer said. "A sick woman needs us."

Hadley grinned and tugged on Spencer's hand once again. "Follow
me."

"Anywhere."

❖

Hadley hadn't been lying. The soup in question came from a tiny
unassuming deli in Franklin Village, about fifteen miles from Venice,
but took way longer to reach in LA traffic. The small shop had a green
neon sign in front that let everyone know they were open until midnight,
and that was a good plan, because there were four people in line when

they arrived at just after ten. The little man behind the counter couldn't be less than seventy years old, and he smiled and nodded to them when they entered the closet-sized shop. There were exactly seven items on the menu board that hung over the register: four different sandwiches and three kinds of soup: vegetable barley, cream of broccoli, and as promised, chicken noodle.

"Slim offerings," Spencer whispered.

Hadley shrugged off the comment. "No, no. Nothing slim about this place. You'll see. That's Saul, and he puts care into everything he does. There's love in those soups and sandwiches, and you can't dilute love just to have more menu offerings. It's not worth the trade."

Spencer shook her head. "I wouldn't want Saul to dilute the love."

"Me neither." She said it as if it would be the most dire of consequences ever. Just thinking about it brought a melancholy expression to Hadley's face. "Good thing that's not our reality."

"Agreed," Spencer said, as they stepped forward in line, and more customers filled in behind them, keeping the room fairly tight.

When it was their turn, Saul smiled at them warmly. "Hello again!" he said to Hadley, as if they were long lost friends. "I never forget a face. You have a pretty one."

"Thanks, Saul. We've met once or twice before. My name is Hadley and we'll need a large chicken soup to go. A friend of mine is sick, and she needs it to get better." He pointed in question at Spencer. "Oh, no. This is my friend Spencer. She's well."

"Hello! I'm glad you're feeling okay," Saul said, and offered her the same warm smile.

"Thank you. Me, too, Saul."

He rang up the soup and packaged it up in a nice sturdy container with a bag full of homemade crackers to go with it. Impressive, and all made with love, apparently. She could get behind that kind of extra service.

"See you soon, Hadley!" he said, handing her a receipt with a wave.

They headed to the door, and Spencer noted that the line now had even more patrons than when they'd arrived. Apparently, lots of people knew about love-filled soup and demanded it. Where had she been?

"You take care of yourself, Saul! Good to see you," Hadley called, waving happily back at him from the door.

This so wasn't behavior she was used to, but at the same time, she was compelled to wave at him herself. And did! What the hell was going on here? "I think you're sucking me into your warm and happy vortex."

Hadley stared at her, her eyes darkening. "That sounds sexy. We should get out of here." And just like that Hadley tossed Spencer onto her head once again. Happy do-gooder one moment and sex vixen the next. She had to learn to prepare for that duality more, realizing Hadley could change it up at any moment.

Spencer swallowed. "Then hurry we shall."

Gia, Hadley's sick friend, opened the door to her apartment with bleary eyes and a red nose. "Hey," she said with that "I have a cold" voice people got. "What's going on?"

Hadley pushed past her and gestured with her head for Spencer to follow. "I brought you some soup and some NyQuil. Oh, and Spencer. Feel like you could eat? You should eat."

Gia took a seat on the couch. "I think maybe I could. You didn't have to go all the way to the deli, though. Hi, I'm Gia. I'd shake your hand, but then you'd get the plague."

"Spencer Adair," she said, with a smile. "Sorry about the plague."

Gia shrugged. "Happens."

"Yes, I did have to go to the deli." Hadley began assembling a bowl for Gia, moving around her kitchen like she owned it. "You need your strength, and this soup will do that. Is Elle staying with you tonight?"

"She is," a voice from behind Spencer said. She turned to see a familiar, radiant blonde enter the apartment and move immediately to Gia. "You don't look so hot." She felt her forehead with one side of her hand and then the other. "Yeah, you have a little fever going."

"She's worse than a few hours ago," Hadley called from across the kitchen counter. "I brought soup!"

"You're a doll, Hadley," Elle said. She turned to see Spencer standing there. "Spence!"

"Hey, Elle. How are you?" she asked, and accepted Elle's hug as it all came together in her brain. Aha! So *Gia* was the friend of Hadley's who was dating *Elle*. She was also the other woman from the corn chip billboard on the 405.

"I'm sorry I bypassed you on the way in," Elle explained apologetically. "I was worried about this one. She tries to act tough when she should really just be a crumpled mess on the floor."

"So true," Hadley said, tag-teaming. "She does that exact thing."

Gia looked at Elle and shrugged. "Not letting it take me down is all."

"I'm the same way," Spencer said. "Sometimes when you give into it, it feels like you lose control."

"Yes!" Gia pointed at her. "Thank you for getting it." She turned to Hadley. "I think I like her."

Hadley grinned and studied Spencer. "Yeah, well, who doesn't? She's a good egg. And a fantastic kisser." Spencer felt the embarrassed blush descend. Elle nodded enthusiastically. Gia laughed. "What?" Hadley asked. "I can't not say so. It's true. You're a kissing genius."

Spencer shoved her hands into her pocket. "Cat's out of the bag now. That's what they call me." She shook her head and grinned, hoping they understood she was joking.

Hadley delivered a bowl full of soup and crackers to Gia and handed the NyQuil off to Elle. "Passing the nursemaid baton."

Elle held up the medicine like a trophy. "Baton accepted. You guys go enjoy yourselves. I'll deal with the less than ideal patient. I heard she enjoys having her hair played with."

Gia smiled lazily from the couch. "I can accept how sick I am now. Just decided. I'm very, very sick."

Hadley rolled her eyes and grabbed Spencer's hand. "I'll check on you tomorrow, G. Night, Elle. You're a saint!"

"And don't you forget it!" she called back. "Spence, we need to catch up soon!"

"We will," Spencer said, around the door jamb.

They didn't make it but three feet outside Gia's apartment before Hadley took Spencer's face in her hands and kissed her, long and good. "I've waited too many hours to do that," she said, with a proud grin.

"Maybe you should do it some more then," Spencer said, with a shrug. "Just want you to be your happiest self."

"You're so thoughtful. I've always thought so." Hadley leaned in and did just that.

"There you two are kissing again," yelled a voice from the courtyard below. "Every time I see you it's kissing central!"

"Isabel," Hadley murmured against Spencer's mouth, before going in for more.

"You need to enter, like, a kissing anonymous program!" Isabel shouted. "Do you want me to look one up for you?"

"Stop harassing Hadley," a quieter, more levelheaded voice said. "She's enjoying herself, and it's about time."

"Taylor, her girlfriend," Hadley murmured again. "I'll introduce you later. Not now. Kissing now."

"Nothing you say registers when you're kissing me like this anyway," Spencer murmured back. "Just so we're clear."

"I'm not clear on anything either. Let's go inside." She glanced down over the balcony. "Night, Izzy. Go harass others now."

"Way ahead of you, ya kissing bandit."

Hadley let them into her apartment, which was decorated in a variety of creams and beiges, accented with subtle touches of sage. She'd gone out of her way to make the space feel elegant and worthy of being photographed. The window treatments alone must have cost her a fortune. But then Hadley put a lot of thought into everything she did. That was the last of her ruminations on the apartment, however, because when she turned back to Hadley, she found her unbuttoning her blouse very slowly, her eyes trained on Spencer. They weren't just any eyes either, they were sexy eyes. The blue had turned noticeably darker and communicated her very clear intentions. The kissing had sent Spencer's libido into overdrive, leaving her skin hot and her blood pumping but the display now had her in a hurry to satisfy it.

They didn't go slow this time, the way they had at Spencer's house. The fire lit hours earlier at Autumn's place raged too hot for that. Clothes came off, lips came together, tongues clashed, and desperation reigned as they went at it in a haze of chaotic perfection. It was no surprise that they slammed into Hadley's dresser (which would probably leave a bruise) as they kissed in the dark on their way to somewhere more comfortable.

"Fudge," Hadley hissed, lifting her foot after banging the back of it against the doorframe.

Spencer pulled her face back and narrowed her eyes. "Fudge?"

"Fine," Hadley said, and then adjusted her vocabulary selection. "Fuck." Only she whispered it, making the word barely audible.

Spencer couldn't believe what she was witnessing. "You're not comfortable swearing?"

"Yes, I am," Hadley said, in the mostly darkened room.

A long pause as Spencer waited her out.

"Okay. No, I'm not. I don't like using swear words. I try to, but fail miserably every time."

Spencer gestured behind her to the living room where Hadley had just seduced the hell out of her with her own version of a striptease. "You can come at me like a very confident sex vixen but you can't say *fuck*?" She kissed Hadley. The dichotomy got her even hotter.

Hadley shook her head between kisses. "They're very different."

"If you say so."

There weren't many words spoken after that anyway as they undressed each other in a flurry. Soft and slow was amazing with Hadley, but fast and furious proved to be just as satisfying.

"Oh, I think there can be more," Hadley whispered, after taking Spencer easily over the edge for her second orgasm. She reached between her legs and stroked slowly.

Spencer grasped her wrist, stopping the unyielding determination that was Hadley Cooper, but not before her hips bucked at the sensitive contact. "No. No, there can't. You've wrecked me. Do you hear me? I'm wrecked and I can't be playing with you anymore."

"If this is wrecked, I'm keeping it." Hadley crawled up the bed, laying partially on top of Spencer. "Your cheeks are flushed and you're glowing. I want to not forget what you look like in this moment." She closed her eyes and went still like a mummy, as if committing all of her energy to preserving the memory. When she opened her eyes again, she shook her head, blond hair all a sexy jumble. "I loved spending tonight with you. Just doing basic things."

"I was not surprised to find out that we're a good team," Spencer said. "And I got to see more of your world, which you fit into very nicely."

"I want to see more of yours," Hadley told her, and traced the outline of Spencer's breast.

"It's not very big. I'm close with my parents and have a pretty kickass best friend."

"Kendra, who helps you put the right moves on your dates."

Spencer laughed and pulled Hadley in closer. She honestly couldn't get enough of her. "Kendra knows romance. I'm still an apprentice."

"No, you're not. Trust me. You've graduated," Hadley said, kissing along Spencer's collar bone. "Will I get to meet your parents?" She paused, closed one eye, as if unsure she should have asked the question. "Do you think I'm jumping the gun? Just flat out say so."

Spencer ran her hands down Hadley's smooth back, until it flared into the subtle curve of her hips. "I don't think you're jumping any guns. I'm sure they'd love to have you over for dinner. My mom is a whiz in the kitchen and my dad loves to mooch off her food whenever the opportunity arises. She's going to make a big deal over you, though. She loves people, especially nice ones."

Hadley's mouth fell open. "I happen to love nice people as well! What a coincidence!"

"I can only imagine the love fest," Spencer said dryly.

"Where's this from?" Hadley asked, running her hand over the tiny scar on Spencer's chin.

"I crashed my bike when I was ten and jammed my chin on the handlebars when I fell. Four stitches."

"Oh, no," Hadley said, seemingly crushed.

"It didn't happen yesterday," Spencer told her.

"Doesn't matter." She leaned down and kissed the scar softly. "I'm sorry that happened to you."

Spencer laughed. "Really, it's okay." She looked down at the side of Hadley's hip. "What about this one? I saw it the other night."

"My neighbor's dog thought I looked like his dinner." When Spencer's eyes went wide, she waved her off. "Just a misunderstanding. We made peace and his owners paid my medical bill. My dads were none too happy, though. Papa scolded them thoroughly for allowing Barracuda to run free. When Papa scolds anyone, it feels like the guilt will never leave. It's a rare talent."

"So, is Papa responsible for the light and sunny disposition?"

"Nope, that would be Dad. He sang 'You Are My Sunshine' to me every night of my life until I begged him to recognize that I was a teenager and didn't need the nightly serenade anymore. At that point, he just followed me around the kitchen singing it until I couldn't take it anymore and allowed him to finish the song."

"Okay, yeah. It's all starting to make sense."

"Hey!" Hadley said, punishing Spencer with a kiss. It felt nothing like a punishment, however. She stared up at Hadley, whose features were highlighted by the gentle moonlight that slanted across the room from the solitary window. Things were happening to Spencer that she'd never experienced. It felt as though Hadley and her smile and her positivity and her whimsical-could-turn-sex-kitten disposition was slowly undoing Spencer's carefully constructed opinions about life. She was slipping into what could only be described as Hadley Land and she was finding that she was more than okay with that reality.

"Does it bother you how different we are? You know, me, cynical and—"

"Driven," Hadley supplied.

"And you, easygoing—"

"With her head in the clouds? That's what you think, right?"

Spencer held her thumb and forefinger close together. "But in a good way."

Hadley fell back onto the bed alongside Spencer and stared up at the ceiling. "I don't know that I'd be into you if you were just another version of me. I mean, can you imagine two Hadleys, each running around in a cow costume?"

"I'm sorry. A cow costume?"

Hadley waved her off. "Details for another time. But no, it doesn't bother me. I think you're meant to find the person who fills in your gaps, who compensates for your weaknesses, and compliments your strengths."

"An interesting take." Spencer tucked her arm behind her head. "Meant to find."

With a finger on her chin, Hadley gently turned Spencer's face so she could see her eyes. "Yes, *meant to find*. Maybe one day you'll believe it, whether it's with me or someone down the line."

"I'm going to meet someone I like more than you?"

Hadley laughed. "I know it's far-fetched. I can't imagine it either." A pause. "Does it bother you that I'm white?"

Spencer lifted her head to fully meet Hadley's gaze. "No. That's just part of you. Does it bother you that I'm black?"

"What? No. Not at all."

"Have you ever dated a woman who was of a different race than you? Just an honest question."

"Nope," Hadley said. "But then again, I haven't dated a *ton* of women. Just here and there. Does that matter?"

Spencer thought on the question. "I don't think it has to."

"Good. Then it won't. Do you know what surprised me about you the first time we were together?" Hadley asked.

Spencer nodded. "That I'm magnificent in bed? Hoping for that one."

Hadley kissed her cheek. "That's a given. But I was surprised how gentle you were, how patient, given how aggressive you are in business. Oh!" Hadley pushed herself up onto her elbow. "And what a snuggler you are. Who would have guessed?"

"Shhhhhhhh!" Spencer looked around to make sure no one had overheard the reputation-ruining declaration. "You can't just say that out loud."

"Yes, I can. I just did. You're the best snuggler, and you don't get tired of it and roll away. You snuggle all night. You're like an Olympic snuggler with gold medals all over your house."

Spencer covered her eyes. "I'm never going to live this down. But yes, I happen to like…getting close."

"Snuggling. Say the word," Hadley teased, circling Spencer's nipple with her forefinger.

Her eyes fluttered closed and she took a moment to enjoy the little hits of pleasure. "Snuggling is fine. I can tolerate it."

Hadley took that cue and cuddled up close, nestling her head in the crook of Spencer's arm. "I will accept that watered down answer… for now." With a heavy sigh, Hadley's entire body seemed to relax into Spencer's, which made sense. She'd had a long and full day.

"Had?" she asked, not believing that someone could fall asleep so quickly and completely after being in the midst of a conversation just moments prior. But again, she was wrong, because Hadley was out like a light. She kissed the side of her forehead and settled in, smiling at the night they'd shared, the kids, the soup, the friends, and God, the fast and furious sex. She tossed her free hand over her eyes and allowed herself to join Hadley in happy slumber.

"Love you," Hadley murmured, minutes later, into her neck.

Spencer's eyes went wide. "What?"

A long pause. "And green beans on the side. I like 'em."

Wait, did Hadley just say what she thought she said? Panic hit. "Hadley, are you awake?" she asked quietly.

"Tomorrow is good," she mumbled. And then more insistently, "Tomorrow!"

"Terrific," Spencer whispered. She settled back in, but it wasn't like she could relax now. She'd been thrown into high alert from those words. Were they moving toward love? Was that what was happening? Was Hadley's subconscious confessing things on her behalf, or did she literally just want some green beans?

Spencer had never been in love before.

She wasn't afraid of what that entailed, but she also knew she and Hadley were still of different mind-sets. How would that work exactly? What would Hadley demand of her and how would she handle it? Those were the questions that kept Spencer up half the night, dancing quietly in the back of her brain until the problem itself was exaggerated in a garish middle-of-the-night hallucination that had Hadley walking down the aisle in a black wedding dress, beaming the way Hadley did, only this version of Hadley looked more like a puppet with scary hair, and

Spencer's heart was beating way too fast as she contemplated whether to stick it out at the altar or run from Puppet Hadley. A trickle of sweat cascaded down her forehead as she stared at Hadley's darkened ceiling, wondering where she could find more air.

Losing the battle, she rolled Hadley to one side of the bed, and spent the night on her own, contemplating, blinking, and wondering just what in the hell she was supposed to do now.

CHAPTER TEN

I think you've found us a winner," Trudy said, two weeks later. She took off her dark-rimmed glasses and regarded Hadley from across the desk in the office they shared. "I was skeptical at first, but Ms. Adair has certainly risen to the occasion with these new samples."

"So, the order's been written?" Hadley asked, clasping her hands in front of her face.

"Here you go," Trudy said, handing over the paperwork. "I'm putting a lot of eggs in this basket, Hadley. I hope this gamble pays off the way you assure me it will."

"Understood. I assume full responsibility for whatever happens moving forward."

"Good. This one is your baby. Don't let me down." Trudy sashayed her way across the small office and grabbed her Louis Vuitton bag. "I have a lunch. I'll see you soon. Oh, and take a look at the new arrivals and organize a plan for a cleaner showcase of the Dena Marie dresses. They're not moving the way they should, and it's likely our presentation."

"I'll get right on it."

Hadley waited patiently as Trudy exited the office entirely and then broke into a silent scream accompanied by festive spirit fingers. Yes, they'd had the go-ahead from Trudy already, but it was different when the order was in hand. It was a done deal now! Spencer's line would move into the store just as soon as the manufacturer could ship the order. She fumbled for her phone and placed the call she'd been waiting to place.

"You're official," she said as soon as Spencer answered.

"I'm in? You're sure? You already had the meeting and everything?"

"Trudy just gave me the paperwork. It's a done deal."

Silence on the other end of the line. Hadley knew Spencer wasn't nearly as demonstrative as she was when it came to expressing big emotion, but knew that this kind of news would rock even her. When she did speak again, her voice was laced with emotion. "I can't believe it," she said quietly. "We're there. This is a big moment for me."

"Enjoy it," Hadley said, tears pooling in her own eyes at the sound of Spencer's vulnerability. "You deserve it."

"I am. I just wish we were together right now, you know. You made this happen just as much as I did."

"I wouldn't go that far," Hadley said. "You put in a little more work, I'd say."

"I want to see you. Can you come to my mom's house for dinner tonight?"

The invitation was one she'd been waiting on since they'd first broached the subject two weeks ago. She grinned at the ceiling and turned in a small circle in the office. "I would love that." Spencer rattled off the address and time as Hadley took notes. "What can I bring? I want to contribute."

"Absolutely nothing. My mother would never allow it. Just you."

"Easy enough. I'll see you tonight, superstar."

"Hadley."

"Yep?"

"Thank you. Just…thank you. If you were in front of me right now, there would be kissing, and hugging, and more kissing."

Warmth hit her chest and spread. "I would hope so. And you're welcome." Hadley clicked off the call on a high, looking forward to the night ahead. Heck, the days ahead! The weeks! She floated out of the showroom to adjust the display Trudy had asked about. She didn't even mind the grunt work. There was nothing that could tear her down from this high.

❖

Spencer grabbed the strainer and tossed in the asparagus, doing what she could to help with dinner, which smelled amazing.

"You're not going to overwhelm her, right?" she asked her mother, who came around the corner in a beautiful yellow dress, one Spencer had designed personally the year prior. "Oh, Mama, you look gorgeous. I love that piece on you! Your photo should go on the website."

"Just a little something to celebrate the last few semi-warm days we'll have for a while. The cold hits next week and never leaves. Plus, this is a big day! An official order for Rodeo Drive, and I get to meet the new woman in your life who's been keeping you so busy lately. It felt like the appropriate day to go all out and wear a nice dress." Her mother grabbed Spencer's head and kissed the side of it with a smack as she passed.

"Stop the manhandling."

"I will not. I'm your mama and will manhandle my child whenever I so please," her mother said calmly, checking on her pot roast.

"She here yet?" her father yelled from the entryway.

Spencer closed her eyes a moment. "What if she had been? You can't come in here hollering. That's embarrassing." She loved her parents to death, but she was now seeing how they might appear to an outsider, and that had her on edge, which was dumb. Hadley loved all people, and that's why she loved Hadley.

What?

God.

Where had that popped up from? Hadley's acceptance of everyone was why she *liked* Hadley so much. Why she was into her. She pinched the bridge of her nose. Better.

"It's our job as your elders to be embarrassing," her mother said, with an authoritative stare. "You'll do it to your kids one day. It's the cycle of life."

Her father strolled into the kitchen wearing his work clothes. Slacks, a short-sleeve button-up, and a sweater vest. His standard. "I look okay. Don't I, Sparky?" He adjusted his vest, and Spencer smiled at how cute he was.

"You look great, Pop."

That's when the doorbell sounded. They all three turned in synchronized anticipation. Spencer held up a hand. "Let me." When she opened the door, Hadley didn't just smile, she vibrated happiness. She wore an A-line purple dress that Spencer just knew her mother was going to love, and had her hair down and swept all to one side.

"For you," Hadley said, presenting Spencer with a bottle of Champagne. "Welcome to the Silhouette family."

"You didn't have to go to any trouble." She met Hadley's eyes and grinned, touched by the gesture. Throwing a glance behind her to make sure they were alone, she stepped out onto the porch. "My parents are lively but loveable. Just know that in case they venture into appearing nosy, which could definitely happen. Did I mention they can be loud?"

Hadley was completely unfazed. "I'm ready."

Because she couldn't help herself, she placed an arm around Hadley's waist and pulled her in. "And they're going to love you." They shared a kiss before Spencer took her hand and led her into the house.

"Well, hello!" her mother said, coming around the kitchen counter with her arms open for a hug. "You must be Hadley."

"That's me," Hadley said, hugging her mother. She placed a hand on her chest and looked all around. "Thank you so much for inviting me. I love your house. Oh, hello!" she said to Spencer's father. "Hadley Cooper."

"Russell Adair. I've heard you're friendly."

"I've been told so."

"And I'm Sonora," her mother said. "Sonny for short. Like the sunshine."

"Which is perfect for your gorgeous dress."

"You think so?" Her mother turned to the side to model it more effectively, slimming a hand down her stomach.

"Looking good, Sonny," her father said, before dashing off to sneak a bite of food, no doubt. Spencer laughed. Okay, this was going well.

Her mother moved to the couch and patted the seat next to her for Hadley to sit. When the two of them were side by side like a couple of best friends, her mother launched in. "Tell me about you."

"Well, I'm a Gemini and a big believer in all things good in the world."

Spencer laughed at what was probably the whitest sentence she'd ever heard. Didn't matter. It was all Hadley.

"I was raised in Calabasas but have come to love living in Venice. It's my home."

"It's beautiful out that way!" her mama remarked. Hadley continued to impart her life story as her mother nodded and oohed and ahhed in all the right places. Her pop hadn't been seen recently, which meant he was still in the midst of raiding the oven. She prayed silently he'd leave enough for dinner. Yet somewhere in the middle of that moment, she felt herself relax. Things felt…natural, as if they would all be just fine without her. She didn't have to direct the conversation or monitor the flow. Hadley was taking care of herself. She could just kick back and enjoy it all. What an odd and wonderful relief that was.

"Two dads!" she heard her mother say, pulling her attention back to the conversation. "Oh, I bet they doted on you."

"You have no idea. I was dressed to the nines just to go out for ice cream. I credit them with my fashion ability, which led me to Spencer."

"Then we might just owe them by the end of all this. Tell me what you think of her."

"Mama!" Spencer said. But she was easily waved off as the two new peas in a pod continued to dish. If they continued at this pace, her mother would like Hadley more than her. Not that she would blame her. She listened as Hadley described her as smart, ambitious, talented, and a knockout.

"Oh, I think you have her pegged nicely," her mother said. "But you forget stubborn, pigheaded, and stubborn again."

"Maybe I should be taking notes. Then again, I'm sensing a theme."

Her mother nodded. "A very noticeable theme."

"You realize I'm sitting directly across from you, right?" Spencer asked.

Her mother scoffed. "As if you didn't know yourself. Hadley, if you ever need a house, you just let me know. I'll drop my commission."

Hadley lit up. "That's a very generous offer. When the time comes, I'll be calling *you*."

"We'll have such fun when we set out to look. We can build in some time for lunch at this new Thai food spot that's getting lots of buzz."

"I love Thai food."

Spencer shook her head. "You're planning a fictitious house-hunting venture in the long distant future. You two just met."

"But we get on!" her mother crowed.

"We get on nicely!" Hadley crowed along with her. Spencer wasn't sure how she felt about their united force but suspected it to be a very positive thing once she'd had a chance to wrap her mind around it.

Her mama popped Hadley on the knee. "The three of us have to stop gabbing now. We have a dinner to eat. Russell! Your fat fingers better not be infiltrating my pot roast." But they weren't. When they came around the table to sit, they found her father finishing up a batch of freshly squeezed lemonade. The kind he used to make for Spencer and Kendra when they were kids.

"Give this a try," he said proudly, and handed a glass to Hadley as if it were his masterpiece he was now vulnerably releasing to the world. She sipped the iced lemonade as he leaned in. "Oh, goodness. That's amazing! What's in that?"

"Can't give away all my secrets," he said warmly, and patted her arm.

"Now you're just showing off," Spencer said. In response, he handed her her own glass and set out one for himself and Sonny, who'd brought the dinner to the table.

They gathered around, took their seats, and joined hands. "There are lots of gods people pray to, Hadley, but we find it's best to pray to just one of them. Feel free to join us."

Hadley smiled and bowed her head as Spencer's mother led them in a short prayer of thanksgiving for the food. What followed was a delicious parade of homemade pot roast, new potatoes, mixed vegetables, and fresh salad (with homemade dressing, of course).

"I can't tell you how long it's been since I've had a meal this wonderful," Hadley said, placing her hand on top of Sonny's. "You've really made me feel special tonight. Thank you."

"Well, if you're special to my Spencer, then you're special to me." They seemed to share a moment before Russell intervened out of discomfort or jealousy. Hard to say which.

"Where's the pie, Sonora? I'll get it."

"Let me help," Hadley said, setting her napkin neatly on the table. She followed Russell to the stove where her mother had left the chocolate strawberry pie to cool. They shuffled about with plates and forks.

Alone at the table, Spencer turned to her mother. "Well?" she asked quietly.

"I don't know why we didn't meet this woman sooner. She's well-mannered, and cheerful, and more likable than anyone I've met in five years."

"So, you're in?" Spencer laughed.

"I see what you see in her, Spencer," her mother said, with warm eyes. "This one is a catch."

"That's what I think, too."

"Don't you get spooked."

"Me?" she asked, knowing full well it was exactly like her. Her mama knew, too.

"*You*," her mother said, pointedly.

"Am I too late?" an out-of-breath voice called from the entryway. "Is she still here? Traffic killed me." Kendra dashed into the living room still wearing her Snoopy scrubs.

"She's here," her mother said happily.

Hadley returned with the pie and placed it on the center of the table. "Hi," she said brightly when she saw Kendra standing there. "I'm Hadley." She moved toward Kendra with an extended hand. "And I happen to be a big fan of Snoopy."

"Me, too! I'm Kendra. The best friend."

Hadley pointed at her. "Who knows all about lighting and music."

"That's me!" A pause. "You look so familiar, though. Have we met somewhere?"

"Well…Rodeo Drive?" Hadley offered.

"Unlikely."

"Venice Beach."

"No, again. Any reason to have been in labor and delivery at any point?"

Hadley's eyes went wide and her mouth fell open. "You're *Nurse* Kendra from Autumn's delivery. She had twins a couple of months ago! A boy and a girl. Ring any bells?"

"Caroline and William!" Kendra exclaimed in adoration. "Two royal names! With the crocheted matching hats."

"Yes! Those were a gift from me. A woman I know makes them. This is amazing." Hadley turned. "Spencer, your best friend helped deliver the twins. She was so supportive and wonderful to Autumn and Kate that day."

"That's Kendra," Spencer said, smiling on. It really was quite a coincidence.

Kendra squinted. "Wait. Were you the one who was humming Brahms for hours after the babies were born?"

"That was me!" Hadley said. "Catchy tune. I still return to it every now and again."

"I hum it every day. It's my work theme song."

A lightbulb seemed to pop on above Hadley's head. "Hey, you should come to theme night next week. I do them once a month at the apartment complex where I live. Just fun reasons to get together and celebrate something festive. This month, I'm doing Winnie-the-Pooh in honor of the twins. Their nursery décor inspired the whole thing. Snacks, music, and anything you want to wear inspired by the Hundred

Acre Wood, of course. Not that you have to dress up to attend. You don't."

"I'd love to," Kendra said. "Just have to check my schedule at work, but I could always trade if there's a conflict. It would be great to see the little ones again now that they're older."

"Oh! Can I come, too?" Sonny asked. "I love Winnie, but Kanga and Roo are my favorite. They're so cuddly and sweet to each other."

"I'd like nothing more!" Hadley said, looking like she'd just won the friend lottery. "Spencer, you can make it, right? Tuesday after work. You don't have to dress up. I promise."

Spencer's heart was overflowing watching Hadley's excitement grow. There was honestly nothing better, and it was becoming her very welcome drug of choice. "How could I possibly miss a nod to the Hundred Acre Wood? Winnie's my guy."

Hadley clapped. "Perfect! It's all decided."

"Now, let's try some of that pie!" her pop said, steering them back to the topic he found most important in all this: food.

Hadley went home with Spencer that night the way she had multiple nights that week and the ones prior. They had gotten good enough to predict their evenings and at whose place they might land based on geography, prompting Hadley to stash an overnight bag in the car just in case.

"You were amazing tonight," Spencer said, once they'd let themselves inside. She was still on a high from how fabulously the introduction had gone, how effortlessly Hadley had fit into her world. "Everyone loved you. I knew they would, but now we have confirmation."

"I hope so," Hadley said sincerely. "They're really fantastic people, Spence. You're so lucky."

"In more ways than one," Spencer said, taking Hadley's hand and kissing it.

"Oh." A pause. "That was really romantic," Hadley said. "That gave me goose bumps."

"Me kissing your hand?"

Hadley nodded. "Like a fairy tale. Is it odd that that's how I feel when we're together?"

"No. We're unexpected, in the way a fairy tale is. I don't think either of us planned on this. On an *us*." They collapsed onto the sofa and she pulled Hadley's feet into her lap. Hadley did love her heels, and sexy as they were, Spencer wasn't one to complain. She removed one at a time.

"An us," Hadley said with a smile, and dropped her head back onto the couch cushion as Spencer went to work on each and every pressure point. It had become a thing they did together, a ritual that she looked forward to. Spencer also fondly remembered that first PG-13 massage on their third date when she'd made dinner for them both. How things had changed. She inched her hands up Hadley's legs to her calves, working out the tension as Hadley once again rewarded her with wonderful sounds of satisfaction. Her thighs came next. Hadley raised her head and met Spencer's gaze. She watched as Hadley's expression shifted from relaxation to full-on arousal over the course of just a minute or two. Spencer slid her thumbs up the inside of her thighs and watched as she bit her bottom lip, and her eyes fluttered closed. She knew all of Hadley's signals now, knew what turned her on the most. There would be no PG-13 foot rub tonight. Thank God. Hadley's hips began to move slowly in a sultry dance against the sides of her thumbs. Spencer pulled her from the couch onto her lap, where she'd have better access. Hadley's lips parted as Spencer touched her fully, her dress pushed up around her hips. A few well-placed strokes and Hadley was gasping for air.

"Take me to bed now, so I can have my way with your body." Hadley followed that sentence up with a finger down Spencer's chest to the dip in her cleavage.

Spencer took in air at the command and shivered at the intimacy of the touch. She craved more. Her body screamed for it, twisting and turning inside. Hadley leaned down and kissed her neck from her collarbone up to her ear. "Are you wet right now?" she whispered. "Does touching me do that to you?"

Spencer nodded, not finding the right words in the haze of lust. She ran her hands up Hadley's thighs again. The movement of her hips earlier had taken Spencer to the brink and left her there. "It won't take much, will it?" Hadley whispered. She was enjoying this. That's what one didn't suspect about happy-go-lucky Hadley. Beneath her easygoing exterior, she liked being in charge, and it was hot as hell.

"Nope," Spencer said, with a shaky smile.

She was true to her word. Once Hadley had her in bed, undressed, and writhing beneath her, all it took was the feel of Hadley's hair across her stomach and the briefest of touches from her tongue before Spencer skyrocketed into a wonderful oblivion. The orgasm tore from her fast and hard.

"Every damn time," she said, in recovery mode. "I'm like this lightweight when you're around. You undo me," she said, hauling Hadley on top. "How do you do it? Tell me every last secret."

"You inspire me. That's all there is to it." Hadley tucked a strand of hair behind Spencer's ear. "Plus, you're sexy for days when you're turned on and pushing against me, desperate and eager. I will never tire of that."

Spencer covered her eyes. "I'd be embarrassed, if I didn't love it so damn much."

"We're good together," Hadley said. "I knew I was attracted to you the second I saw you, but I couldn't have predicted *this*."

"Who could have? I was just minding my own business, being a kick-ass designer in a rough world, and then there, out of nowhere, you appeared in my life." Spencer smiled and tickled Hadley's back softly. "Did you ever make those cookies for Elle?"

"Only like eight batches."

"I'm going to buy her a boat. A yacht. I am surprised to find out that the overly peppy girl from English class would one day change my life so drastically."

Hadley stared at her. "Don't underestimate the power of peppy people. Have I taught you nothing?"

Spencer crossed her heart. "Never again. Trust me."

Hadley kissed the underside of her jaw. "Tell me again about you being the kick-ass designer in the rough world."

Spencer laughed. "You're making fun of me. You're supposed to be the nice one." Hadley laughed as Spencer flipped their positions.

"Tomorrow we need to talk about the order and timing. Remind me."

"I can't believe you're thinking about work right now."

Hadley slid her hands between their bodies and cupped Spencer's breasts. "I'm a multitasker," she murmured. "Oh! And don't forget about theme night next week."

Spencer opened her mouth to answer but was caught in a wave of pleasure that silenced every part of her. Better to just enjoy the ride.

❖

Hadley woke first the next morning and slipped out of bed, careful not to disrupt Spencer. That wasn't a tall order because Spencer, she'd come to learn, slept like the dead, especially after sex. She hopped in the shower and went about getting herself ready for the day as Minnie Mouse looked on. "You're a very social cat. I admire that about you," Hadley told her. Minnie seemed to accept the compliment and leapt onto the bathroom counter. "That's even better. I can see you easily now and your cute black ears." Hadley glanced around at the same travel case she'd been lugging back and forth between Spencer's place and hers for the past few weeks. They hadn't shown any signs of slowing down, so maybe she'd just leave a few of the more essential items at Spencer's place for convenience and duplicate them back home.

Once she was dressed and ready to take on the day, her next task was an easy decision: French toast before she headed into Silhouette. She checked in on Spencer, who smiled up at her groggily from bed. "Good morning," she said, in her raspy, sleepy voice.

"Hey, you," Hadley said, kissing her softly. "Feel like sleeping some more? You can."

"Not after I've seen what's waiting for me." She sat up and buried her face in Hadley's neck, wrapping her arms around her waist. "You smell so good."

Hadley grinned. "It's that hibiscus shampoo you love."

"I identify it entirely with you now."

"Good. Gonna start some French toast if you think you have the ingredients. Thoughts?"

"It's likely. Can I help? I suck at it, but will try."

"No need. I make killer French toast and am planning to dazzle you. I got this," Hadley said, proudly. "Plus, making breakfast always gets my day started right. Drives my motivation forward."

"Then I'll hop in the shower and meet you in the kitchen soon. Hey, I meant to ask you, want to do dinner tonight? I know a fly little place I've been meaning to show you. Sangria to die for."

"You had me at fly and sangria and you."

"It's a date." They shared a final kiss and Spencer hopped out of bed.

Hadley got to work, humming a tune as she prepped the toast and located the syrup and powdered sugar. As she waited for the pan to heat, she registered that Spencer had been out of the shower for several minutes, and would likely be able to tell her whether she wanted orange juice or apple. She rounded the corner to the bathroom, and saw Spencer standing there in her towel, taking in all of Hadley's belongings on the counter. The drawer she'd stashed some of the more important things in stood open with Spencer looking down into it. Concern and unease was written all over her face.

Hadley felt her face heat. "I'm sorry. I thought since I was here so often lately, that maybe I could just leave a few things. That was stupid."

"Oh." A pause. "It's not stupid," Spencer said, attempting to recover and failing. Hadley had already seen the concerned look on her face and that overt discomfort still lingered. She could see and feel it in every essence of Spencer's being, no matter how hard she tried to shove it aside. Spencer was officially freaked out.

"I shouldn't have been presumptuous," Hadley said, humiliated now. "I'll just…here." She went about organizing her things, as a hot blush spread, making her feel ridiculous. She reached across Spencer, accidentally knocking over the small bottle of perfume, which then knocked over her hairspray, which she clumsily snatched and shoved into her bag.

"I don't need you to do that. It just caught me off guard."

"No, no. I get it. Why wouldn't it? It's not like it's something we talked about. I made the leap and that was overzealous. I see that now." The embarrassment was upon Hadley in full force, and she just wanted to gather her belongings and remove them from Spencer's space. She was dumb to have taken that kind of liberty.

Spencer reached for her wrist and stopped her progress. "Stop it. I don't want you to pack it all up. I just needed a minute to adjust and I have. I'm all good now. See?" She pointed at the forced smile on her face. Didn't matter. The damage was done. Spencer's reaction had pretty much slashed her to bits, but in the spirit of harmony, Hadley propelled herself beyond it. She was capable of rising to any occasion and this one was no different.

"Yeah, I see." It was all she had in her. "No big deal."

"We're fine," Spencer said, kissing her cheek.

"Yep. Fine," Hadley said back. "French toast should be ready in ten."

"Thank God. I can't wait."

But the damage was done. They never did regain their easy give and take, and when it was time to head out for work, Hadley did something she never ever did. She lied. "Hey, about that dinner tonight? I just remembered, I promised Isabel we could get together. It slipped my mind entirely. Can we raincheck?"

"Oh. Okay, cool. Then we'll do it another night this week."

"Great. I'll call you or—"

"You can call me."

"Perfect."

"Yeah." A pause. "Hey, have a good day at work." Spencer kissed her lightly on the mouth and searched her eyes as if trying to ascertain their current status, which is the opposite of what Hadley wanted. She didn't need Spencer to feel sorry for her or go out of her way to make Hadley feel comfortable. She was a big girl and would take care of herself. Always had.

When she reached her car, she fumbled blindly for her phone. *Anybody free tonight for a chat?* she typed into her friends' four-way group text. It was her own version of *mayday*, and she hoped her friends would be there for her. It wasn't until later that day when Isabel texted back that she'd be working late, and Gia apologized but had a date night planned with Elle, and Autumn didn't respond at all that Hadley burst into tears alone in her office, wondering how she'd gotten herself and her heart so far entrenched, feeling things for someone who may never be able to reciprocate the way she wanted her to. Not only that, but she felt very alone in the world, with no one to confide in.

"Had, you okay?" Daisy asked, peering at her around the corner.

"Oh, yeah." She straightened automatically and pretended to lean down for something in her bottom drawer, wiping her eyes as she went. "It's just that my allergies have been unbearable lately, you know. Fall is brutal when it creeps in."

Daisy reached for a tissue and carried it over to Hadley. "Here you go. For the allergies."

"Thanks, Daisy."

"Hey, I know you're my boss, but you're honestly the best boss I've ever had. If there's anything on your mind, or if there's anything I can do to make your day better, just say the word, okay?"

The kindness generated a small light in the center of Hadley's chest that spread out slowly. She'd needed that. "Thanks, Daze. I'm okay, really. Now even better."

Daisy nodded. "Good. We're all closed up and set for the night. I'll see you tomorrow?"

"You most certainly will." She stood and gathered her belongings.

"I plan to have fewer allergies." She slung her arm around Daisy and they walked out together to greet dusk in LA. This time of day, Rodeo was a little slower, with cars headed home and shops closing for the day. Some people would return to their families and start dinner. Others would head out to meet for drinks or a date. Hadley headed home quietly alone. She hadn't heard from Spencer all day, which was rare for them. Maybe she was every bit as off-kilter as Hadley was. Maybe she was reconsidering everything. Who really knew?

With her spirits low, Hadley quietly got out of her work clothes and slipped into yoga pants and her old threadbare Dodgers sweatshirt. She ate in silence at her kitchen table and then slipped off to bed early, feeling more lonesome than she could ever remember. She let her thoughts turn to Spencer as she drifted off, her smile, her dry wit, and her kind heart. She was everything Hadley wanted, and apparently, exactly what Hadley couldn't have.

She'd have to learn to reconcile that. Settle for less or run screaming for the hills. The weight of her eyelids and the stress of the day whisked her away from all of it. At least temporarily.

CHAPTER ELEVEN

The rainy October morning seemed fitting. Hadley had woken to a text message from Spencer that said simply *Good morning, Beautiful.* Those words should have left her glowing, and in a small way, they managed to put a smile on her face. But she was concerned and not feeling at all like herself. She shuffled her way to Pajamas in her yoga pants and sweatshirt, not needing to dress for work for a couple of hours. She accepted her mocha gratefully from Autumn, who'd returned to work three days a week, juggling the kids between her schedule and Kate's until a nanny started the following month. But Hadley was just going through the motions.

"Why isn't Had saying anything?" Isabel asked Autumn, from across the table. "Have you noticed that Had has stopped speaking?"

"I haven't," Hadley said simply. But she couldn't look them in the eye. Emotion circled and bubbled and reared its relentless head. There would be no tears. None at all. But she lost the battle the moment the thought occurred to her, and became a big blubbering mess.

"Oh no, sweetie," Autumn said, coming around the table. "What's going on? Why are you sad?"

She waved Autumn off as the tears pooled and fell, hot and plentiful. "I'm just being stupid and extra emotional." She swallowed the lump in her throat. "Maybe I'm on a PMS kick. Ignore me. Put a plant in front of me or something. Go back to whatever you were talking about."

"We were talking about strangers dancing in their cars when they think no one is looking," Gia pointed out. "I think we can press pause."

"I don't like it when you cry," Isabel said. Her face was pulled in and she seemed alarmed. "Tell us what's going on. Autumn, make her tell us, so we can make it stop."

Hadley tried to smile, but with Autumn's comforting arms around her, it never quite manifested. What was it about someone being nice to her in the middle of a difficult time that just unleashed the emotion in one big whoosh? "I'm just having a rough couple of days. I think Spencer's afraid of commitment, and that may never change no matter how strong my feelings grow for her. I was a wreck about it and then you guys blew me off last night when I needed someone, and the world just felt very, very big. I felt small." She shrugged, not sure how else to categorize it.

The three of them exchanged glances and seemed to sink lower in their chairs. Isabel turned to Hadley soberly. "That was fucked up of me. No workday is more important than you."

"Thanks, Izzy." Hadley sniffled. The words helped.

"Same. You would have dropped everything for any one of us," Gia said. "On a dime."

Hadley nodded her appreciation.

Autumn stared at them sadly. "I fell asleep," she said, as if it were the most horrific of admissions. "Kate watched the kids, and I just passed out and missed the text entirely. I'm an awful friend," she said in horror.

It was Hadley's turn to put her arms around Autumn. "You are not. Do you hear me? You are an exhausted friend." Still holding Autumn, she glanced across the table at Isabel and Gia. "Just hearing you care is enough for me, okay? Everyone is forgiven automatically."

"Shouldn't we at least get more of a lecture?" Isabel asked. "I don't feel properly punished."

"Yeah," Gia said. "Call us a few names."

Isabel nodded. "Slam your fist on the table. Take away *Ms. Pac-Man*."

"Malign our families."

Hadley winced. "That seems extreme. I don't want to do any of that."

Autumn sat up, regaining her composure. "Well, at the very least, tell us about the trouble with Spencer. Let us weigh in and help."

"I can do that." Hadley obliged and recounted the events of the prior morning. Hearing it all played back made her feel slightly ill and embarrassed all over again. "Did I overreact?"

"Your emotions are yours, which makes them valid," Isabel said.

"That sounds like code for I'm a crazy person."

"You're not crazy," Autumn said. "You were completely in the right to feel slighted. You're someone who places a high value on your relationships, and it makes perfect sense that you'd want the same back from someone you were falling for. You *are* falling for her, aren't you?"

"You wouldn't be crying if you weren't," Isabel pointed out.

Hadley blinked back the returning tears. "I am. I feel it happening more and more with each moment we spend together. We're so different, but that's what has me so enraptured."

"Then don't you dare discount what's happening," Gia said, speaking with an intensity Hadley was not used to. "You always shove your own feelings aside for everyone else's. You go out of your way to do nice things for others and to make the world a better place. You take the burnt piece of toast or the bad seat just to ensure others are happy. Do not compromise."

Isabel nodded. "You're deserving of so much, Had."

"Is she falling for *you*?" Autumn asked gently.

Hadley asked herself the question honestly. "I think she is. I also think the concept terrifies her. For example, she seems to do much better when we stay at my place. She relaxes, but when I come too far into hers, the walls go up. I dropped by out of the blue one afternoon when she was working, and you'd have thought I'd stolen her cat." Hadley shook her head. "You should have seen how out of sorts she looked. She always recovers. But it's there."

Her friends exchanged a concerned look, which only validated her worry.

"I felt like I had intruded, which is how I felt yesterday morning, too. I don't want to intrude on anyone's life. I want to share in it." She sighed. "Why in the world did I think falling in love would be amazing?"

"It can be," Gia said. "You just have to sort out the issues first."

"Does Spencer know how you feel about her?" Autumn asked. "That you're falling in love with her?"

Hadley shook her head. "We haven't discussed love. I don't want her bolting on me."

"Bolting or not, maybe it's time to show your cards," Autumn said, and squeezed her hand. "Then Spencer knows exactly what she's responding to."

Isabel slowly raised her hand.

"You, there," Autumn said, calling on her. "With the dark hair and pale, pale skin. What say you?"

"Thanks, formerly pregnant lady." She turned to Hadley. "I

remember what that's like, to be Spencer. When Taylor and I first started up, I was scared out of my mind. I was so careful about every little thing, and always waiting for the other shoe to drop, that it was hard for me to fully let go of myself and allow her in. I panicked. Couldn't believe what we had wasn't going to just disappear and crush me. To this day, I can't imagine what made her stick around and wait out my neurotic bullshit, but she did. She waited me out. Maybe that's what Spencer needs. A little bit of patience."

It made sense, and it had worked for Taylor. She'd be thrilled if she and Spencer found their way to being their own version of Isabel and Taylor, who were so in love it radiated off them wherever they went.

"Or just leave every damn item you own all over her place and indoctrinate her by fire," Gia said, smoothly. "Or there's always kneecaps. Just say the word."

Autumn turned to Hadley. "Talk to her."

"I will." Hadley smiled at her friends. "Thanks, guys. Very good advice. All of it." She turned to Gia. "Maybe not the kneecaps."

"Just file it away," Gia said. "It's here if you need it."

❖

Spencer couldn't work. She couldn't think. She couldn't function. She'd tried many times over, to no avail. All she knew was that she'd inadvertently hurt Hadley and hadn't been able to concentrate on anything else since. She'd sent her that good morning message hours ago, only to receive nothing back. The memory of the look in Hadley's eyes when she'd walked in on Spencer discovering her stored belongings haunted her. She never wanted to see her look that way again, which meant something had to give. She had to be forthcoming with Hadley. Honesty was the only way to go, she told herself, as she paid the exorbitant parking fee at the lot near Silhouette. Even if that meant revealing every vulnerability she had, every hang up, and each conflict of emotion, because there were many.

She opened the door to Silhouette and found a rather posh, serious-looking girl with a red updo adjusting the dress on a mannequin wearing sunglasses. She turned regally to Spencer and regarded her as if trying to sum up her purpose on Earth. "Hello," she said, breaking into a languid smile. "Please come in."

"Thank you," Spencer said.

"I'm Miranda. What can I help you find today?" the woman said.

"Spencer. And Hadley."

"I'm sorry?"

"I was looking for Hadley Cooper?"

"Spencer Adair," she heard another voice whisper behind her. This voice carried excitement and seemed a great deal friendlier. She turned to see a second woman, with shorter brown hair and a contagious smile, approach. "Hi, I'm Daisy. Big fan of your designs and thrilled to know you'll be one of our designers soon."

"Thank you," Spencer said. "Me, too."

Suddenly the Miranda chick seemed a great deal warmer. "How lovely," she said, beaming at Spencer. "Can I get you a refreshment? A glass of Chardonnay, perhaps?"

"Just point me to Hadley if she's around?"

"Right this way!" Daisy said, and marched Spencer toward the back of the store and up the handful of stairs to the sitting area. There she saw Hadley working with what appeared to be a mother/daughter combo. "Thanks," Spencer whispered to Daisy. "I can take it from here." Daisy nodded and returned to the retail space below. Spencer watched Hadley from a distance, a little nervous, but also fascinated to see her in her element.

"I'm thinking if you went with the blue and added a jacket, something casual, and a pair of killer shoes, then this outfit is going to slay," Hadley told them. The mother looked on, dubious, as the daughter turned to the side and studied herself in the mirror.

"I think I'm down for slaying."

"Sophia, I'm just not sure about all the skin showing. The neckline and the shoulder glimpses don't sit well with me."

Hadley pointed at the mom. "I know exactly where you're coming from. Why don't we give that jacket a try now and see?" She shuffled through a nearby rack of clothes she'd likely pulled for the fitting. That's about the time her eyes landed on Spencer. "Oh. I didn't see you there. Hi."

The mother and daughter turned. Spencer smiled. "Hi, everyone. I don't mean to interrupt."

"Friend of yours?" the mother asked, nodding to Spencer.

"Yes," Hadley said. "This is Spencer Adair. She's actually an up-and-coming designer. You'll be seeing her line in the store soon."

"Impressive," the obviously rich woman said.

"What's less impressive is what an ass I can sometimes be," Spencer said pointedly.

The woman squinted, intrigued by the bold comment. "Is that so?"

"It is." Spencer walked farther into the room. "I have the best of intentions and then they fly right out the door anytime anything scary happens. Can you identify with that?" she asked the daughter, who stared at herself in the three-way mirror.

"All the time," she said. "You should see me on the first day of each semester. I'm a lunatic with no direction."

Hadley looked at her clients in hesitation and back to Spencer. "Spencer, you don't have to—"

"I'm actually here because I did just that. I acted like a lunatic to Hadley here, who didn't deserve it." Both mother and daughter swiveled to Hadley, who smiled at them nervously. "She's pretty great."

"We love her," the daughter said.

"Not a hard thing to do." She met Hadley's eyes and watched as she softened. "I'm finding that out firsthand." She pulled herself from the weighted moment. "I vote yes on the outfit and the jacket, by the way."

"That's three votes. We'll take all of it," the mother said, standing.

Hadley grinned. "I'll have Daisy ring you up at the desk, and I'll meet you down there with boxed packages shortly."

As the mother passed Spencer, she waggled her finger just shy of her face. "You be good from now on. Understand?"

"That's the plan."

When the daughter disappeared into the changing room, Spencer walked slowly to Hadley. "I'm sorry I crashed your fitting."

"You seem to have won some fans in the process," Hadley said conservatively.

Spencer still couldn't tell where her head was. "No, I'd say those are your fans. I'm just a supporting player, who happens to be very, very sorry."

Hadley allowed Spencer to take her hand.

"I want you to have a drawer."

"You don't have to say that."

"And if you outgrow it, I will clear space in my closet."

A pause. "But that petrifies you. Can we just admit that?"

Spencer sighed, not wanting to lie to Hadley, ever, if she could help it. "You're not wrong. It turns out that maybe I have a few more issues to sort through than I'd planned on. But I'm working through them. I want to."

Hadley didn't say anything, making it feel like the jury was about to deliver a verdict on the most important of cases. "Okay. That's important to know."

"I should have been more open with you about all of it. I promise to communicate more, even when it's hard." They paused for the daughter to pass through the room. Hadley smiled at her. "Be right down."

"Take your time," she said, allowing her arm to trail along the railing as she descended the stairs, smiling back at the both of them knowingly. Hadley laughed. Once the girl turned and they were fully alone, Spencer didn't hesitate. She kissed Hadley, willing everything she felt for her to flow into their connection. Hadley murmured pleasantly, and relaxed into the kiss, holding Spencer in place with a hand to the back of her head.

"My toes are wiggling," Hadley said, coming up for air. "Dammit. I love it when my toes wiggle, but I have to finish that sale. Then maybe there can be more wiggling. Later."

"I'll live with later." She cradled Hadley's cheek. "I'll let you get back to work, then. As for tonight, don't make plans." She stole another long, lingering, hot as hell kiss that she could carry with her throughout her afternoon. "I'll call you later."

"Okay," Hadley said with a small smile.

Good. Yes. She needed to see that smile. They were going to be okay.

At least it felt like they *might* be.

Isabel sashayed into the courtyard wearing Winnie-the-Pooh ears, a red crop top, and Wonder Woman bikini bottoms. Hadley squinted at her mid-punch pour. "Izzy! What in the world?" She scurried over to her.

"What?" Isabel asked casually, hands on her mostly bare hips.

Hadley pointed at her. "You're half dressed!"

Isabel scoffed. "I'm Pooh. You said we should embrace the theme, and I'm embracing it. Actual Pooh wore no pants, if you remember, so you should consider yourself lucky. Sexy-Wonder-Woman-Pooh is better than Naked-Pooh. I'm confident you'll agree."

"Oh, dear," Hadley said, grateful that the twins were too young to be scarred.

"I dig your Tigger outfit, though!" Isabel said.

Hadley grinned. "Really? I put most of it together myself. Rented the feet and tail, though!" She turned in a circle to showcase her orange and black ensemble.

Isabel offered her applause. "Rockin' it as always, Had. Gonna steal some grub and camp out on the couch."

"Enjoy!" Hadley sang after her and continued to organize the snacks.

Outside of Sexy-Pooh, Hadley's Winnie-the-Pooh theme party was off to a promising start. Not only had most of the Seven Shores dwellers chosen to attend, but they'd contributed gifts for the twins' room and decorations to Hadley's already detailed party. Bonus! Because the weather was crisp and cool and sunny for fall, she'd chosen to stage the gathering in the courtyard, stealing what time she could before the sun went down. The snack table overflowed with cozy baked goods and a variety of punch flavors all geared around her theme.

"What do you think of all this?" she asked Will, who wore his Winnie onesie. He smiled at the colors as she bounced him from one attendee to another to say hello. "Hey, buddy, those are my whiskers," she told him, when he got a little handsy. "Tigger needs his whiskers."

She surveyed the space and her variety of guests. Gia, Autumn, and Isabel drank the "honey flavored" punch, as Kate whisked Carrie around to the different interactive stations. There was Pin-the-Tail-on-Tigger, Help Pooh Find His Pants, and her own personal favorite, cupcake decorating, manned by Larry Herman himself. If only he would quit demanding that people stay realistic in their frosting designs. Barney had already quit the activity altogether and stolen two handfuls of unfrosted cupcakes in artistic protest of Larry's rules. Conversely, Elle's Pin-the-Tail-on-Tigger station consistently held a steady line. But then, everyone lined up for time with Elle.

"My, my, my! Just look at this!" a new voice said loudly, from the gated entryway.

She turned and beamed at the sight of Sonora entering the courtyard with Spencer. She wore Kanga ears and a fluffy apron which was perfectly coordinated to Spencer's subtle nods to Roo, including ears, whiskers, and a blue shirt! They'd made such an effort that Hadley almost couldn't contain herself.

"You came," she said, rushing over to Sonny, who gave her a hearty squeeze.

"Told you I wouldn't miss it. It's too fantastic an idea! I don't know why we don't have more parties just because. Makes the world brighter."

"I agree," Hadley said.

"Wait! I'm here, too!" Kendra yelled, racing in behind them. "I suck at parallel parking." She wore a Tigger T-shirt and an "Oh, Bother" baseball cap.

"You look fabulous," Hadley said, and hugged her promptly before directing her immediately to Autumn, Kate, and the twins for a lively reunion. Sonny headed off for refreshments, which left Hadley and Spencer on their own, making eyes at each other. They were still finding their footing after the other morning, but with Spencer close by, Hadley was pretty much putty.

"Babe, you did an outstanding job. Just look at this place," Spencer said, looking around. "It's the best kind of fall festival."

"Just you wait for next month. A Monster Mash! I've already picked up a few scary props."

"But isn't Halloween *this* month?" Spencer asked, quirking her head.

Hadley widened her eyes. "My creative whims cannot be controlled by a calendar."

Spencer laughed and held up her hands. "I should have anticipated that."

The gathering went much later than they'd anticipated, with folks getting comfortable as the stars took over for the sun. Kendra carried a sleeping Will into the apartment for Autumn, who kept the video monitor with her at all times. Spencer took on the challenge of getting Carrie to sleep and, once again, shocked them all with her speed in doing so. "Can you move in?" Kate asked, accepting the little girl delicately from Spencer.

"What if, in addition to a salary, I tossed in free coffee?"

"Incredibly tempting," Spencer said, taking Hadley's hand. "And it would get me closer to Hadley, which is a bonus."

"Nicely done," Autumn said, pointing at her. She winked at Hadley as she passed.

"This woman is a gem!" Larry Herman declared from across the courtyard, grabbing everyone's attention. He pointed directly at Sonny, who smiled in appreciation.

"We're going shopping next week for potential investment properties," she informed the curious group. "I know of a few pocket listings that Mr. Herman might be interested in."

Hadley made her way over to them. "Larry, that's fantastic news! Did you know Ms. Sonny is Spencer's mother?"

Larry eyed Spencer and then Sonny. "I can forgive that." He turned abruptly and made his way back to his cupcake station, where he began to pack up the remaining few.

"Don't bother, landlord-dude," Barney said, and grabbed the last four cupcakes as he ambled to his apartment door on the first floor. "Rad gathering!" he called to Hadley by way of thanks. She sent him the hang ten sign, which he happily returned.

"He just stole all your cupcakes," Kendra pointed out in confusion.

"That's just Barney," Gia said. "He does what he wants and dances around while he does it. We like him for his consistency, even if he's a tool."

"That's all true," Hadley said. "Plus, he'd give you the shirt off his back if you needed it. Well, maybe not Larry, but the rest of us."

"Aww, then I like him," Kendra said. "He must have really wanted those cupcakes."

"I could bake him some," Sonora said, showcasing her generosity. Spencer came from really good parents. Hadley was now positive.

After such a laid-back, fun evening, everyone began to gather their belongings and hug their goodbyes. Gia and Elle headed out for Elle's place, as they planned to wake up and train on Hermosa Beach before heading off to Portugal for a tournament in the coming days. The days of settling for less on tour seemed to be a thing of the past. Elle had recaptured the number one spot, and Gia temporarily embraced her number two ranking. That is, until she could overthrow Elle. The two couldn't be stopped. Sonny and Kendra also took their leave, hugging Hadley many times over for inviting them to the event. The sleepy parents joined their kids, and Isabel, Spencer, and Hadley remained in the courtyard.

"So, what are we gonna do now? The three of us," Izzy asked, in all her half-clad glory. She placed her hands on the hips of her superhero bikinis and looked from Spencer to Hadley. They stared back at her. "I'm just joshin' ya." She clapped them each on the shoulder. "I have plans with Taylor, so you two can suck as much face as you want. As you were."

Once they were alone, Spencer didn't hesitate. "You are the

sexiest Tigger I've ever seen, and I have never once expected to utter that sentence."

Hadley tugged the front of Spencer's T-shirt. "You know how to flatter a girl." She shrugged. "I might have been checking you out tonight. Can't say for sure."

"Now you're just teasing me."

"My place?"

"I'd give anything to stay, but I didn't bring anything with me. I could run home and come back, or you could come to my place."

Hadley looked skyward. She'd not stayed at Spencer's since the unfortunate drawer incident. "You sure you want me all up in your space?"

"I will sell half of my possessions to make room for yours if it gets you over there tonight."

Hadley laughed. "Someone is in the mood."

"When it comes to you, I'm *always* in the mood. You pretty much own me in that sense. But I'd be thrilled to just watch a TV show with you, or we could sit out here and talk."

Hadley stared at Spencer as heat flamed and flickered between them. "Your place it is. Let me change and grab a few things."

Did she go inside and put on her sexy jeans and tight-fitting black top that made her look a little bit wanton? Heck yeah, she did. Hadley fluffed her hair, smiled at the result in the mirror, grabbed her overnight bag, and descended the outside stairs to Spencer, who waited below. Upon seeing Hadley, her lips parted and she seemed struck. Oh, yes. She'd achieved her intended effect.

"Oh, man," Spencer said, finally.

"Shall we?" Hadley asked, with a grin. She walked past her on the way to Spencer's car, working it the whole way. Sashay, sashay, repeat. She was going to work her va va voom and enjoy every decadent minute of it.

❖

The rules of the road took on new meaning as Spencer attempted to navigate her way back to her apartment with Hadley next to her in the passenger seat, affecting her in so many indescribable ways. She found herself breaking those traffic laws and accelerating past the speed limit simply to get them there sooner. Hadley was driving her crazy, the way she'd leaned back in the seat, crossing her legs and showcasing the black heels she'd selected for their journey of just over nine miles. Lord help her. Midway through the ride, Hadley leaned forward to retrieve her bottle of water, only to reveal a glimpse of cleavage as it pressed against the tight black shirt. She sent Spencer a knowing smile, making her wonder if it had been on purpose. Spencer swallowed and forced herself to keep her eyes on the road and ignore the blood that left her brain for other places. They'd be there soon enough, and then all bets were off. Just drive. She shifted uncomfortably in her seat, tapping the steering wheel, chewing the inside of her lip as a distraction.

"You might be speeding a tad," Hadley said quietly, pointing at the speedometer.

"Sorry," Spencer said, easing off the gas. She tossed Hadley a look. "Apparently I feel like taking risks to get you home a little faster."

"I could occupy your mind in other ways if you want."

"That could be helpful. Yes. What do you have? Anything."

Hadley tilted her head in thought. "I could tell you all the things I want you to do to me once we get there."

"Not helping." Spencer swallowed. "Now who's endangering lives?"

"Not me." Hadley shook her head. "I was just using my imagination. Trying to help alleviate yours."

"Sure you were." Spencer exhaled slowly. "Your imagination."

Hadley nodded. "And let me tell you, it is going to delicious and unexpected places. I think you'd enjoy them."

Spencer gripped the steering wheel that much harder. Eyes firmly on the road. Aching ignored. "Tell me."

"I feel like being taken tonight. Do you think you can do that?" Out of the corner of her eye, she saw Hadley trail a finger down her neck as she asked the question.

Spencer nodded. "I remember the first time I wanted to do that very thing. Visualized it even. At Notes, the jazz club I took you to."

"That was a good night. I wanted you then, too, but was too scared to do much about it. Where would you have touched first that night? If we had."

"Your breasts. Definitely."

"With your hands?"

"Yes, at first. Then my mouth."

"You know what I think?"

"I have ideas."

"We need to go back to that jazz club now that we're acquainted."

Spencer laughed, which broke some of the tension, but not for long. Realizing how much fun she had with Hadley, how she kept Spencer guessing and on her toes, it just made her hot all over again.

They arrived in front of her complex at long last. Mr. Wannamaker, her kindhearted upstairs neighbor, sat on his balcony looking out. She didn't know if he could see them. She didn't care. The second she put the car in park, she leaned across the console and crushed her mouth to Hadley's, who moaned quietly, matching her intensity. Hands were moving in a flurry of desperation. Hers to Hadley's breasts. Hadley's to the back of her neck, where she held her in place and lightly sucked on Spencer's tongue that was firmly in her mouth. Spencer readjusted, slamming her shoulder into the steering wheel. "Ow," she mumbled. Hadley leaned across the center console but took the gearshift to the side of her ribs in the process.

"Yikes," she yelped. She refocused, shifted a knee beneath her, and pulled Spencer forward by her shirt for another wild kiss. As they crashed back against the passenger side door in a painful tumble, Spencer sucked in air.

"This car is too damn small. Why didn't I buy an SUV?"

"You'll know for next time," Hadley said, breathless. Undeterred, they separated and exited the car from opposite sides only to come together again in front of the vehicle, all hands and mouths and passion on unabashed display. "Inside," Hadley whispered through their kissing. "Now."

They tried to enter the building like respectable humans and backpedal from the show they just gave unsuspecting Mr. Wannamaker, but their efforts were fruitless. They took breaks on the way to Spencer's door to kiss and grope and lose themselves in the overwhelming gratification. Spencer kissed Hadley up against the door to her apartment, smiling as Hadley gently bit her tongue, all the while fumbling to unlock the damn door. "You're turning into a biter," she murmured happily.

"Is that a problem?" Hadley asked.

"Hell no." She glanced to her left at the sound of shuffling.

"You okay down there, Spencer?" Mr. Wannamaker yelled.

They froze, and stared at each other, eyes wide. Hadley broke into a giggle. Spencer grinned and covered her mouth. Finally, "We're fine! Sorry about that, sir."

"Just making sure no one got hurt," he yelled back. "Tricky kids aren't watching where they're going," she heard him mumble.

In that moment, the apartment door gave in to the click of the key and fell open behind Hadley. They spilled into Spencer's living room, stumbling to find their footing. Hadley failed and crashed onto the floor in a fit of laughter. Spencer joined her there, the whole thing just too ridiculous. "We're not good at car sex," Spencer finally managed. "Now we know."

"The worst!" Hadley couldn't stop laughing. "That poor guy was probably so confused and then maybe alarmed."

"It's the most action he's seen in weeks, I'm sure. Clumsy or not."

Spencer crawled over to Hadley and looked down on her. "Can I say that you look just as good on this floor as you do in any car?" Hadley pulled Spencer to her so she was fully on top. She let her weight settle, knowing how much Hadley liked it. Her eyes fluttered and she shifted her hips to fit against Spencer more snugly.

"Maybe we're good at floor sex," Hadley offered with an innocent blink. "We honestly don't know."

"I hate not knowing things," Spencer said, kissing Hadley. Savoring it.

"Would be wrong to not find out."

She pushed Hadley's top up and ran her nails across her smooth skin before freeing her of it altogether. Hadley nodded and bit her lower lip. Spencer shoved her bra up over her breasts so she could see them. The jeans came down past her knees. Those fantastic heels? They stayed on. Spencer didn't delay. She knew what she was after, and pushed inside, overcome by how wet Hadley already was, how ready. She began to move, her hips propelling her hand.

Hadley moaned and turned her head to the side. "More."

"Yeah?"

"Definitely."

Spencer obliged and drove more firmly, pulling sounds she hadn't heard before from Hadley. God, it inspired her own arousal in ways she couldn't have fathomed. She kissed Hadley's bare stomach and licked her way down to her thighs which parted further, asking for more attention. Hadley said her name over and over as Spencer pushed into her. Her hair pooled beautifully around her face as Spencer drove harder, circling her most sensitive spot with her thumb, watching Hadley's face, reading her cues until she gasped and gave in to the climax, shuddering and bowing. She cried loudly, her hips still moving feverishly against Spencer's hand. Spencer reached up and cupped Hadley's breast hard as she rode out the final waves in glorious sharp thrusts.

"Are we still here?" Hadley asked, limp and smiling and so hot in those heels.

"I think so, but I'm not entirely sure." Spencer crawled up the rug until she lay alongside Hadley, breathless and feeling satisfied.

Hadley's eyes went wide. "Oh, no. Do you think Mr. Wanna-something heard me?"

"I'm going to go with most definitely."

Hadley covered her mouth. "I was loud."

"You were wonderful and fucking hot as sin. We have to have floor sex more often if it's always like that."

"Don't say it like it's over," Hadley said. "Floor sex is merely on break." She slipped a hand between Spencer's legs and squeezed gently.

She resisted the urge to come right then and there through her jeans. She was already that close.

"Lucky for you we have all night."

Spencer smiled at Hadley, flushed, beautiful and nearly naked. She removed her remaining pieces of clothing, kissing her in between. "The bed's just around the corner, you know."

Hadley unbuttoned Spencer's pants.

"Oh. We're not making it off this floor, are we?"

Hadley grinned. "Not a chance."

After they were exhausted, fulfilled, and wrapped naked together in a blanket from the nearby couch, Spencer drifted off to the most wonderful dream. They were strolling hand in hand through an endless meadow. Hadley stopped to pick a flower and smiled up at Spencer, so full of life and kindness that Spencer's heart was set to burst. "Have I told you today how much I love you?" Spencer asked.

Hadley looked to the sky in contemplation. "Why don't you tell me again just in case."

"I love you, Had." She kissed her cheek and met her gaze. "So damn much."

CHAPTER TWELVE

S pencer was late.
    She'd worked in her apartment until the last possible second, getting caught up in her latest creative surge and sketching each image like a maniac as it appeared to her before realizing distantly that, damn it, she had a lunch date with Dez and that overseas contact he wanted to put her in touch with. She'd forgotten all about it and now she was behind the power curve. She had just enough time to make it once she threw on appropriate going-out-in-public clothes, then floored it the whole way there. Now that things felt like they were in a better place with Hadley, she could try and focus on business. Yet playing catch-up had screwed her this time.

    She made it to Redbird for lunch to find Dez and the woman already seated and having drinks. She took a moment in the entryway to catch her breath and find her "this is for business" smile. "Hello, everyone. I hope I'm not too late," she said, accepting a kiss on the cheek from Dez when she arrived at the table.

    "Not at all," he said. "We were early. Spencer Adair, meet Claudette Fournier."

    She turned to the woman with a smile in the same moment that the name registered. Not possible. Claudette Fournier was second in command at Bertrand, the French label people couldn't get enough of lately. They were just starting to make waves in America, but she followed the trades, and they'd taken Europe by storm in just a short time. Bertrand shows were packed. Impossible to get tickets to. Surely, this was not *the* Claudette Fournier. She studied her. Dark hair pulled back into a sophisticated bun, makeup done to perfection, and a killer Bertrand pantsuit. All signs pointed to yes.

    "Pleased to meet you," Claudette said with, yes, a subtle French accent. "Desmond has shared a great deal about you. I know your work and feel as if I already know you somewhat."

"You're very kind," Spencer said, taking her seat. She sent Dez a what-the-hell look that he either ignored or didn't see.

"Thank you," Claudette said, conservatively.

"Claudette's in charge of operations for Bertrand. They're based out of Paris."

Spencer nodded, allowing him to relay information she already knew and using the time to gather her thoughts.

"She heard rumblings about you from Trudy Day's circle and asked for an introduction. What she didn't realize was that I was already looking for a way to put the two of you together in the same room."

"I know Bertrand well. I own several of their pieces." Spencer didn't supply that she'd had to save up for months, and that one of those pieces had been a lavish Christmas present from Kendra. "I'm also an admirer of your work. Bertrand's work. The whole label. I watch the shows on YouTube as soon as they're made available."

"It seems we have a common eye," Claudette said, with a smile. Where was this all going? Spencer wasn't sure, but she was eager to find out.

They ordered and Spencer shot Dez another look. He smiled confidently back. He always seemed to have a plan and stayed two steps ahead of her. It's why she took him on as a partner. She was the creative to his strategic, and that balance had worked wonders for the brand in the past. She owed him a kidney for this caliber of introduction, however.

"Why don't we get started talking about how you two might work together?" Dez suggested.

"Us?" Spencer swallowed. Work together? "I'd love that."

"I would, too." Claudette said, folding her napkin onto the table. "I've known Trudy for years, and she has a keen eye. But perhaps, in this instance, she should have held her cards closer to her vest. Desmond is another friend who knows me and what I like. He showed me your spring line earlier this week when I asked."

Spencer nodded, words failing.

"It's very good. Unique. It made me go back and look at your past work. Also quite good."

"Thank you," she managed. "I'm proud of my designs, but I think this year might be my best yet."

"You should be more than proud. You should come to Paris." She sipped from her wine glass.

Spencer looked from Dez, who raised his eyebrows at her subtly, to Claudette, who maintained her mildly interested, calm demeanor. "I love Paris."

"Everyone loves Paris," Claudette said, with a wave. "It's Paris. But I'm not speaking about a visit. I'm speaking about a job. With Bertrand. Are you interested?"

She took a sip of water to calm her nerves. Dez smiled knowingly. "I don't understand. What kind of job?" she asked.

"We'd like to absorb Spencer Adair and feature it as a smaller collection under the Bertrand label. But you are young and quite green when it comes to large-scale design. I'd want you in Paris with us so we can work with you, develop your talent."

"I'd still be designing?" It was like her brain couldn't keep up with the words that were spoken at the table.

"Yes, of course, my darling. You are a designer. That's what you were born to do. It's my preference that you design for us. In Paris."

"What about my line? I already have a major order from Trudy."

Dez leaned across the table. "Not a problem. We cancel the order. Fine print in the contract protects you. I made sure before you signed. Trudy Day will find her next top designer somewhere else."

But this wasn't about Trudy Day, whom she couldn't care less about. This would affect Hadley. No, no, no. This was all happening too fast. It felt like she couldn't make her feet touch the floor, no matter how fast she ran to catch up. She needed clarification, and time, and air. She took another sip of ice water, resisting the urge to crunch a big piece of that ice and relieve the nervous tension that billowed and bunched. "When would you want me in Paris?"

"Can you be there next week?" Claudette asked. "We'd be happy to help with all of the arrangements. I know it's short notice, but the fashion world moves fast, as you know."

Another sip of water as images of the Eiffel Tower, Parisian cafés, and the most fantastic runway shows dazzled. "I don't know. Can I have some time to think on this? Make sure it's the right move for me professionally?" She was crazy not to instantly leap, but there was a bigger picture to consider.

Claudette sat back in her chair and smiled as if what Spencer had said was cute and should be humored. "Of course, my dear heart. Let me know soon. I think we can do a lot for each other, Spencer. You're a diamond in the rough."

"I have to agree. I think it's a fantastic match," Dez said. "But it's a big change and would require some renegotiation of the business and the way it's set up."

"In other words, our partnership," Spencer said.

"Among other things, yes."

"There'll be plenty of time for negotiating," Claudette said, with a wave of her fork, indicating that Spencer would be taken care of.

And there it was.

Spencer didn't finish the rest of her lunch. After that rattling offer, she couldn't.

Two hours later, her mind still ran in spastic circles. The excitement, the terror, the downright confusion brought on by such an unexpected opportunity had left her in a hurricane she couldn't see her way out of. Designing for Bertrand? She couldn't in a million years have predicted a chance like this would come her way. In design school, it would have been a Cinderella story that professors wowed their incoming students with, dangling it in front of them like bait.

She'd made waves in the online retail space, big waves, but this was different. This was the big leagues. She paced her kitchen, picking up Minnie and setting her back down again only to repeat the process eight more times in anxious nonsensical patterns. Her cat must have thought she was crazy, and maybe she was, for not immediately jumping at the opportunity she'd been presented with. She was a nobody who was now the It girl, exploding onto the scene, and she had to choose which path would be best for her.

On one hand, how could she ever turn down Claudette and Paris and the opportunity to design at the top level where she could learn from the best? She'd passed on an internship in Paris years ago and never stopped regretting that decision. On the other, she was actually doing quite well on her own, bolstering the Spencer Adair label right and left. Her life in LA was blossoming both personally and professionally. But it was Hadley herself that had changed everything in so many ways in just the couple of months she'd known her. Spencer always thought they had so much more ahead of them. But if she headed off to Paris permanently? Where did that leave them?

She didn't sleep that night, but then she didn't exactly expect to. The next morning, she had to speak to Hadley and knew just where to find her.

The Cat's Pajamas was virtually on fire with customers buzzing in and out of the shop on their way to a million different places. The long line stretched nearly to the door, full of suited-up business types and beach bums alike. It really had a whole separate vibe in the morning, embracing the hustle bustle. She easily located the table with Hadley, Gia, and Isabel just as Autumn sat down to join them with a tray of pastries. Their Breakfast Club was just getting started.

Gia was the first to spot her. "Well, well, well," she said, as Spencer approached the table. "A designer in our midst."

Everyone turned, and Hadley broke into a smile that communicated both excitement and curiosity. "Hi," she said, gazing up at Spencer. "This is a nice surprise. Want to sit?"

Spencer shook her head and opened her mouth.

"Spencer, I hear congratulations are in order," Autumn said with a grin, halting her progress. "Your line on Rodeo Drive? I can't even imagine. Amazing."

"Thanks," Spencer said, with a slight hesitation. Everything felt so up in the air that she wasn't sure how to behave. "I couldn't believe it myself either."

"You're a champ," Isabel said.

Gia, who wore surf trunks and a hoodie, raised her coffee. "Elle is over the moon. She feels she had some part in all of this."

"Well, she did," Hadley pointed out. "A big part."

Gia pointed at her. "Which is why baked goods keep arriving on her doorstep."

"Among other reasons, but yes," Hadley said, beaming. "I don't anticipate that stopping, by the way. Every time I think of Spencer's line coming into Silhouette, I start a new batch of brownies for Elle like some kind of Pavlovian soldier."

"If it makes her a little slower on her board, all the better for me," Gia said with a competitive smirk. "Keep sending the brownies. I need her number one spot."

"You're awful," Autumn said.

"Please." Gia scoffed. "Guess who winds up eating most of them? Her name isn't Elle."

"So, are you pumped?" Isabel asked Spencer. "This is like the designer Olympics, right? Rodeo Drive, I mean. The Hunger Games of fashion."

"It's a fantastic opportunity. I'm lucky in a lot of different ways," Spencer said, looking at Hadley, which pulled a collective "aww" from the group. She and Hadley exchanged a smile until something in Hadley's expression changed. She seemed to intuitively know that Spencer was out of sorts and gave her a nod. She knew with just a look.

Hadley stood and addressed her friends. "On that happy note, I better dash. Time to change for work. I'm opening today. Come with me, Spence?"

"Right behind you." She waved at Hadley's friends. "Sorry for crashing."

"You're welcome at Breakfast Club anytime," Autumn said.

They said their goodbyes and Spencer followed Hadley out of the shop and to the adjacent courtyard of the apartment complex.

"Hey," Hadley said, holding tightly to her hand. "Are you okay?"

Spencer nodded. "I'm okay, but my head's a mess with a meeting I had yesterday. I needed to talk to someone about it and honestly? There's no one I really want to discuss these kinds of things with as much as you."

"Okay," Hadley said, concern creasing her features. "Want to talk to me while I get ready for work?"

Spencer nodded. But just seeing Hadley, being in her presence, reaching out and touching her, centered Spencer in unimaginable ways. The Hadley Effect, as she called it, was powerful.

Hadley had already made her bed for the day, as she did within a half hour of waking up most any day of her life, but Spencer flopped down onto it anyway, enjoying the scent that was all Had. She grabbed a pillow and held it against her as Hadley dressed with the closet door open. "Talk to me," Hadley said, as she selected a top.

"Have you heard of Claudette Fournier?"

Hadley slipped the top over her head and shimmied into it. If Spencer weren't in such a state of disarray, they'd have to pause this whole thing for a quickie before work. She swallowed the always present impulse. Hadley studied her. "Everyone's heard of Claudette Fournier. Why?"

"I had lunch with her yesterday."

"Shut the front door and come back in and shut it again. You did not." Hadley's attention shifted entirely to Spencer. She was half dressed for work, wearing a chic designer black shell and blue yoga pants and flip-flops, straddling her worlds.

"It was the craziest thing. Dez, the business partner I told you about? He set it up and made the introductions. But get this. She wants me to design for Bertrand."

Hadley shook her head and squinted as if not fully understanding. How could she? Spencer wasn't sure she understood herself.

Hadley moved toward her, pants in hand. "She wants to bring you on board? At *Bertrand*?"

Spencer nodded.

Hadley blinked as if the world had shifted. "That's...amazing. That's such a huge compliment, Spence. Do you understand the gravity of Claudette Fournier recognizing the value in your work? Babe, this is awesome." Hadley plopped down next to Spencer and took her face in her hands. "Big things are happening for you, and you deserve every minute of it. I want to kiss you senseless in congratulations."

"Claudette heard my name when Trudy dropped it. Trudy heard my name because of you."

Hadley's eyes sparkled. "Then I will happily pat myself on the back when I'm done making out with you."

They shared a kiss. It meant everything to Spencer that Hadley was so happy for her. But she didn't yet know the whole story.

"Are you going to do it?" Hadley asked, tracing her jaw.

Spencer stood and put some distance between them. How was she supposed to work in the next part with Hadley smiling at her, touching her? No, she needed courage to push through, and that meant space. "I don't know. If I did, there would be ramifications, which is why I'm here. To put the cards on the table."

Hadley squinted from where she sat on the bed. "Cards. What kind?"

"No deal with Silhouette if I take the job."

For a moment, Hadley didn't say anything. "Wait. That part's a done deal. The order's in and accepted."

"Apparently there's an out in the contract. Dez made sure, just in case."

"But we planned all of our ordering for the season around your line. We dedicated space for you. We'd be in an awful position. I would be." It was Hadley's thinking out loud voice, which she was entirely entitled to.

"I know."

"Spence, no. You can't pull the order now. It's my neck on the line. I vouched for you with Trudy."

"I know that part, too."

Silence reigned. Hadley wrapped her arms around her midsection and nodded several times, lost in her own thoughts, working it all out like a math problem.

"Hadley." Big blue eyes met Spencer's. "This is not an easy situation for me."

She nodded. "I understand. I'm just in a difficult spot myself."

"What can I do?"

Hadley stood and faced her. "Honestly? Don't pull the order. I went to bat for you."

"Which I appreciate more than you'll ever know, but this is business, right?"

"It's also *me*. Don't I deserve a little consideration?"

"Of course you do." Spencer dropped her head back and stared at the ceiling. "I don't want to put you in a bad position, Had. I would never want to do that."

"Then don't. I understand this is a great opportunity, but don't discount what you have going. You're creating a name for yourself, and this is just further proof that people are noticing. If you design for Bertrand, it's their brand you're enhancing, not your own."

"That part hasn't escaped me. But how do I say no to this?"

Hadley held out her hand. "I'm not sure."

Spencer crossed her arms. "I haven't told you all of it."

Hadley blinked as if not believing there was more. "Okay."

"The job is in Paris."

"Paris," Hadley whispered. She swallowed and stared at the floor. "So, you'd be moving?"

Spencer nodded. "I would have to. On the flip side, I'd be designing alongside some fantastic mentors and they wouldn't drop my name completely."

But it was like Hadley couldn't hear her anymore. "I don't know what to say. I need to get ready for work."

"Can you tell me what you're thinking first?"

"I'm thinking I feel ill." Hadley stared at her, dejected, sad.

It felt like Spencer had been hit with a two-by-four. She couldn't stand that anything she'd said or done had put that look there.

"I'm also thinking I should get to work. It sounds like I'm going to have some cleanup to do if I want to save our season and likely my job."

Spencer moved to Hadley and placed her hands lightly on her waist. "I didn't say I was taking the offer."

Hadley smiled up at her wanly. It killed her. "You didn't have to."

Spencer dropped her hands. "I'm not going to. Decided."

Hadley studied her. "I don't understand."

"You don't have to anymore." Spencer kissed her hand. "You're right on all counts. I just needed to see your face, hear your voice to be reminded of where I should be, and that's here with you. I don't want to go anywhere." She kissed Hadley, who kissed her back, and before she knew it they were kissing their way to the bed. Clothes came off in a fury and they made love with a new urgency that morning, as if seeking to reassure each other and reaffirm what they had after the difficult conversation. Spencer needed that connection and reveled in it that morning, holding Hadley close.

"I don't want to go to work. I want to stay here with you," Hadley said, touching Spencer's face.

"I'm not going anywhere," Spencer murmured into Hadley's hair. "Okay?"

As she held on to her tightly, Hadley nodded and kissed her softly. "Are you sure? I need you to be sure."

"Yes." Spencer kissed her again. They lay like that for the next few minutes, staring into each other's eyes, sharing soft touches, not wanting to separate. She didn't allow herself to think about the offer, or the confusion, or even her professional future. She gave herself permission to get lost in Hadley, her favorite place to be. The rest would work itself out, and she would be okay. There would be more opportunities like this one in the future. She closed her eyes and inhaled the scent of Hadley's fresh hibiscus shampoo. There would be other chances, wouldn't there? She opened her eyes and studied the paint pattern on Hadley's ceiling and wondered one thing: Why did everything have to come at such a significant price?

Chapter Thirteen

Hadley felt Daisy watching her as she worked quietly at the retail desk, adrift in her battling emotions. She used the numbers in front of her as a distraction. She glanced to her right at Daisy and then went back to sorting the receipts from the day before. Daisy didn't waver. "Did you need something, Daisy?" Her tone came without her usual patience and she hated that. It felt like her emotions weren't exactly hers to control, and she hated that, too. In fact, she hated everything about today.

"Not so much, no," Daisy said, delicately. "I just wanted to remind you that I sorted those last night, remember? You asked me to."

Hadley nodded once and let the folder drop in frustration. "Right. Okay, great. I just wasted a half hour. Good to know." She passed the folder to Daisy and moved onto the showroom floor, which seemed crowded and uncomfortable. "We have too much out here," she said, to no one in particular.

"Sales have been down," Daisy offered.

"I know sales have been low," she said calmly. "But that doesn't mean we can let the inventory clutter the space. If anything, that's likely the reason. Help me thin some of this out for a more pleasing aesthetic?"

"Of course," Daisy said, dashing over. They worked steadily for the next two hours, pausing only to assist customers, until the store was looking sharp, elegant, and pristine once again. The solid work and achievable goal kept Hadley sane and out of her own tortuous head. Well, as much as possible.

"Had? You doing okay today?" Daisy asked, once they were alone again.

Hadley forced a smile and leaned against the sales desk. "Have you ever had one of those days where it felt like the day was having you? You just watched as the world took you down?"

Daisy grimaced. "They're the worst."

"They are."

"I don't know if it will help, but I ordered in milkshakes from an app on my phone. Chocolate with Oreos for you. Banana nut for me. Thought maybe you could use a pick-me-up. I know I could."

Hadley wasn't sure why, but the kind and thoughtful gesture was the little push that did it, causing her, right there in the middle of her place of business, to burst into tears. "I'm sorry," she said, resorting to windshield wiper hands. "I don't know why I'm crying. I mean, I do, but I shouldn't be doing it. At least not here. Maybe don't watch."

Daisy's arms were around her immediately, and their warmth and stability helped her work her way back to a place of control. "I'm going to take a minute in the office," she finally told Daisy.

"All the time you need. I'll drop that shake off when it arrives."

Hadley squeezed her hand. "You're a really good person, Daisy. I'm lucky to have you."

Daisy blushed. "Thanks, Had. I feel the same way."

Hadley was battling two very distinct emotions and, once alone in her office, she let them go to war. She was likely in love with Spencer and wanted nothing more than for her to stay right where she was and explore a life with Hadley. God, she wanted that for them so badly it physically hurt. Yet Spencer had shown signs of discomfort as things between them progressed. She didn't fault her for that, but it didn't change the facts. What was more, Spencer had a life-changing opportunity placed in front of her. Hadley stood, crossed her arms, and walked the small length of the office. If she gave it all up for Hadley, what then? Would she resent her down the road and always look back at this time in her life and wonder "what if?" Of course she would. Not only would she be the girl who stole a drawer, she'd be the girl who stole her future. No. Not okay. She couldn't be the one to stand in Spencer's way, as much as she hated what that meant for her own life and what she would lose personally.

"Shake's here," Daisy said, and placed the Oreo goodness on her desk.

"Thanks, Daze. I need this." She picked up the shake and went to town, eating her feelings without delay while part of her began to loosen her grip on something wonderful. It's what you did for people you cared about, and she more than cared about Spencer.

She loved her.

As she made her way to Spencer's place a few minutes later, she didn't permit herself to remember their hours lying in bed, cuddling, laughing, and talking. She didn't envision the amused smile Spencer got on her face when Hadley said something overly whimsical or how she'd tuck the hair behind Hadley's ear while she listened to her tell a story. She also didn't dwell on the high she'd been on ever since their first big bang kiss, when she knew Spencer was different from everyone else she'd ever dated. If she did those things, she wouldn't make it through the next part of this.

"Hey," Spencer said with a grin, as she opened the door. "Come in. Minnie was just smacking me around like a bitch while I tried to retool my website."

"Well, that sounds like a win-win." Hadley smiled and allowed Spencer to steal a kiss as she passed. She touched her lips, holding in that kiss for just a moment longer.

"You got off early."

"Daisy had things under control, and I wanted to see you."

Spencer surveyed her living room. "Ignore the mess. It's another shipping day."

"It's very you," Hadley said, taking her hand and leading her to the couch. "Do you know what else is you?"

"What?" Spencer asked with a tilt of her head. She immediately pulled Hadley's feet into her lap, removed her pumps, and went to work, massaging away the stress of the day. The familiar ritual only made things harder.

"Designing in Paris."

Spencer paused her progress and looked up at Hadley. "I already told you I'm not taking it."

"That's a mistake and we both know it."

Spencer pulled her face back, squinting. "Where is this coming from? Just this morning you begged me not to."

"I know. I fully realize that, but I was caught off guard and leading with emotion which, you've probably realized about me, is my default."

"I happen to like your default."

Hadley pulled her foot back and sat up straight. She had to organize her emotions to fit her logic on this one and not the other way around. It was too important. "The more I think about it, the more I realize that you have to do this for yourself, Spencer. You'll regret it if you don't.

I saw the look in your eye this morning. You were trying to find that common ground, anything to make it happen. I'm here now to tell you that it *can* happen. It should."

Spencer didn't say anything, appearing to take it all in. She rolled her lips in as she contemplated. "Yeah, but I can't leave now. We're just getting started."

That one was harder and the reality sliced at Hadley, painful and raw. "I don't want to be the person who stood in your way, who kept you here, and I would very much expect you to feel that way about me down the line. Think about it. How could you not?"

Spencer inched across the couch until she was next to Hadley. "Okay. Come with me, then."

"To Paris?" God, she'd like nothing more. Paris was her dream city and she hoped to make it there one day for a visit, but to move there permanently? Her world was in LA. Her job, her friends, her dads. Everything.

"I don't know how to just pick up and leave. The babies were just born. Everything is here." She deflated into resignation. "This is your path, Spencer. I'm not so sure it's mine."

Spencer blew out a breath. "This whole thing just sucks. I wish I'd never gone to that lunch in the first place."

"Don't," Hadley said forcefully. "The timing isn't ideal, but this is the rest of your life you're talking about. And me? You said it yourself. Maybe I'm just one in a series of important people who will be in and out of your life." Those weren't just words to Hadley. The truth was clear. Spencer wasn't as sure about the two of them as she was, and that had certainly factored in to her decision to let go.

Spencer shook her head. "I didn't know you when I said that. I didn't know us."

Hadley nodded, accepting the explanation but not fully believing it. The idea of Hadley long term made Spencer nervous, and if the decision had to happen now, she couldn't allow Spencer to make the wrong one.

She leaned in and kissed Spencer, slow and romantic. Her chest ached, her stomach clenched, and she wanted more than anything to be selfish and hold on to what she had. If she said the word, Spencer wouldn't go. That would be a mistake.

"Maybe you'll tell me all about Paris someday."

Spencer nodded, lost.

Hadley could identify.

They just had to get through this hard part, right? Goodbyes hurt the most. Hadley stared at Spencer, her Spencer, who was so very beautiful and smart. "You remind me of this space captain in a book I'm reading. Captain Janika."

"You've mentioned her."

"Because she's someone I admire. She set out for the unknown, without any knowledge of what she would find there. By the end of the series of books, she was a hero. That's you."

Spencer brushed away the now apparent tears. "I don't know about all that. I'm a nobody."

"I do," Hadley said, commanding herself to brighten. "And you're not anymore. You're Spencer Adair and you're going to do great things. I can feel that as plainly as I can feel how much this all hurts right now." She stood, and Spencer followed. "No," Hadley said, and held out a hand. "Maybe don't walk me out. Let me remember you here, just like this. The hero about to head out on her journey." She headed for the door, holding in her emotions with everything that she had. She wanted to hold Spencer, to kiss her, to spend the night, and many more, right there with her. While it felt like Spencer was meant for *her*, she apparently wasn't meant for Spencer.

"Had," Spencer said.

She turned back.

Spencer seemed to struggle with the words, opening her mouth and closing it.

Hadley smiled and touched her heart. "I already know." They stared at each other and Hadley let herself out of the apartment.

❖

The next few days were a whirlwind for Spencer. There were papers to sign, flights to book, plans to be solidified, and her apartment to pack up. The flurry of activity helped keep her focus on what was ahead, because if she looked side to side, she would likely come apart and scrap the whole idea. Never in a million years would she imagine she'd let someone in the way she'd allowed Hadley in. She was grateful now to know that was possible but couldn't quite imagine anything coming close to what Hadley made her feel.

Was she convinced she'd made the right decision? Not at all. But Hadley had a point. She'd always wonder, and life was too short for regrets. She was trying to lead with her head and not her heart, the way she'd led life up until this point. It had served her well in the past, and she should stay the course.

Damn if it didn't hurt, though.

Two days before her plane was set to take off, her parents threw her a small gathering in her mother's backyard. Family and friends she'd known since she was small mingled in the yard drinking fresh lemonade à la Russell and beers of the world. Her father and mother battled over the grill, serving up chicken, hamburgers, and hot dogs for anyone who stepped on up.

"I can't believe I'm not going to see you until Christmas time," Kendra said. She bit into her hamburger halfheartedly. "I'll be sittin' on that damn porch alone."

"That's only a couple of months from now," Spencer pointed out. "It'll give you time to miss me and make a big deal when I show back up."

Kendra scoffed. "You'll be so homesick, it'll be you making the big deal." She imitated a weeping Spencer, her arms outstretched. "Kendra, thank God it's you! Put me back together again so I'm whole." She continued to blubber into her beer.

Spencer laughed, knowing it was a very possible outcome. She'd spent her entire life in LA. Leaving it now felt necessary but awful. No more weeknight dinners with her parents, or porch sitting with Kendra. She didn't let herself think on her more recent happiness, but Kendra went there anyway, pushing on the bruise.

"I can't even imagine what you're going to do without Hadley. She was the sunshine in your Cheerios."

Spencer felt the corners of her mouth pull downward. "I asked her to go with me."

"Get out. You did?"

"I think she actually considered it. If I had pushed, she might have agreed. She would do that for me."

"So why didn't you push, then?"

"Me and my stupid hangups have disappointed her several times already. What if we got there and I couldn't get past them?"

"You're afraid of your own damn demons, huh? Poor, damaged Spencer. Lots of people's parents get divorced, you know."

"I do, but this is bigger than that." She paused, lemonade halfway to her mouth. "I wouldn't want that to be me and Hadley after I've begged her to come to another country with me. I would hate myself for doing that to her if I wasn't sure."

"How are you not sure?" Kendra practically yelled.

Spencer glanced around to see who had taken notice of their conversation. "I'm sure I'm invested in Hadley, but what if something along the way were to change. Not just for me, but for her. It could happen, Ken."

Kendra shook her head. "Once again, you discard the idea that it might *never* end, cuz you're a bonehead who's too stubborn for her own good. Maybe Hadley is better off without you."

"Hey!" Spencer said.

"Only kidding and you know it. Hi there, Ms. Mary!" Kendra said, waving at their elderly across-the-street neighbor. "How's that little dog of yours getting on?"

While Kendra was occupied with Ms. Mary, Spencer proceeded inside to see if she could find something harder to spice up that lemonade. Her talk with Kendra had inspired a knot in the pit of her stomach that she needed to do something about. Her mother kept the liquor on the top shelf of the walk-in pantry, and if she remembered correctly—

"Jesus in heaven!" she practically shouted. She dropped her lemonade and watched it run straight into the pantry and pool at the feet of her parents, who'd been making out right in front of her eyes! They broke apart slowly when interrupted.

"Sweetheart, what have I told you about taking the Lord's name in vain?" her mother asked, smoothing her dress casually like they'd just walked out of Trader Joe's.

Spencer pointed from her mother to her father, who dabbed the lipstick from his mouth. "You two don't look nearly guilty enough for what I just walked in on." She covered her eyes and then uncovered them, realizing that you couldn't shield your eyes from a sight that happened moments before. She heard the sounds of mingling outside, and realized that her parents were in here sucking face during her party! *Her* parents! Her *divorced* parents who were better off divorced! She stepped inside and closed the pantry door behind her. "Is someone going to explain to me what's happening?" Her heart hammered away and her brain was firmly in the overdrive category.

Her father gestured for her mother to go ahead.

"Your pop and I have been meaning to talk to you for a while now. We've found our way back to each other. It just took a little while to admit it."

She glanced from one of them to the other. "As in, how long? How long have you been carrying on like this?" She gestured around them. "In pantries?"

"Two years?" her father asked.

"Two and a half," her mother said, more firmly.

Spencer shook her head in anger. Her world slid wildly off-kilter as she reexamined every dinner and family gathering they'd had in the past two and a half years with new eyes. "Why wouldn't you have said something to me? This is pretty important information to who I am as a person. It affects me."

"We weren't exactly sure what our status was," her mother said, "and didn't want to upset your world unnecessarily."

"And this is better?" Spencer asked, exasperated.

"But we know our status now," her father said, taking her mother's hand. "Facebook official. We're in love."

"Don't put this on Facebook." She looked to her mother as the words registered. "In love?"

Her mother nodded and shrugged. "He's a coot, but I love him. Can't help it."

Spencer scrubbed her face. "So, what? You're moving back in together?"

"Not until we're married," her mother said firmly, as if Spencer had lost her damn mind. "Hooking up is one thing. Shacking up is another. We have the Lord to think about."

Spencer blinked at them.

"We were thinking when you were home for Christmas, we might have a small ceremony. Make it forever then."

Forever. Spencer grappled. "I don't even know what to say. This is so bizarre."

"Say you're happy for your old man and his lady," her father said, and clapped her on the shoulder. "We are."

"In fact, never happier," her mother said. "We were meant to be, plain and simple. Just took us a while to settle in and realize it. Get comfortable." She hooked a thumb at Spencer's pop. "He still annoys the hell outta me. But that's part of it, too, I suppose."

Spencer replayed the first part of that sentence in her mind. *Meant to be.* It registered. Maybe it was possible. A pause. "Okay, then. This will take some getting used to. Um, gotta rewire my brain somehow." She made circles with her hands near her head. "I'm gonna get back out there and see to the guests." She grabbed a bottle of Kentucky whiskey for reinforcement. "You guys coming?"

"In a minute," her mother said, and sent her father sexy eyes.

Oh, good God. She opened the whiskey and poured.

What in the world had she done to deserve this? But as she returned to the party, something in her loosened and a small smile took shape on her lips. Her parents were not only happy, but they were happy *together*. She could leave them for Paris knowing they had each other's back. They'd keep each other company in ways she politely chose not to imagine. She sipped her now hard lemonade and exhaled, refusing to be jealous. She reminded herself who she'd always been, and what her priorities still were. Strangely, she didn't feel like that same person from before. She wasn't sure how to cope with that reality other than to focus on the good.

Life had a lot of exciting things in store for her.

She just had to keep her eyes trained forward, as she'd done a million times in the past. She'd get there. She would, too, no matter how daunting it sounded. *Stay the course, Spence. Stay the course.*

CHAPTER FOURTEEN

The pastries had been scarfed, the coffee sipped, and everyone began to shuffle in their seats, checking their phones as they looked ahead toward their respective days. All signs that Breakfast Club was winding down. Hadley, for one, had a lot on her to-do list: orders, delivery, and the negotiating of some important vendor contracts for the upkeep of the building. The less glamorous side of fashion. She let her mind linger on those mundane work tasks as long as possible, a tactic she'd developed over the last few weeks, ever since Spencer had left for Paris. It had been good for her self-preservation. Well, what little there was. Going through her day with a conscious sterility was her new normal.

Just as she reached for her bag, Autumn exchanged glances with Gia and Isabel, who each gave her a silent nod. She set the bag down again. Interesting. Hadley watched as Autumn sat a little taller in her chair and tucked a strand of curls behind her ear. "Before we go, Had, I think we'd all like to check in on you."

"On me?" she asked. "Why? What did I do?"

"You haven't done anything wrong," Gia said, with kindness in her eyes. "You've just not been yourself lately."

Hadley scoffed, knowing full well she was downplaying, but not willing to concede. "Not sure what you mean. Yes, I've been a little sad that Spencer left, but I'm still me."

"You're robot-you," Isabel said forcefully. "And it's killing my soul. You don't smile. You don't joke. You never gush, and you're our resident gusher. You barely contribute at Breakfast Club, just nodding along like someone's programmed you to do so, and it makes me so sad I could melt. I mean, when was the last time we had an 'Oh, my dear goodness'? I can't even remember the last time!"

Autumn held up a hand for Isabel to throttle back. "I think what

Isabel is trying to say, in maybe extra-dramatic terms, is that we're all really worried about you."

Hadley nodded. "I appreciate that." She didn't expand or explain herself further. She didn't have the capacity. Deep down she *felt* like the robot version of herself and wasn't sure how to get out from underneath that without completely falling apart. She hadn't shed a tear over Spencer. She couldn't or it would all come tumbling down, and then where would she be?

"And?" Isabel asked.

Hadley blinked. "And I'm managing."

"Yeah, but you're not Hadley," Isabel said.

"Look, guys, I'm doing the best I can, okay?" She retrieved her bag and stood. Her tolerance fell to an all-time low. "I'm sorry that I'm not as cheerful as I normally am. I'll work on gushing over you all more later."

"No. Wait," Gia called to Hadley, as she headed for the door. "That's not what we meant. There's nothing to apologize for."

"Okay. Then I'm not sorry," Hadley said, with measured control. "Just trying to get by, guys."

Gia nodded sadly. Isabel stared at the table in defeat and Autumn looked at her with so much sympathy that Hadley had to turn away or risk losing it entirely.

"I'll see you all later," she said over her shoulder, and hurried the hell out of there.

Silhouette, while the best place to distract herself from the memories that tended to tap her on the shoulder when she least expected it, was still not a stress-free environment. When she'd explained to Trudy that they wouldn't be getting Spencer's order after all, the exchange had been heated.

"What do you mean she's now designing for Bertrand?"

Hadley lifted one shoulder. "Claudette Fournier offered her a job, and Spencer pulled the order."

"The hell she did," Trudy said, and rifled through the papers on the desk. "We have a contract."

"With an out," Hadley said, pointing to the second page, fourth paragraph. "She's taking it."

Trudy turned to Hadley and removed her glasses, dropping them on the desk with a thud. "I put this in your hands."

"I realize that."

"And now I'm hugely disappointed. What do you suppose we do

now? We're late on any kind of replacement and will be waiting in line now behind everyone else for inventory from our standard designers."

"I realize that. I'm sorry."

"Sorry doesn't help anyone, Hadley. Does it?" Trudy made clicking sounds with her mouth which is what she did when she was too furious to vocalize. "Why don't you take the rest of the day off, while I try to sort out your mess?"

"Let me do that. I can call around and reorder—"

"Oh, I think you've done quite enough, don't you? Lesson learned." She made a show of dusting off her hands. "I'll handle all the big decisions from here on out. You can ring up sales. How would that be?"

Hadley nodded. She swallowed any further response to the demoralizing declaration, collected her things, and returned home, where she stared at the wall for a short period before retreating to the solitude of her bed. The awful day at work was one thing, but her inclination was to call Spencer and tell her all about it. The fact that she didn't have that luxury any longer cut deeper than any guilt trip Trudy could lay at her feet. No tears, however. None.

Now that it was weeks later, she'd gotten better at the stoic maneuvering. If her friends didn't care for it, there was very little she could do for them. When she arrived at work after the semi-intervention at Breakfast Club, Hadley was shocked to see Daisy dressing a mannequin in the green skirt and top from Spencer's collection. It didn't add up. She surveyed the room, surprised to see most all of Spencer's clothes on display.

"Why do we have these?" she asked Daisy, as she touched the fabric from the military jacket she was so fond of.

Daisy moved closer and glanced around to make sure they were alone. "From what I could piece together from paperwork and overheard conversations, Spencer Adair didn't pull the order in the end. I heard Trudy on the phone a couple of weeks back. Something about Spencer negotiating with Bertrand to fulfill all existing orders and Bertrand finally giving in and allowing her that leeway."

Hadley nodded. Spencer had gone to bat for her, even after they'd said goodbye. Her heart ached and pulled, but she pushed past it. "Fantastic. I'm sure she's going to sell well. A coup for us. Did the FedEx representative stop by yet?" she asked, back to business as usual as she headed back to the office.

"No. Haven't seen him."

"Great. Let me know when he's here."

Daisy smiled. "Will do."

"Appointments today?" Hadley asked.

She quickly flipped through the schedule. "I have three before lunch."

"I'll make myself available on the floor shortly."

"Thanks, Had," Daisy said, and went back to work.

Just a regular day. Her life itself wasn't all that much different from before Spencer Adair had walked into it. The difference was in Hadley herself. Now that she knew what it was to have that person who she longed for and shared so much with, it was hard to revert to a life barren of those overflowing feelings. She felt like a cleared-out, desolate warehouse. She missed Spencer, and not just the role she filled in Hadley's life. She missed Spencer herself. The way she tolerated Hadley's wild hairs and spontaneous whimsy with a secret smile hidden away, or the way she looked after Hadley kissed her when she wasn't expecting it, or showcased her sarcastic charm with a dry quip that came out of nowhere. That didn't even touch on their amazing sexual compatibility, or the tenderness they shared late at night afterward. Spencer had opened her eyes to a part of life she'd always hoped for but had never quite experienced. Now that she had, how was she supposed to settle for less without this kind of fallout?

No. Spencer was her big bang, and now she was gone. That's all there was to it.

She scrubbed away the feelings and focused on the here and now. Better to be numb and barren than experience the depth of her loss at full volume. Yep. Safer to feel nothing at all.

❖

Paris was turning out to be everything Spencer had always imagined it would be. Well, outside of the rain there'd been so much of. She'd been in town six weeks and was beginning to find her footing at Bertrand. She'd been given her own office with a high-end drafting table and a handful of assistants she could call upon should she need anything. It was entirely different from anything she was used to, and flattering, too. Did she feel like a fish out of water? Hell, yes, but Gerhard (pronounced with a hard *G*, apparently) had taken her under his wing for mentoring.

"Let me see," he said of her sketches, one afternoon. He tossed his blond hair out of his eyes in a dramatic fashion as he studied her work. "Yes, yes, definitely yes, no."

"You don't like the burgundy?" she asked, taking the offending sketch from his hands.

"The texture is not to be loved," he explained in his French accent. "It makes me feel heavy. Sad. Blah." He made a show of looking weighed down and depressed. "The rest is so light. Find your lightness, Spencer."

"Gotcha. Good note," she said, and returned to her table. Throughout her work weeks, she called on him with questions about the process, timeline, and structure of Bertrand and even where to find something comparable to coffee creamer. Honestly, the transition had been a smooth one. Claudette, herself, had even stopped by to welcome Spencer and see if there was anything she needed. There actually wasn't. They had taken care of her, and then some. These people were the real deal.

The company had arranged for a small one-bedroom apartment for her not far from their building. She could walk to work or take the metro just one stop. How easy was that? In her time there, she'd adventured to cafés, bookstores, and all the expected tourist sights. Sitting across from the Eiffel Tower late one night with a latte in one hand and a warm chocolate chip cookie in the other, Spencer tried to marinate in the beauty of the city. The beauty she knew innately was there. She could see it easily enough with her eyes, but she was having trouble feeling it. She thought back to the walk she took with Hadley on the canals, and how being there with her, looking down at the "duckling gentlemen" that swam past, had her on such a high. It was because she saw them through Hadley's eyes. When she was with Hadley, she saw—no, *felt*—the beauty in most everything. What an amazing gift that was.

At a loss, she took out her phone, needing to reach out and connect with someone. While she wanted more than anything to call Hadley, maybe Kendra could talk her through her rough patch. She dialed and waited, only to have the call roll over to voice mail. She listened to the outgoing message, so familiar, and such a strong reminder of home. She clicked off the call with a sigh and stared off into the night feeling more cut off from the world than ever.

She decided to walk as she ate her cookie, smiling at the couples cuddled together to fight off the November cold. They took selfies with the tower and laughed and kissed and did all the things Spencer might have rolled her eyes at just a year ago. Now she felt physical pain square in the center of her chest as a result of acute jealousy. She imagined taking one of those photos snuggled up to Hadley, inhaling the gentle scent of her hibiscus shampoo.

She tossed the cookie and headed home.

She had Paris, yes, but did this version of Paris even matter in the larger scheme? Everything came with a price, but sometimes it was simply too high. The cold wind blew and she pulled up the hood of her jacket and contemplated her life, her future, and her place in the world. She glanced back at the shimmering tower and blinked, looking to it for guidance, feeling pulled in a million different directions.

Everything she thought she knew felt so very foreign to her right now. She nodded to the tower, turned, bowed her head, and walked what felt like the very lonely streets of Paris.

❖

Hadley sat among various piles of her childhood belongings, taking a moment as her gaze passed over each toy, trinket, or book from her past. Her dads had continued their decluttering process now that the house had officially been remodeled and asked Hadley if she wanted to retain any of the nostalgic items for herself. She'd made the trip to Calabasas for dinner with the dads, and now that the homemade pizza (courtesy of Papa) had been consumed, she sat quietly with the remnants of her youth stacked around her like protective walls. The old Hadley would have struggled to part with that tennis trophy from high school, as it held such sentimental value and reminded her of a much simpler time. She glanced over at the music box with the puppies on top that she'd play each night before bed until she hit the seventh grade when she'd decided it was, sadly, too juvenile, only to resume the practice one short year later. The old Hadley wouldn't have parted with the music box for anything. The current version of herself, however, saw the value in letting go and not holding on to things too tightly.

"So, what are we saving?" her Papa asked, drying off his hands from the last of the dinner dishes.

She glanced around. "Nothing. Let's just donate it all. I think that would be for the best."

He stared at her. "I don't think I heard you correctly. Either that, or you're an alien being taking the form of my daughter who likes to hold on to anything with sentimental value."

She shrugged, and a melancholy heaviness settled right on her chest. "Just traveling a little lighter these days. That's all."

He nodded and shoved his hands into his pockets. He was always the more reflective parent, never rushing to any one conclusion, and she saw him working something out as he approached and took a seat next to her on the floor of the garage. "This about the girlfriend in Paris?"

She attempted a smile that didn't quite make it. "Maybe. I don't know." But she certainly knew. She wasn't the same anymore, and that made complete sense. The months she'd spent with Spencer had been that impactful.

He gave her knee a quick pat. "Tell you what. I'm gonna box up a couple of the more important items. You know, just in case you change your mind."

"I won't," she said, more firmly.

"Then I'll do it for me." He picked up the music box and turned it to her. "I always had a soft spot for these puppies here anyway."

She smiled at him wanly. "Whatever you want."

"Well, I definitely want this music box." He glanced behind him at the door leading into the house. "Your dad has a chocolate cheesecake he's just pulling out of the fridge. We can indulge him if you want."

She didn't have a lot of words, but nodded and followed him inside and into the kitchen. It felt good to be back at home with her dads, and for just a little while, she let herself be propped up by the comforting walls of that house and by the men who'd given their everything to raise her. Chocolate cheesecake wouldn't magically rewind the last few weeks of her life, but it certainly wouldn't make anything worse.

Her dad pulled her into a silent hug as she passed, and Papa sliced her an extra-large piece of cheesecake. The three of them ate together around the kitchen table. It wasn't like their typically raucous, fun-filled times together, but the quiet solidarity would have to do.

❖

Isabel held the door open for Hadley as she entered Pajamas just past seven that next morning. Autumn had her mocha already on the table, which meant that she would win the angel in heaven prize for the day. Hadley blinked and gestured behind her to Isabel. "Why is she being the door person?" she asked Gia, who was already seated.

"Who knows? Maybe she's writing a courteous character into her next episode and needs to experience it firsthand. Hard to say with writers. They're puzzling. She opened the door for me, too."

Hadley nodded and took her seat as Autumn joined them. Isabel, however, remained at the door. "She's being weird," Autumn said. "Can we officially say that, as a group?"

"Maybe not." Hadley glanced back at her with a confused shrug. "She's expressing herself...via door. She's greeting your guests. Nothing wrong with that, really."

"Except that it's weird," Autumn reiterated. "We all know it."

Gia sat forward. "Isn't that their assistant? Scarlett somebody, who works on the show?"

They all turned to find out. It was in fact Scarlett. Isabel greeted her and directed her to their table. "Hey. Scarlett's joining us today," Isabel called.

"Hi, Scarlett!" Hadley said, forcing herself to brighten.

"Hi," she said, waving at everyone. "Sorry to crash. I'm bumming a ride." Autumn leapt to her feet to secure Scarlett a coffee just as Taylor arrived. She gave Hadley a squeeze as she passed and took a seat, looking elegant in a white and black pantsuit, calm and in control as always. Isabel joined them finally, which meant she'd been waiting for Taylor all this time. Okay, that was cute. Hadley passed her a smile as Isabel took the seat next to her. She returned it, shyly.

"How are the twins?" Taylor asked eagerly, as everyone helped themselves to baked goods. Hadley zeroed in on the croissant, because light and flaky and warm was worth the calories these days. Bring 'em on!

"Learning how to manipulate others," Autumn said. "I've never been prouder."

"Amazing!" Taylor said, as the rest laughed along. She turned to Gia. "And I hear *you* just had a fantastic finish at the Hawaii Women's Pro."

"You heard right!" Gia beamed. "I finished second, which I will happily accept. Elle was third, but we're not discussing that right now." She winked at her friends.

"Well, congratulations," Taylor said, beaming. "I caught some of the highlights online."

"What about you?" Isabel asked, turning the tables on Taylor. "Tell them about agility."

Taylor laughed. "It hardly compares, but we thought it might be fun to get Raisin into a few agility classes. See if he can hold his own and get a little exercise along the way. He's spending way too much time lounging on the couch in my office. We haven't started yet, but that's on tap for when it's warmer."

"Adorable," Hadley said. "He's so smart. He'll be the star and have a million different girlfriends in the class."

"What if we also thought about making things more permanent when it gets warmer?" Isabel asked. She laced her fingers together nervously and everything in Hadley went still.

Taylor turned to her. "What do you mean?"

"I love you," Isabel said simply.

Taylor turned until her entire body faced Isabel. "I love you, too," she said, with a hint of curiosity in her voice. She studied Isabel as if unsure what she was getting at.

Autumn and Gia exchanged a wide-eyed glance.

"I plan to always love you," Isabel said, continuing. "I'm a fucking mess when it comes to expressing myself eloquently."

"No, you're not," Taylor said, and reached for her hand.

Isabel smiled. "But I knew that here, among friends, I would be at my best." She tossed a glance at Scarlett. "I asked Scarlett to come, by the way, because I know she's important to you and I wanted her to be here when I asked you to spend forever with me. Hi, Scarlett."

Scarlett waved back. Autumn covered her mouth. Hadley squeezed the sides of her chair as hard as she could. Gia sat forward, and Taylor welled up. None of it stopped Isabel, who Hadley was so proud of she could burst.

With a shaky hand, Isabel pulled a box from her pocket and opened it. "I don't know if this is the perfect ring or not, but I thought it was pretty amazing, and that made me think of you. You've completely changed my life for the better in every way possible. You make me want to wake up early in the morning just to see you sooner."

Taylor didn't hesitate. She cradled Isabel's cheek. "I could say the same back to you. All of it."

"I'm sorry this isn't more grandiose or happening on the side of a mountain or something, but this just feels more like us."

Taylor nodded her agreement through the tears.

"I want to marry you, Taylor. More than I want to break every *Ms. Pac-Man* record. More than I want an Emmy. More than I've ever wanted anything." Her hands continued to shake and she took a deep breath. No one at the table moved. "Taylor Andrews, what do you say? Will you marry me?"

It was the triumph of all triumphs! No matter what happened now, Isabel had done it. She'd conquered her fear head on and had the most earnest and sincere of moments to show for it. She wore her heart on her sleeve, and her words were everything. Hadley felt them down to her very core. They turned to Taylor in anticipation. Perhaps she was aware that taking a pause was simply good pacing for storytelling. Regardless, she remained silent for several long, excruciating moments.

Finally, when Hadley was ready to slink to the floor in suspense, she gave Isabel her answer. "I will happily marry you, Iz. In fact, it's pretty much all I've thought about doing for a year now."

The table instantly erupted in applause and wrapped arms around each other as Isabel and Taylor stood and fell into a romantic kiss. Hadley *loved* that Isabel had chosen Breakfast Club for her proposal. It was so very her, and that made it perfect.

"And you invited my best friend," Taylor said through tears, and pulled Scarlett into an embrace as the others took turns hugging Isabel.

"You did it," Hadley said, in her ear. "Best proposal ever."

"You really think so?" Isabel asked, her eyes overflowing with vulnerability. "It was okay?" she whispered. "I wasn't sure."

"Without a doubt." Hadley touched her heart. "It got me right here." As everyone dried their eyes and posed for photos with the happy couple, Hadley knew that something had come unfastened inside her. She kissed Taylor's cheek, said a quick goodbye to all of her friends, and made a hasty exit. She'd barely made it onto the sidewalk before the tears hit fast and heavy. After holding the emotion back for weeks, it assaulted her now with an intensity that almost brought her to her knees. She held a hand across her midsection and walked directly to her apartment, stopping for no one. She choked on the ambush of sadness, twisting uncomfortably against the pain she'd avoided for so long. Once inside, she leaned against the closed door and slid to the floor. She'd yet to make a sound, but that first sob was upon her in a matter of moments and it racked her through and through. She cried for what was, she cried for what she'd lost and what she would likely never have. She'd done the right thing in sending Spencer to Paris, hadn't she? Why did it feel like such an awful decision now? She took out her phone and through blurry vision stared at the photos she and Spencer had taken together over the months since they'd met. It was too much. She pressed the phone to her forehead. What had been the point if they weren't meant to be together in the end? Why bring Spencer into her life?

There was a knock on the door behind her. She did her best to wipe her eyes but with the tears continuing to fall, she was less than successful. Better to just ignore it. They'd go away. Only they didn't. Another knock.

"Had. Open the door. I'm not leaving."

She closed her eyes. Gia. "Not a great time." The words were stilted and her voice cracked when she said them.

"I know it's not. That's why I'm here."

She couldn't face Gia right now, not when she was so raw and ripped apart. "I'll call you later, G, okay?"

"No, not okay." She heard Gia slide down the outside of the door, which left them sitting back to back, separated by just that slab of wood. Hadley turned her head to the side and rested it against the door. Knowing Gia was on the other side actually did bring an unexpected comfort. "If you don't want to talk to me, just listen, okay?"

Hadley nodded, not that Gia would know.

"I've been where you're at right now. It's the worst place, and you start to second-guess everything and yourself. Nothing that was important to you before really matters, except that other person. Am I close?"

Hadley nodded again.

"I'm going to imagine that your silence means yes. If that's what you're going through, Had, and it's hard to know because you've been so bottled up, you have a decision to make."

"What decision?" she heard herself ask, eager for any kind of lifeline or guidance at this point. She was floundering and not sure how to right herself any longer.

"Whether to push through this pain to the other side or to do something the hell about it."

She turned and faced the door, her emotions firing. "What am I supposed to do?"

"That's for you to decide."

Hadley blinked and nodded. She pushed herself into a standing position. She could continue her new sad existence or take back what it was she wanted. She opened the door to find Gia standing outside, waiting. "I have to go to Paris," Hadley said, with calm determination. "If that's where Spencer is, that's where I have to be."

Gia stared at her. "Well, you've always loved the city."

Hadley practically fell into Gia's waiting hug as the tears came again. She wasn't so quick to let go either. "Thanks, G," she mumbled. "I don't know what this means for my life here or how I'm going to make this work, but I have to try, right? Maybe we're never going to ride off into the sunset together, but being with her for even a small amount of time is better than not at all."

Gia nodded. "If Spencer is what you want, you definitely have to try."

"I'm terrified."

"I know."

"But I have to do it, right?"

"You have to follow your heart. That's exactly what you would tell me to do."

Hadley took a deep breath, and noticed that, with a sense of direction on board, even a scary and less than ideal one, the tears began to recede. She could breathe again, if only a little bit. Now it was time to get her world in order for what could be a very big leap. This was either the smartest or the most reckless thing she'd ever done. Didn't matter. The gamble was worth it.

"If I do move to Paris, will you and Elle visit me?"

"Please. Just try to keep us away from the wine and baguettes at your place."

Hadley grinned and geared up.

Here goes nothing...

CHAPTER FIFTEEN

A utumn held up Hadley's black and white plaid coat. "This one is definitely going."

Hadley squinted. "You think? I already packed the red plaid. I don't want to be known as the girl with all the plaid once I'm in Paris."

"There can never be too many plaid coats," Autumn said, emphatically. "What are you even thinking right now?"

"I know. I know. You're right. Toss it in the suitcase."

Autumn did as Hadley asked, using her super-specific, space-saving packing technique that involved rolling the clothes into tiny clothing-burritos. She straightened with a hand on her hip. "We're running out of space."

Hadley waved her off. "It's just a preliminary trip. If things go well, I'll hire a company and send for the rest. I don't need it all in one go-round. Have to see what she says first, right?"

"Yeah, but she asked you to go with her."

"True. But it's been a while since then. We haven't communicated. I don't know where her head's at."

Autumn sighed. She took a seat on the bed and ran her hand across the suitcase fondly. "What am I going to do without my Hadley if you move to Paris?"

It felt like a gut punch, because what would she do without her Autumn? She joined Autumn on the bed and snagged her hand. "We're gonna FaceTime like crazy, for one."

Autumn laughed through her melancholy. "We are. Thank God for technology."

"And I'll be back for the important holidays. Gotta get my Pajamas fix somehow, right?"

"I don't know how you'll survive each morning without it. Well, except for all of those amazing Parisian cafés. They know how to roast a good cup there. You heard it here."

"Nothing will hold a candle to Pajamas coffee, you hear me?"

"Bless you for saying that." Autumn gave her hand a squeeze. "And now I should probably check on Kate and the twins. She might have them running drills by now. Will's obsessed with her turnout gear's suspenders."

Hadley laughed. "Well, who isn't? Thank you for the help. I'll stop by later to say, you know…goodbye." She said that last word delicately and with less volume. It was a hard one. Her flight was far too early the next morning to disrupt any of her friends. She'd see them each that evening for a brief farewell. Nothing too drawn out. She wasn't sure she could take it. Plus, it wasn't goodbye forever. Just for right now.

"I'll be around," Autumn said quietly.

She let herself out and Hadley got back to the last of her packing. It wasn't long before there was a knock at her door. She expected Autumn, who'd likely forgotten something, but found Larry Herman staring at her in shock from her doorstep.

"Hi, Larry," she said, smiling up at him.

"Is it true?" he asked, solemnly. He wore his traditional brown pants, blue shirt, and striped tie. "You're leaving?" The guy looked like a kicked puppy. She deflated. She hated seeing him so dejected.

"It's true. I'm heading to Paris tomorrow. I'm not sure if I'll be back. Don't worry about the rest of my lease. If I can't sublet, I'll pay it out."

He studied his shoe. "She's that important to you, Ms. Adair?"

"She is."

The admission seemed to make him shrink further behind his tie. "What is it about her that you like so vehemently?" he asked.

And there they were. Hadley had known for some time that Larry had certain feelings for her. She'd hoped they were superficial, but maybe it was time to be a little more straightforward with him, for his own sake. She took a deep breath. "I'm in love with her."

"Oh." A long pause. "Love."

"You've always been a good friend to me, Larry, and I value our friendship, but I'm afraid that's all we can have."

He raised his gaze to hers. "I understand that. Just…do me a favor. Be happy, okay?"

"Thanks, Larry. I'm trying."

"She doesn't know how lucky she is," he said, and turned to go, head hung low.

"Larry, wait. How about a hug goodbye?"

His cheeks colored, and after a moment he nodded and extended one arm. Ignoring that, she put her arms around his neck and gave him a firm squeeze. "You're a good guy, Larry. Be nice to these people around here, okay? Do it for me. They're your friends."

He seemed conflicted. His brow creased dramatically, as if an internal battle waged. "Even Ms. Chase? Because that one is just out of—"

"Even Ms. Chase," she said slowly.

"Very well." He nodded hesitantly and headed down the stairs. She'd miss that quirky guy, as frustrating as he could be. Alone now, she stepped onto the second-story sidewalk and stared out over the railing to the courtyard below. She would miss Seven Shores, too, so very much. She watched the waves crash just above the roof, dusted with the colors of the setting sun. The courtyard stood empty, which allowed her to envision all the great times they'd had out there, from theme nights to late night talks and water balloon fights in the summer. She placed a hand over her heart in honor of the friendship she'd found there that she'd never let go. She might be leaving, but these women would travel with her in her heart.

"Gonna miss this place," she said, and stood there for one final, long-lasting look. She blew a kiss to the buildings that were so much more than that to her and headed inside. She had a big trip ahead of her.

❖

"No, no. I don't think we can make that work." Claudette leaned back in her elegant desk chair and stared at Spencer like she'd just asked for her own personal elephant.

"I had a feeling you would say that," Spencer said. "You want me here in Paris to learn the company culture, to work under the mentorship of someone like Gerhard, and truly live the brand."

"All very important. Now you understand."

"I understand entirely, and I'm more than grateful for the chance to work under the Bertrand label," she said, as respectfully as possible.

"Then why are you asking to return to California?"

She took a deep breath and prepared to state the rest of her case as the sounds of incoming emails pinged like an electronic symphony on the computer behind Claudette. All a reminder of a successful business running itself as they sat in those very chairs. Somehow that only added to the pressure. She swallowed, and began. "I can do all of those things if I design from Los Angeles, and I'm more than willing to travel to Paris whenever you need me for face-to-face time, to go over samples, sketches, all of it. I don't mind the travel. I welcome it."

Claudette eyed her. "This is the kind of opportunity that most young designers would kill for. Yet you are unhappy."

"I'm not unhappy with the job, but I guarantee that you'll get better work from me back home, in my element."

Claudette sat forward, incredulous. "You're homesick? This is *homesickness*?" She said the word like it was the most offensive of weaknesses.

"It's more than just that. I left a lot unfinished, and—"

"Then you should see to it," Claudette said, head held high. "Bertrand will release you from your contract."

It was a blow. Spencer's eyes fluttered closed. Those were not the words she was hoping to hear. "Isn't there some sort of compromise we could come to? I was hoping that after we talked—"

"You either want to be here or you don't," Claudette said, icily. "There are too many others waiting for your job for me to hesitate. This is an insult."

Silence hit and stretched. Spencer shifted uncomfortably at the decision in front of her. The ramifications of throwing it all away would be huge. But what she had waiting behind door number two felt so much more important. It had taken her a lot to fully understand as much, but she had.

"In that case, I'm sorry. I'll turn in my badge and keys to the front desk."

Claudette didn't say anything as Spencer excused herself from the office with an uncomfortable feeling in the pit in her stomach. In fact, she felt more than a little nauseous. As she walked the length of the hallway, however, something interesting happened. With each step she took, that sickening feeling gradually fell away until all she was left with was an overwhelming sense of relief and excitement for what was to come. She closed her eyes and took a deep, fortifying breath. It was time to be honest about her feelings and reclaim what she so desperately missed. She just hoped Hadley would be open to what she had to say.

If not, then what? God, she couldn't think about that. Not now. She had to pack.

❖

It was ten that night when the friends gathered at the now-closed Cat's Pajamas one last time together. Hadley had made a point of saying her personal goodbyes to Kate and the twins earlier that night. That had been hard. She couldn't imagine months going by before she saw the little kiddos. Would they be crawling by then? Talking? Would they forget all about her? She tried not to dwell on all she'd miss. Next, she'd caught Elle in the parking lot on her way back to her house, and Taylor had been nice enough to stop by personally with a going-away gift for Hadley, a journal with a photo of the Eiffel Tower on the cover—extra thoughtful as always. She'd miss them all no end. Thank God for technology and social media that would hopefully keep her plugged into their lives.

However, standing there in the dimly lit coffee shop with Isabel, Autumn, and Gia brought with it a new kind of sadness. These three, she couldn't imagine life without.

"Do you have snacks for the flight?" Autumn asked, nervously moving toward the storeroom for baked goods in case Hadley said no.

"I do. I packed a very detailed and varied bag of snacks just like you told me to."

"And your book?" Gia asked. She always paid attention to what installment Hadley was on.

Hadley smiled. "Yes. The new Captain Janika is prepped and ready to accompany me overseas."

"And you're sure about this?" Isabel asked. "As in big bang times a thousand?"

Hadley smiled. "You have no idea how sure."

"Where's your connecting flight?"

"Newark," Hadley told them. "I have a two-hour layover and then it's straight on to where all the magic happens."

They stared at each other in silence, recognizing the importance of this moment. Isabel shifted uncomfortably and Hadley's eyes crowded with tears. "Well, I don't want to hear about too many wild nights without me."

Gia shoved her hands into the pockets of her jeans. "Wouldn't be the same anyway."

"We won't let theme nights die, either!" Autumn said. "I already have several ideas for the months ahead. Gonna make you proud."

Hadley grinned through her tears. "Thanks, Autumn. I'll need photos."

"Pshhh," Isabel said. "You will not. You'll be there with us. We're gonna FaceTime you in."

"I would love that. Oh!" She reached in her bag. "I almost forgot. I have a card for each of you. Nothing major and you can read them later. Just a few words from my heart about what you each mean to me. What this group does." The tears were falling freely down her face now. Looking at her three best friends, she could see that she wasn't alone in that department.

"I look like such a loser when I cry," Isabel said, accepting her card.

Gia elbowed her. "Shut up. I'm the idiot."

"Well, *yeah*," Isabel said, followed by another elbow. "No one is disputing that."

"And I look amazing tear-streaked," Autumn said, with an angelic grin. She waved like the queen through her tears. That earned a laugh, which helped break the tension.

"Well…I guess this is it." Hadley smiled, opened her arms wide, and her best friends came together in one big hug. "You guys look out for each other," she said, in the midst of the giant group squeeze. "No one let Autumn work too hard. If Gia beats herself up about how she finishes in a tournament, you guys remind her how amazing she is. Keep an eye on Izzy. She gets in her own head and self-doubt creeps in and that's stupid. Pull her out of it at every chance."

"Yes, ma'am."

"Got it."

"We won't let you down."

She released them and wiped her tears quickly. "Okay, no more of that," she said forcefully. She pointed at them. "Fast is better, so I will just say that I will see you all very soon. You hear me? Only a handful of weeks until I visit at Christmas."

"Safe travels, Had," Autumn said.

She nodded, blew the three of them kisses and, with focused determination, made herself walk out of the shop. She glanced back up at the logo, that crazy cat playing his guitar, and smiled fondly at what felt like the end of an important era.

In the midst of it all, she was so very grateful.

❖

Spencer strolled the concourse of Newark Liberty International Airport, perusing the windows of the various shops and wondering if she should eat a full meal before boarding the plane that would whisk her back across the country to Los Angeles. Just the thought gave her a twinge of nervous energy in her stomach. She'd stick with a snack and bottle of water.

Waiting in line to pay, she smiled as she was overcome with the familiar scent of Hadley's hibiscus shampoo that used to drive her wild. Someone in the store must also be a fan. She smiled at the reminder and took that as a sign from the universe that she was on the right path. Took her long enough, but she'd made it. The Hadley kismet didn't stop there. As she walked to her gate, she spotted a woman from behind who reminded her so much of Hadley, even down to the way she walked. She laughed. Okay, she got it, cosmos! She had Hadley on the brain and shook her head at the series of signs directing her path.

She checked her watch. With another half hour to boarding, she placed a quick call to her mother, who'd be waiting on a status update.

"You almost here?" her mama asked, as soon as she clicked on to the call.

Spencer laughed. "You know I have another few hours. Just letting you know I'm on time."

She heard a rustling and then her pop's voice. He must have grabbed the phone. "I'll be picking you up in the blue SUV. Not gonna bring your mama's car because it's cramped and it smells like flowers all the time."

Spencer smiled. "Yes, sir. That makes total sense. I'll look for the SUV."

"Here's your mama."

"My car doesn't smell like flowers," she said forcefully. "That's a baked cookie air freshener, and he knows it. He's just trying to make trouble because he's old and bored."

"Doesn't smell like any cookies you've ever made before," she heard him say in the background.

"Would you be quiet? I'm talking to our daughter. Hush now."

"Fine. I'll just work my puzzle and let you two gab away."

"Praise Jesus at last."

Spencer sat there and let the two of them bicker as they always did, no longer freaked out by their reunion, but rather, enjoying it very much. So much of life was about perception. Simply in changing hers, Spencer saw so much of the world differently, including her parents and their relationship. They really *were* meant to be together. She was lighter with this new outlook, happier, and ready to explore the world with new eyes.

Waiting in line to board her flight, she stared across the concourse at a similar line of people at the gate diagonal from hers. They were headed to Paris, just like she had been, weeks prior, when everything in her had been so focused on the wrong things. She smiled at them, mentally wished them well on their journey ahead, and handed her boarding pass to the gate agent. She was LA bound and couldn't be more excited.

❖

As Hadley waited patiently in line for a cab, she took a deep inhale. That was Paris air in her lungs. Did she mention she was in Paris? Because she was. This was Paris. With her in it. Hadley Cooper in Paris! Not caring who noticed, she twirled a few times as she stood in line because she felt like it. "I'm in Paris," she said, by way of explanation, to the man in front of her. The best part of all of this was not Paris, however. It was that she was on her way to see Spencer, who she missed more than she could wrap her mind around, and who she hoped would be happy to see her. That trumped everything, even the monumental day when she met her favorite city in person.

She got to try out her rudimentary French in the cab as she asked to be taken to the address she had for Spencer. Luckily, the driver also spoke English, which helped their navigation and small talk. She was small talking with French people! This was big!

"I am Victor," he said, as they drove.

"Oh, nice to meet you. Hadley Cooper. I'm from the United States. Los Angeles."

"Hollywood!"

"Yes," she said. "Lots of movies made there."

"You like my city?" he asked.

"I love it! It's every bit as beautiful and as busy as I was expecting. Fast paced."

"Yes, very, very busy. You need a bicycle."

"I can see that!" She marveled at how many people chose biking as their method of transportation. Definitely energy efficient. She'd be looking into that.

"You like bread?" he asked.

A little random, but Hadley went with it. "Yes, I love bread!"

"Right there," he said, pointing out a quaint little bakery as they drove past. "Best bread in Paris. Warm croissants with chocolate."

Hadley's mouth watered because croissants were her weakness in life. She started to thank him for the spot-on recommendation, but stopped. As they turned the corner, there it was. The symbol of the city she'd dreamt about since she was a child, the Eiffel Tower itself! She couldn't quite believe this was real. She glanced down at her lap to the Eiffel Tower journal Taylor had given her, then back up at the real thing right in front of her, looming large and beautiful. The best welcome she could imagine.

"Come back for a photo with your love, yes?"

Her heart grew. "I will definitely be getting a photo," she told him. "At least, I hope."

"And here we go," Victor said. "That one. There."

She stared up at the tall structure. Spencer's apartment building, it turned out, was right in the heart of everything, which had to be so exciting for her. She could walk to the outdoor market, the florist, and even to the tower itself. Bertrand was treating Spencer right.

"*Au revoir*, Victor." Hadley handed him the fare with a smile. "Thank you for the recommendations."

"Anytime, my sweet. Enjoy my city. *Au revoir*."

Hadley watched the cab drive away, then turned to the building in front of her. Her nerves flew into overdrive at what these next few minutes might bring. Nope. No time to entertain her worst fear, that Spencer would tell her that they were probably best as they were and to go home. Maybe she'd even met someone in Paris, which was entirely possible. Someone exotic and sexy and way more sophisticated than Hadley could ever be. Sigh. Why did she have to go there? Hadley gave her head a shake to rid it of the awful idea, though it wasn't the first time it had occurred to her. It was possible she'd waited too long, but there was no turning back now. She'd come here for one reason, and one reason only, and she planned to follow through. All she could do was speak from her heart and hope that Spencer's offer still stood. She made her way into the building and located the door on the second floor that belonged to Spencer. *Here goes nothing*. She knocked. And waited. And knocked again. It seemed no one was home. She'd considered calling first, but somehow the idea of just showing up felt like part of the grand gesture she'd imagined.

The Bertrand offices weren't far away. In fact, a quick search on her phone showed they were walkable. Couldn't hurt to see if Spencer was available. The workday had to be coming to a close, given that it was approaching dusk in Paris. Surely, designers came up for air at some point. After quickly orienting herself with a map on her phone, she decided to set off for the Bertrand building. You know, just in case.

She hadn't traveled more than two blocks when her phone buzzed with an incoming text from Autumn.

Um, Had? I think we have a problem.

Moments later a photo arrived. She squinted, trying to understand what she was seeing. Yep, that was a photo of Spencer waiting in line for coffee at Pajamas.

What? No.

Hadley stared.

Mayday!

What in the world was going on?

She scrutinized the photo to be sure it was Spencer. It was. Right there in Autumn's coffee line, which meant she wasn't in Paris at all. She was in *Venice*? Hadley blinked as her world ran off the rails. A minute later, her phone rang. Autumn.

"What's going on?" Hadley asked. "I don't understand."

"Let me pass the phone to someone who might be able to explain."

"Hadley."

She closed her eyes when she heard the velvety voice she'd know anywhere. "Spencer, what are you doing in Venice?" she asked, mystified.

"The question is what are *you* doing in Paris?"

"I'm here for you," she said quietly. "I should have been here all along."

Spencer laughed. "Well, that's perfect because I'm here for you, where I never should have left."

Hadley stared up at the darkening Paris sky. "We're ridiculous."

"I'm ridiculously in love with you, is what I am."

Hadley turned it around. "You are? No. You don't have to say that. We can pick up where we left off. Open minds, remember?"

"I don't have an open mind anymore. Mine's decided. I love you, and I flew all this way to tell you so."

Hadley couldn't keep up. With the utterance of the three words, her mind regressed to a jumble of information while her insides turned to wonderful mush. She'd dreamt of the right person saying those words to her and it had just happened. While she stood on the streets of Paris no less! Okay, she was alone, but this was still Paris, darn it!

"Victor drove me to your apartment, which is so close to the Eiffel Tower that I couldn't believe it, and then I went to find you at Bertrand, but you're apparently drinking coffee with Autumn instead, and I love you, too!" It all came out in a joyful, euphoric run-on sentence that she hoped made at least a little bit of sense to Spencer, who she swore she could hear smile through the phone.

A pause. "Sounds like we're a couple of kids in love," Spencer said, and it felt like Hadley's heart took flight. "We should really be in the same city for this moment. We have to plan better."

"I promise to try if you do," Hadley said, laughing. "What now?"

"I parted ways with Bertrand. I don't work for them anymore."

"Oh, no."

"No, it's good. I'm moving back to LA. In fact, I already have. The brand was taking off before I left, and I want to see what I can do with it on my own. Maybe you can help me with that. You offer great advice."

"You're going to kill it!" Hadley ran a hand through her hair in happy disbelief. "This is the most amazing news I've ever heard."

"She's back for good!" Autumn yelled in the background. "Come home already! I have a mocha with your name on it."

Hadley grinned. "I'll find a flight."

"No," Spencer said. "Stay there. Please. You've always wanted to see Paris. I'll come to you. We can make it our first real vacation."

"No. You don't have to do that. Really? You would want to travel all the way back?"

"I would do anything to see Paris with you. We can hold hands, stroll the streets."

"And take a photo with the Eiffel Tower?"

"Are you kidding? We'll take ten."

❖

Spencer sat in the back of her cab as it wound through the downright cold streets of Paris, wondering why in the hell she wasn't feeling the fatigue she should be after back-to-back international flights. There was only one reason. She was about to lay eyes on Hadley for the first time in weeks and was close to leaping out of her skin from the pure exhilaration. She smiled at the pedestrians who snuggled further into their jackets as the wind whipped around them, tousling their hair and making one gentleman lose his cap entirely and chase it down the sidewalk as his friends laughed. She made a mental note: no hats tonight.

Twenty minutes later, she arrived at the Shangri-La where, at her encouragement, Hadley had reserved a full-on suite with Spencer's credit card, complete with a terrace and an Eiffel Tower view. Hadley deserved that and more. She wanted this trip to be a memorable one and would go out of her way to see that happen. She planned to pamper Hadley and show her Paris in style. If there was a time to splurge, this was most definitely it.

Who was she kidding? Spencer would find a way to rope the moon in everyday life if Hadley asked her to. Everything felt different now that she'd been honest with herself about who she was and what she wanted. The sky was the limit for the two of them.

With luggage in hand, she knocked and waited. The door opened and there she was, like a long-needed drink of ice water: Hadley, in person, at long last. Spencer took a moment to absorb the sight and enjoy every second of their reunion. Hadley wore jeans and a navy sweater which highlighted the blue of her gorgeous eyes. Her hair was down and she looked more radiant than Spencer remembered. She skipped right over the shy part where they would chat and smile and get used to each other again. Nope, none of that damn getting reacquainted nonsense. She moved to Hadley and had her by the waist in seconds, walking her into the room as Hadley laughed.

"Oh, my dear goodness. Hi," Hadley said, as she was virtually carried inside. "You're finally here." She took Spencer's face and kissed her and kissed her again and again. "I thought you'd never get here." *Kiss.* "Time was moving too slow. Like a turtle in peanut butter."

"Same. Trip took"—*kiss*—"too"—*kiss*—"long." Spencer released her. "You don't know how happy I am to see you. A turtle in peanut butter?"

"Yes, that's a thing. And I do, too, know, because I'm just as happy." Hadley pressed her forehead to Spencer's. "Let's neither of us move away again."

"Ever," Spencer said. "You heard it here."

Hadley smiled. "Sounds permanent."

"Because it is *very* permanent. You were right. Happily ever after is real, and I'm staring at her."

Hadley paused. "Do you mean it? We don't have to leap fully if you're not ready. We can go slow."

"I've never meant anything more in my life. There will be no more slow. Where you go, I will follow."

Hadley shook her head in surprise. "I don't understand. What's changed?"

"Are you kidding? What's *changed*?" Spencer laughed, glanced at the ceiling and back to Hadley again. "You. The second I met you everything changed. Everything down to the damn sidewalk seemed brighter and more exciting. Things are now infinitely possible that I didn't think were before. All from *you*. I just needed a smack in my head to understand that."

The words seemed to carry a large amount of weight for Hadley. Spencer watched as she sifted and sorted through them. After a pause, a smile started slowly on Hadley's lips and blossomed into the most beautiful beam Spencer had ever enjoyed.

"I love you," Hadley said quietly.

Hearing the words sent Spencer on a high. Would they ever sound normal, or mundane, or casual rolling off the tongue? She couldn't imagine that. Hearing "I love you" from Hadley would always undo her, and she looked forward to each and every time. She was up for future dismantling.

"I love you, too," Spencer said, and let the words float in the air, delicate and important. She stared at the woman who was lit up brightly from the inside out. Hadley glowed in every possible way as she leaned in, kissing Spencer unhurriedly and communicating so much in the process.

"Come onto the balcony. It's freezing, but you have to see this."

Spencer followed, holding Hadley's hand. Her breath caught as she saw the tower, lit up for all the city to see in the encroaching darkness. She'd seen the tower at night many times now, but tonight was different. She didn't just see its beauty, she felt it. Standing there with Hadley, knowing how much she loved the city, it meant so much more. A surge of emotion hit and she pulled Hadley's lips to hers. Right then and there, they kissed with the lights of Paris twinkling behind them. The wind, the cold, none of it mattered.

"That might have been the best kiss of my life," Hadley said, finally. "No, it *was*."

"Was there toe-curling?" Spencer asked. "I like it when that happens."

Hadley nodded. "Ten toes a-curling."

Spencer's entire heart turned over in her chest. "Please tell me we can order room service and see what other things we can make curl? I love a challenge."

Hadley blushed and followed her back inside. In moments, she was on the phone ordering strawberries, chocolate, and Champagne. While she spoke in the best French she could, Spencer looked on, removing one piece of clothing at a time, while Hadley watched in captivation. By the time she hung up, Spencer was in lingerie on the bed waiting for her.

Hadley sat next to her and placed one finger on her cheek. "There's a sexy woman, who I happen to be in love with, waiting for me in bed in the center of Paris." She tapped her cheek.

"What would Captain Janika do?" Spencer asked, sweetly. She ran a hand from her breast to her stomach and watched as Hadley swallowed noticeably.

She closed her eyes and opened them. "Captain who?"

Spencer laughed. "Kiss me. You own my heart, now own the rest of me."

Hadley didn't hesitate.

They came up for air only briefly when the room service arrived. Hadley answered after hastily stepping into her robe, which she quickly dropped as she returned to bed.

"Disneyland on fire," Spencer murmured.

The chocolate and strawberries made a nice addition to their fun. Spencer dipped a strawberry and ran it down Hadley's body, chasing the results with her tongue as Hadley moaned quietly, moving her hips. Tasting Hadley herself was much sweeter, and she relished taking her to the brink only to pull her right back in.

"You are torturing me, and it's wonderful," Hadley said, back arched in their now-darkened hotel room. The outline of the Eiffel Tower was still visible through their window and offered the small amount of illumination which Spencer used to navigate. She took her time and worked slowly, touching, caressing, and making love to every inch of Hadley Cooper.

When they were happy and tired, Hadley pulled her into her

arms where they lay as sleep hovered. "What do you think we'll do tomorrow?"

"I want to walk the streets with you. Explore. Find a café and do nothing but watch the world go by."

She felt Hadley smile up against her cheek. "That sounds like one of the best days of my life." She paused and looked down at Spencer in her arms. "I'm starting to imagine a lot of those ahead."

Spencer crawled up the bed until she lay face-to-face with Hadley. "It's not imagination anymore. It's our life, and it's only just getting started." She reached across Hadley. "Chocolate-covered strawberry?"

"Yes, please."

They stayed up most of the night talking, catching up on all the things that had happened since they'd parted, and when the sun came up the next morning and drenched the suite in its magnificent show of color, Spencer snuggled further into Hadley, lost, happy, and sure.

EPILOGUE

Summertime

No two people had ever looked more beautiful. Hadley was sure of it.

As Isabel and Taylor walked hand in hand down the beach together to the sound of a solo violin, Hadley was a goner. Remembering to breathe in the midst of all of this beauty would be a task. The brides were barefoot and each carried a single white calla lily, which perfectly accentuated the simplicity of the dresses Spencer had designed for the ceremony. Isabel's dress was more casual in nature, short and lacy with an asymmetrical hemline and V-neck. It was amazing how accurately the dress captured who Isabel was—part of Spencer's talent. Taylor's dress was longer and fuller and fell just above her bare feet. While also white, it transitioned into a beautiful light blue ombré as the fabric neared the hemline. They held hands and gazed at each other as a photographer snapped a photo.

The wedding on Venice Beach was a small affair, attended by just a handful of friends and family. Instead of assembling and sitting formally, everyone stood, looking on, as the sun met the water and the rings were prepared. The sunset arrived on time and did not disappoint, haloing the couple in amazing pinks, oranges, purples. Hadley squeezed Spencer's hand just in time for the vows, her very favorite part.

"Isabel, you are the most unexpected gift," Taylor said, as she held Isabel's ring in her hand. "Never once did I imagine my life could be as full and wonderful as it became the moment you walked into it. I hope, with all I have, that you will continue spilling coffee on my belongings, encouraging me to eat junk food, and challenging me, making me think, and coloring in my life until the end of our time on

Earth. I love you, and with this ring promise to continue loving you always. I vow to support you, stand by you, and be there for you even on the most difficult of days. In fact, it's the most natural thing I could imagine doing. You're my everything." Isabel's hand shook as Taylor slid the ring onto her finger. They exchanged a watery smile.

Okay, it was time! Hadley knew Isabel was nervous about this part and willed all of the courage in the world her direction. "You got this," she mouthed, and squeezed Spencer's hand extra hard to punctuate. Isabel nodded back and accepted Taylor's ring from the officiant. "I have no idea what you're doing with me," Isabel blurted, pulling an unexpected laugh from the guests, as well as Taylor. "Seriously. You may have the wrong girl." Taylor shook her head. "But since you're still here, I'm not about to let you get away. Taylor Andrews, you are the kindest among kind, the smartest among the brilliant, and the most beautiful woman on the planet. If you hadn't agreed to marry me, I don't know where I'd be. This is infinitely better. I've never been so excited to wake up each morning as I have been since you came into my life and changed it forever." This time it was Spencer's turn to squeeze Hadley's hand. Their gazes collided in warmth. "I guarantee there will be more coffee spilling and swear words at the most inappropriate of times." She held up the ring in pledge. "But there will also be continued love, and tenderness, and kindness, and loyalty. I'm yours forever, Taylor. My heart beats for you." There were tears running down Taylor's face, just as there were Hadley's. She rejected the tissue Gia offered her and embraced the happy emotion.

When it was time for the brides to kiss, the small group of guests erupted in applause. Will, in his tiny little man suit, burst into tears at the shock of noise. Spencer graciously took him in her arms and shushed him back to calm with her soothing words, as Autumn bounced a dressed-to-the-nines Carrie, who it turned out loved clothes and who babbled away constantly these days.

"That was a game-changer ceremony," Spencer said, as they waited for the variety of photos to be taken after its conclusion.

"What do you mean, game changer?" Hadley asked.

She shook her head in awe. "I've never seen one so sincere, so meaningful. All the weddings I've been to were stuffy and inside a church. This one was so heartfelt and honest and *them*. I want ours to be more like that one. Like *us*."

"Ours?" Hadley asked, as she accepted a glass of Champagne from Scarlett, who was on pouring duty.

"Yes, ours," Spencer said, leaning in for a kiss. "And we probably shouldn't wait too long either. Though my mama is gonna want to be very involved, and that's gonna be a whole separate can of worms."

"My dads, too. Get ready. They've had ideas about my wedding since I was nine."

"Good thing they all get along."

Hadley grinned at the recent memory of her dads playing corn hole in pastels at the last Adair outdoor cookout. They'd all had the best time and stayed up well past midnight on the Adairs' back patio, getting to know each other and drinking wine.

"You don't let her get away again, you hear me?" Sonny had said over her shoulder to Hadley, once they were alone in the kitchen. "That child doesn't know what's good for her all the time. But you? *You're* good for her."

"Aww, Sonny," Hadley said, and pulled her into a hug. "That means a lot to me."

"You know what means a lot to me? You and my daughter so happy together. I've never seen her like this, all breezy with grins, and it's all because of you. I knew it the minute I saw the two of you together in my living room. So, listen, if I have anything to say about it? You're not going anywhere."

"We are in agreement, because I plan to stick around."

"Good! Now will you help me carry this sangria outside? You grab the glasses. I'll grab the goods."

"Yes, ma'am. I will happily do that for you."

Since returning to LA, things between her and Spencer had only continued to blossom. With the new line selling remarkably well at Silhouette, Spencer had been able to take a breather from the world of fast-paced online sales and pay others to handle that end of the business for her. Instead, she spent her days and nights dreaming, designing, and meeting with retailers to build the brand. Not surprisingly, Bertrand rethought their offer and extended Spencer the opportunity to work from LA.

She turned them down flat.

"There's too much I want to do to answer to anyone else's artistic vision at this point," Spencer explained the week prior, as they'd moved another box into Hadley's—correction, now *their* apartment.

"You don't need anyone else at this point. I think you made the right call," Hadley told her.

"You do?" Spencer asked, dropping the box and snagging Hadley by the waist. "You think I was right? Say it. Say I was right."

"Sometimes you're right."

"Damn right I am."

"You're cute when you gloat."

"Prove it."

The constant touching and kissing really got in the way of their move-in process but, honestly, Hadley wasn't complaining.

She smiled at how wonderful it was to have Spencer with her for good each night. Not to mention, with Minnie Mouse around, the complex still had a resident mascot. Fat Tony would be moving with Isabel and Taylor out of Seven Shores and into a gorgeous house they'd purchased and upgraded just blocks away in Venice. With Isabel mere moments away, Breakfast Club would remain intact!

"Time for cake!" Isabel's dad called, pulling Hadley back into the hubbub of the wedding. They gathered around the one-tiered cake with flowers cascading over the side as a clap of thunder hit loud and ominous overhead. Everyone looked skyward at the foreboding cloud above.

"Uh-oh," Taylor said. "We should likely hurry."

"It'll hold out," Gia said confidently, with a shrug.

Elle nodded her agreement. "We see those guys all the time on the beach. They never amount to anything."

But thirty seconds later, the heavens opened up just as Taylor fed Isabel the first bite of cake. While it may have been human instinct to duck under the tablecloth, or run for cover, no one on that beach made a move to go anywhere. Instead they looked to each other and smiled and laughed while passing out soggy cake—which they happily ate. The hired violinist didn't bid them farewell, but rather popped an umbrella in the sand and continued to play a variety of recognizable covers.

Because she couldn't help herself, Hadley started to dance in the downpour. Her feet were covered in wet sand, her hair was drenched and her dress clung to her body, but underneath it all, she felt celebratory and free. Moments later, Spencer joined her, followed by Autumn and Will, who tried to catch each drop. The rest of the attendees must have thought it looked like fun, because a full-on dance party cropped up on that beach.

Hadley had never seen anything like it.

She twirled Gia as she danced past. She dipped Elle. She spun

Kate unabashedly. Finally, she kissed Spencer even though she could barely see her through the summer shower. "I love you," she said.

"In the rain, on a train," Spencer said, and kissed her again. "Side note, we're going to have to work harder to top this wedding now."

Hadley nodded at the truth of that statement as Spencer pulled Autumn into her arms for a spin. The rain continued and the music played on. Puddles splashing, guests laughing, and brides kissing would be the subjects of the epic photographs they'd look back on later.

They had a time like no other time. Isabel and Taylor had never looked happier as they kissed in the rain, surrounded by their friends and loved ones.

For Hadley, it felt like they were all, at last, coming into their own. The Breakfast Club, her best friends, had assembled together two years ago, each in the midst of a search. Whether it had been for career, family, love, or self-confidence, they'd each made their own way and found what they'd long been looking for. They were fuller people now, bursting with color and rich with knowledge and life experience. But Hadley understood that not a single one of them could have arrived where they were now without the help, support, and friendship of the others.

Now their Breakfast Club was a little bigger, and on its way to more and more members. She almost couldn't take it. "I love you, Venice!" Hadley yelled to the waves, hands extended in the air. Her soul soared, her heart sang, and her life could go in so many different directions. As long as Spencer was there, too, she was ready to buckle up for that ride.

She turned back to her friends, who pulled her into their circle as the rain continued and Isabel showed them all how to shimmy, to comedic results. The day had been an epic one and would go down in the history books as one of the most memorable of their lives.

They were still talking about it when Elle announced she was pregnant a year later while holding hands with a beaming Gia. They brought it up again the night Isabel won her first Emmy for writing a key episode on *The Subdivision*. When Will started walking and flirting with little girls at the coffee shop, Autumn warned him that beach weddings tended to get crazy, so he should think that one through. The day of Spencer's first major runway show when she proposed to Hadley in front of hundreds of people, she promised her a wedding that she'd never forget…with maybe just a little less rain.

The journey of life was a winding road that never seemed to hint at what lay ahead. Regardless of where it took them, or what happened, their little group would travel that road together, coffees in hand, theme nights at the ready, and beach gatherings galore. There was no doubting they'd show up for each other. You could count on it, rain or shine.

About the Author

Melissa Brayden (www.melissabrayden.com) is a multiaward–winning romance author, embracing the full-time writer's life in San Antonio, Texas, and enjoying every minute of it.

Melissa is married and working really hard at remembering to do the dishes. For personal enjoyment, she spends time with her Jack Russell terriers and checks out the NYC theater scene as often as possible. She considers herself a reluctant patron of spin class, but would much rather be sipping merlot and staring off into space. Coffee, wine, and donuts make her world go round.

Books Available From Bold Strokes Books

Against All Odds by Kris Bryant, Maggie Cummings, and M. Ullrich. Peyton and Tory escaped death once, but will they survive when Bradley's determined to make his kill rate 100 percent? (978-1-163555-193-8)

Autumn's Light by Aurora Rey. Casual hookups aren't supposed to include romantic dinners and meeting the family. Can Mat Pero see beyond the heartbreak that led her to keep her worlds so separate, and will Graham Connor be waiting if she does? (978-1-163555-272-0)

Breaking the Rules by Larkin Rose. When Virginia and Carmen are thrown together by an embarrassing mistake, they find out their stubborn determination isn't so heroic after all. (978-1-163555-261-4)

Broad Awakening by Mickey Brent. In the sequel to *Underwater Vibes*, Hélène and Sylvie find ruts in their road to eternal bliss. (978-1-163555-270-6)

Broken Vows by MJ Williamz. Sister Mary Margaret must reconcile her divided heart or risk losing a love that just might be heaven sent. (978-1-163555-022-1)

Flesh and Gold by Ann Aptaker. Havana, 1952, where art thief and smuggler Cantor Gold dodges gangland bullets and mobsters' schemes while she searches Havana's steamy red light district for her kidnapped love. (978-1-163555-153-2)

Isle of Broken Years by Jane Fletcher. Spanish noblewoman Catalina de Valasco is in peril, even before the pirates holding her for ransom sail into seas destined to become known as the Bermuda Triangle. (978-1-163555-175-4)

Love Like This by Melissa Brayden. Hadley Cooper and Spencer Adair set out to take the fashion world by storm. If only they knew their hearts were about to be taken. (978-1-163555-018-4)

Secrets On the Clock by Nicole Disney. Jenna and Danielle love their jobs helping endangered children, but that might not be enough to stop them from breaking the rules by falling in love. (978-1-163555-292-8)

Unexpected Partners by Michelle Larkin. Dr. Chloe Maddox tries desperately to deny her attraction for Detective Dana Blake as they flee from a serial killer who's hunting them both. (978-1-163555-203-4)

A Fighting Chance by T. L. Hayes. Will Lou be able to come to terms with her past to give love a fighting chance? (978-1-163555-257-7)

Chosen by Brey Willows. When the choice is adapt or die, can love save us all? (978-1-163555-110-5)

Gnarled Hollow by Charlotte Greene. After they are invited to study a secluded nineteenth-century estate, a former English professor and a group of historians discover that they will have to fight against the unknown if they have any hope of staying alive. (978-1-163555-235-5)

Jacob's Grace by C.P. Rowlands. Captain Tag Becket wants to keep her head down and her past behind her, but her feelings for AJ's second-in-command, Grace Fields, makes keeping secrets next to impossible. (978-1-163555-187-7)

On the Fly by PJ Trebelhorn. Hockey player Courtney Abbott is content with her solitary life until visiting concert violinist Lana Caruso makes her second-guess everything she always thought she wanted. (978-1-163555-255-3)

Passionate Rivals by Radclyffe. Professional rivalry and long-simmering passions create a combustible combination when Emmet McCabe and Sydney Stevens are forced to work together, especially when past attractions won't stay buried. (978-1-63555-231-7)

Proxima Five by Missouri Vaun. When geologist Leah Warren crash-lands on a preindustrial planet and is claimed by its tyrant, Tiago, will clan warrior Keegan's love for Leah give her the strength to defeat him? (978-1-163555-122-8)

Shadowboxer by Jessica L. Webb. Jordan McAddie is prepared to keep her street kids safe from a dangerous underground protest group, but she isn't prepared for her first love to walk back into her life. (978-1-163555-267-6)

Racing Hearts by Dena Blake. When you cross a hot-tempered race car mechanic with a reckless cop, the result can only be spontaneous combustion. (978-1-163555-251-5)

The Tattered Lands by Barbara Ann Wright. As Vandra and Lilani strive to make peace, they slowly fall in love. With mistrust and murder surrounding them, only their faith in each other can keep their plan to save the world from falling apart. (978-1-163555-108-2)

Captive by Donna K. Ford. To escape a human trafficking ring, Greyson Cooper and Olivia Danner become players in a game of deceit and violence. Will their love stand a chance? (978-1-63555-215-7)

Crossing the Line by CF Frizzell. The Mob discovers a nemesis within its ranks, and in the ultimate retaliation, draws Stick McLaughlin from anonymity by threatening everything she holds dear. (978-1-63555-161-7)

Love's Verdict by Carsen Taite. Attorneys Landon Holt and Carly Pachett want the exact same thing: the only open partnership spot at their prestigious criminal defense firm. But will they compromise their careers for love? (978-1-63555-042-9)

Precipice of Doubt by Mardi Alexander & Laurie Eichler. Can Cole Jameson resist her attraction to her boss, veterinarian Jodi Bowman, or will she risk a workplace romance and her heart? (978-1-63555-128-0)

Savage Horizons by CJ Birch. Captain Jordan Kellow's feelings for Lt. Ali Ash have her past and future colliding, setting in motion a series of events that strands her crew in an unknown galaxy thousands of light years from home. (978-1-63555-250-8)

Secrets of the Last Castle by A. Rose Mathieu. When Elizabeth Campbell represents a young man accused of murdering an elderly woman, her investigation leads to an abandoned plantation that reveals many dark Southern secrets. (978-1-63555-240-9)